"I'm falling in love with you," I admit, once we've stopped kissing long enough for me to catch my breath.

"Good, because I'm already in love with you," he replies, with a satisfied smile flickering across his face. "I've never known anyone like you, and I can't get enough of you."

I trace the contours of his beautiful face. "That's how I feel about you too. I'm not sure I like it because it makes me feel vulnerable. You could so easily hurt me, but denying how I feel about you isn't making my feelings disappear.

"And to be honest I don't want them to. I like how alive I feel around you. You make me feel powerful and desirable, special and protected. As if I can do anything and yet stay secure in the knowledge you will be with me if I need your help. And even if I don't."

With a slight snort of laughter, I shake my head. "I think I'm more than falling in love with you. I believe that train left a long time ago, I just didn't realize it. I am in love with you."

Praise for April Hollingworth
Double Magick in the Falls

"This story grabs you by the paranormal throat from every angle! Witches, Vampires, Weres, Shifters, even Zombie cops."

~Lori Marsh

~*~

"Oh my! This is the first book in the Candi Reynolds series. It is a unique world created by the very brilliant mind of April Hollingworth."

~Pamela Talley

~*~

"I love when I can smile, laugh, and experience surprise while reading, and this book did all of those and more."

~Stalking Nerd Girl Official

~*~

"It grabbed my interest and kept me turning pages long into the night with its quick pace and snappy dialogue."

~Author Christine Elaine Black

~*~

"I love April's writing because her characters have humor and smarts about them."

~Anne Gonsalves

The Prophecy

by

April Hollingworth

The Candi Reynolds Series

The Prophecy

Cover Art by *Debbie Taylor*

The Wild Rose Press, Inc.
PO Box 708
Adams Basin, NY 14410-0708
Visit us at www.thewildrosepress.com

Publishing History
First Black Rose Edition, 2016
Print ISBN 978-1-5092-0892-0
Digital ISBN 978-1-5092-0893-7

The Candi Reynolds Series Book 2
Published in the United States of America

Dedications

First of all, I'd like to give a huge thank you to Deb Burchfield for beta reading and critiquing this for me. Seriously, I hope you didn't get too much of a headache. You know the word I'm on about, but I won't mention it.

To my family, for always supporting me and looking forward to my books. Guys, I seriously love you all.

And to you my readers, who let me know you're looking forward to Candi's next journey. I hope you enjoy reading it as much as I have writing it.

~*~

To my editor extraordinaire, Lill Farrell,
thank you for believing in me
and for making this journey go so much smoother.

~*~

And finally to Debbie Taylor of DcaGraphics
for once more bringing my cover to life.
Seriously, your talent is amazing.

Chapter 1

As I awake in the comforting warmth of Victor's embrace, I allow myself a moment to snuggle closer to him. Until I remember, it's the morning after the full moon, the morning after the club incident, where my best friend, Alsatian shapeshifter Jasmine, and werewolf Detective Kheda McKnight had almost become the latest victims of Beatrix and Sarah Sullivan.

The sisters had until their arrest worked for *The Protectors,* a sadistic group who kill supernaturals who associate with others, romantically, outside of their own species. Nice, I know, right? Apparently, *The Protectors* had caught wind of the fact they were keeping trophies and had sent a killer after them to frame them for additional murders. Their way of cleaning house.

Feeling rested and in desperate need of a good run, I extract myself from Victor's warmth, dragging my long red hair off my face, pushing it behind my shoulders, so it fell like a thick curtain cascading down my back. Climbing from the bed, I retrieve last night's clothes to put on again, until I can get home and change into fresh ones, and quietly pad into the bathroom to get dressed.

Transforming into wolf form, I re-enter the bedroom. I sit and stare at Victor, the most beautiful vampire I have ever met. Okay, he's also the only one

I've met, but wow, he is truly gorgeous. His sleep-tousled jet black hair makes him look young and innocent in his slumber, the usually taut muscles in his jaw, relaxed. His ridiculously long thick black eyelashes fan the tops of his high cheekbones, and his delicious lips, full and sensual, and oh so talented, curl slightly upwards, making me want to transform back into human form so I can kiss him awake.

I drink in the sight of him. A feeling of contentment settles inside of me. My breath gently blows some hair back from his forehead. I press my wet nose to his neck. Unable to resist, I give his cheek a quick lick and watch as he slowly opens his amazing silvery green eyes.

"Very funny, Candi," Victor mumbles, he reaches out with one hand to wipe his neck and cheek while the other reaches out to give me a scratch behind my ears, which makes me shiver in delight and my tail give a happy thump.

"Why are you in wolf form?" he asks, as I skip backwards out of his reach with a little whine of regret, before looking at the bedroom door. He climbs from his bed looking for something to pull on to cover his nakedness. Spotting a pair of tracksuit bottoms, he drags them on. He heads over to me my jaws open wide, and my tongue lolls out from the corner, in a huge wolfish smile, as I happily watch him.

"No point grinning at me, Candi. As long as you're in wolf form, we are not doing anything," Victor mutters, as he tiredly swipes a large strong hand across his face, then around to the back of his neck and gently massages it, as if he's releasing tension there.

Victor opens the door. As I run past him and down

the stairs, I hear him let out a jaw-breaking yawn. As a vampire associating with me, a werewolf and a witch, it would get us both killed if we're caught. To be without Victor is impossible—I would rather die—yet the thought of any harm coming to him leaves me feeling physically sick. Since we've only known each other for a month, these intense feelings are scary as hell.

My parents were murdered for loving each other. My mother was a witch, and my father a werewolf. Glancing at Victor, I understand exactly how my parents felt, and he is worth the risk.

Other supernaturals born from parents of mixed heritage are born with either their mother's or father's abilities. Some are born with no magical abilities, in which case they're cruelly known as a dud. I am unique, as I was born with both my mother's witch powers and my father's wolf magic. Leaving me with double magick, the only one of my kind. They even wrote a Prophecy about me!

Though I have no idea what it says or where it is. Victor's sire is the keeper of the book of prophecies. He left a note saying he'd hidden the book and was leaving clues for Victor to find it, in hope he could achieve what he couldn't, finding me.

Thinking about how he found out I was the one from the Prophecy makes me smile, even though his pub was burnt down and most of his staff and some customers killed. Okay, not a great memory. But remembering the shock, wonder, and joy on Victor's face, as I transformed into a wolf and ripped out the throat of the witch who was trying to kill me, gives me a warm fuzzy feeling.

He'd thought I was about to die. So had the witch

who had put a binding spell on me, preventing me from using witch magick to protect myself. What can I say, my abilities are unheard of. Now all we have to do is find the actual Prophecy and stay alive. Easily enough in theory, but in reality, with maniacs wanting to kill us…Ahh, we'll figure it out. I hope!

Reaching the bottom of the stairs, Victor runs his fingers along the front door to open it, and with a quick press of my body to his leg, I take off toward the woods. I badly need a run. Because Victor's door is imprinted so only he can open it (a vampire safety precaution), I had to disturb this wonderful man from his slumber. I feel guilty about it for a second. After all, the view had been totally worthwhile. A happy yip escapes from me as I run in happy remembrance of such a wonderful view.

****

My paws beat a rhythmic tattoo into the ground. My heart beats in sync with each thump and lift as I run through the forest. My large stride quickly and efficiently eats up ground, as the wind ruffles my fur and I dodge low-hanging branches. My tongue lolls happily from pure enjoyment of the moment; all my worries are left behind.

A slight twinge of guilt tries to infiltrate my brain for being in wolf form this morning when leaving Victor's, but I brush it off with slight impatience. I'd see him later, and he hadn't seemed to mind. I carry on running through the woods. Instead of going over the bridge, I carefully descend the slight hill into the stream and up the other side of the bank. Crouching low, I glance around to make sure no one has spotted me and then dash into the safety of the woods, leading to my land.

With a little leap, I dash off through the woods and arrive home. Looking up at the Old Winters House, I'm pleased to see the tree cutters are getting rid of the branches and trees overshadow the house. And the carpenters are fixing the porch. I whisper a silent thank-you for the dog flap in the back door as I silently sneak around to it. Seeing the coast is clear, I bolt to the backdoor and squeeze inside.

My wolf form is not small; then again, no werewolf's exactly small as we're all larger than the average wolf or dog. Thinking of Kheda's wolf form, I come to the conclusion there's no way in hell would he fit through the dog flap, as his wolf is huge. With that thought, I let a snort of laughter escape me as I tumble through the dog flap and skid across the floor in an ungainly heap. Turning, I give the door a disgruntled look. If I can't get through it in a hurry, then it's useless to me. I quickly cast a spell of expansion over it, customizing it, so all shapeshifters with an open invitation into my home will be able to use the dog flap, no matter their size.

I transform into my human self, quickly strip out of last night's clothes, and empty my pockets. I dump my dirty clothes in the washing machine. I'll add more clothes to it later before turning it on. I walk into the kitchen, down the hallway, up the stairs, and straight into my bathroom. I quickly shower and dry myself, head into my bedroom to drag on underwear, low rise black jeans, a black tank top, black boots, and a black leather jacket, before brushing my long fiery-red hair. Leaving it down to dry naturally, I collect a hair bobble and pop it on my wrist. Once my hair has dried, I'll tie it up.

Heading into Jasmine's room, I collect some clothes for her and remember Kheda will have some clothes here too. After bagging up Jasmine's clothes, I go into Kheda's room, where I'm surprised to see how neat the room is. The bed is pristine with not a wrinkle in sight. His suitcase is in a corner, and after a quick glance around, I realize he must be living out of it. Heading over to it I flip the lid and pull out some jeans, t-shirt, socks, and boxers before closing the lid and bagging his clothes in with Jasmine's.

Chapter 2

My stomach rumbles loudly, and I debate getting something to eat here or going out for breakfast with Victor. I decide to head back to Victor's; afterwards, we can go together to the hospital. Hopefully we'll bring home Jasmine and Kheda. Quickly collecting my phone, keys, and wallet, I distribute them between my jacket pockets, then jog downstairs, unlock my front door, and exit, startling the carpenter who's fixing my porch.

"Hey, you're doing a fabulous job," I inform him, and then I lock my door, descend the porch stairs, and stride toward my car. Unlocking it, I climb in, put the bag of clothes behind the passenger seat, and then drive to Victor's house.

I zip along my road over the bridge, past the burnt-out shell of Vlad's Bar, only slowing down to take the next turn on the left leading to Victor's house. Pulling up, I climb out and turn to the sound of the front door opening.

"Hello, beautiful," he says in his rich dark chocolate voice as a little smile plays across his luscious lips, making my knees tremble in anticipation. Stiffening my knees, I give him a smile in return before crossing over to him.

"Hey, you. I'm starving. Shall we head out to get something to eat?" I ask, raising an eyebrow in query.

"Sure. I'll just get my coat and wallet, and then I'm ready," he replies, before quickly dragging my body against his. Lowering his head, he gives me a thorough kiss. With a groan of acceptance, my body softens against his hard angles. My lips open wide as I claim his tongue and suck it greedily into mine.

Our teeth knock together in our need to get closer, until I drag my mouth from his, panting and sucking great gulps of oxygen into my deprived lungs. Which I notice he takes great pleasure in watching, as my breasts rise and fall.

"Go and get your things." I laugh, as I watch him ogling my breasts. I wait outside as I don't trust either of us to behave if I go inside. My stomach gives a yowl of annoyance at being left unfed for so long. Giving it a distracted rub, I turn back to my car and climb in.

"So where to?" I ask Victor, once he's climbed into my car. I drink him in, making a brilliant impression of a woman deprived of water. Wearing faded blue denim jeans that hug him in all the right places, but loose enough he needs a leather belt to prevent them from slipping lower on his narrow hips, a dark green t-shirt that clings to his lean muscular frame, and a black leather jacket over it. On his feet, he wears those black trainer boots I like. I must find out what they're called and if they make them in women's or at least in my size. With a sigh of appreciation as a feeling of contentment washes over me, I drag my gaze away from him.

"How about Cynthia's Café," he replies, watching me through hooded eyes as a pleased smile curls his lips.

I like the fact he watches me and wants me as

much as I want him. My stomach lets out a yowl of protest, making him laugh.

"We'd best be heading off before your stomach decides to eat itself!"

"Yeah, I am famished," I smile, as I rub my stomach again. Once we're both belted, I reverse and drive off to the café, my mouth watering in anticipation of their coffee. I drive along the streets, feeling relaxed in the comfortable silence. A glance shows me he is lounging in the passenger seat, a slight smile pulling on his sensual lips, making me want to nibble the corner…

"Eyes on the road," he informs me, a sensual rumble of laughter erupting from his chest, spreading across my skin, like chocolate lightning, deliciously dangerous and totally sensual.

Finally, we arrive at Cynthia's Café. I breathe a sigh of relief when I find a space to pull into. I've just put the car in neutral and switched off the engine when he unbuckles my seat belt, dragging me from my seat onto his lap to kiss me. A squeal of surprise escapes me to my great mortification. I mean seriously, I squealed. Talk about a turn off, not that he seems to mind!

"Ow, ow, ow," I yelp in surprise.

"What's wrong?" Victor demands, as he glances around as if he expects someone to jump out at us.

"Gear shift," I wince, as I awkwardly lift myself from it, shift position, to move more onto his lap, giving my leg a rub where it had dug into me. My legs feel like they're getting tangled, so I heft myself back onto my own seat with a disgruntled grimace. I realize he is laughing, as he watches me trying to get comfortable. My stomach gives another yowl of discontent, making me choose to exit the car altogether.

Seriously, I'd better get myself fed before my stomach gets louder or makes any more embarrassing noises!

****

I quickly lock the car as Victor meets me around my side, and together we enter the café. I'm surprised how quiet it is. I notice the officer who'd interviewed me after the bar massacre, observing us as we enter. Ignoring him, I head for the counter and check out the menu. My nose twitches in satisfaction as it's assaulted by the heavenly smell of coffee. I quickly order a breakfast bagel and mocha, while Victor orders an Americana before paying, and we head to the back of the café.

With a snort of laughter, I walk off. I feel his hand link with mine as he pulls me to his side, stating our claim on each other in the most quiet and sweet way. And I don't care who sees! I know, stupid of both of us, as we both know how dangerous our relationship is. Coming to a screeching halt, I turn and gape at his puzzled expression.

"Are we in a relationship?" I blurt out in surprise making him burst out laughing. I faintly hear sighs of appreciation from the women in the café as his rich baritone washes over everyone.

"Yes, Candi, we are most definitely in a relationship," he states before pulling me into his embrace and kisses me so thoroughly my knees go weak. I wrap my arms around his neck and kiss him back, before drawing away. He wraps an arm around my waist, helping me into a seat at one of the back tables. I notice the silence that has descended upon the café, and everyone is watching. I also note quite a few of the women are giving Victor looks of longing, while others glare at me as if they're getting ready to rip my head off. Except for Officer Jesse James who directs his glare at Victor. He stands up, collects his coffee and breakfast, and heads over to our table.

"May I join you, please?" he quietly asks me. "I have something I wish to discuss with you," he hurries on, plastering a friendly smile on his face as he avoids looking at the vampire beside me.

"Ah, well…" I stammer in surprise, then stare in confusion as I hear Victor say, "Sure, take a seat," inclining his head to the chair nearest Jesse. I cock my eyebrow inquiringly at him wondering what the hell is going on. My only answer, a gentle squeeze of my fingers as he looks at me, with a gentle smile full of promise.

"How can we help you, Officer?" Victor enquires, watching the young officer intently. "Ah, our order has arrived," he interrupts, before Jesse can do more than open his mouth. "Thank you," he says to the waitress as he accepts his coffee.

"Thanks, this looks delicious." I beam at my hot buttered bagel, scrambled eggs, crispy bacon, and mocha. I hear him stifle a laugh at the adoring look I'm giving my food.

"So how do I get you to look at me like that?" he murmurs into my ear, his breath fanning the side of my face and tickling my ear, which he takes a quick nip at.

"Decorate yourself in delicious food with coffee on the side," I blurt out with a snort of laughter, not thinking of what I'd said until I see Jesse's jaw drop and hear Victor burst into delicious laughter. I feel heat encompass me as I blush fiery red from embarrassment. "I didn't…"

"No, no need to say anything else," sooths Victor, with a wicked smirk spreading across his face as he traces his long fingers over my arm.

I feel his touch through my sleeve. Heat spreads through my body, shooting down to the junction between my thighs, where it pools in anticipation. I watch Victor's nostrils flare as he catches the scent of my desire, and to my horror, I notice Jesse's flaring too. A low and threatening growl erupts from Victor as he realizes the officer is breathing in my arousal, as if it's a gift or an offer.

"Sorry, I didn't mean…" he stammers, before coming to a halt, unable to finish his sentence. "Sorry. Look, the reason I wanted to talk to you is because of the Prophecy," he hurries on, in apparent terror of Victor attacking him at any second. Until he glances at me and squeaks in a petrified breath.

The mirror on the opposite wall clearly shows our table, and I see what he sees when he looks at me. My eyes are blazing violet swirls of raw energy. My expression one of steely hardness, a warrioress sitting before him. He gulps in genuine fear and lust.

"You have no right to sniff at me," I snarl, my lips curling back over my teeth as I point my finger at him. Sparks of violet energy crackle in restrained power along my fingers, begging for release as they lick and curl around the brands on my hands and arms, curling along the black rose and lace tattoo.

"I'm sorry," he gulps, quickly lowering his gaze as my wolf glares out at him from the violent thunder of my magick. He obviously hadn't realized I'm a dominant wolf but had assumed, since I'm mainly a witch, my wolf would be lower in the pack hierarchy. I watch him as he gulps in fear, realizing I'm an alpha wolf and he's royally screwed up.

The scent of his fear rises and assails our noses giving off a sour smell, making my nose twitch and my wolf chuff in satisfaction. I start eating my cooling breakfast. I catch Victor gazing at me in the mirror, a smile spread over his face as pride shines from him. I decide to ignore him too, though I can't help pleasure rippling through me. There's nothing better than a strong man being proud and comfortable of a strong woman.

A lot of men hate being around alpha women, as if a woman's strength and independence belittles them, making them less somehow. It takes internal strength in a man not to feel threatened and to know a relationship is a meeting of souls, each other's strengths supporting the other. I should've known he wouldn't be threatened by me. I have never met a man like him before in my life and am delighted and curious to see where our relationship will take us.

"What did you want to talk to us about?" he casually enquires, sipping his coffee.

I glance up curiously at Jesse; to be honest, I'd almost forgotten why he was sitting in front of us. My wolf has retreated, pleased with herself now she's put him in his place.

"You've heard of the Prophecy, I'm assuming?" he asks, trying to get himself back on even footing.

"What of it?" Victor raises his mug and takes another sip of coffee, giving nothing away.

I don't say anything, just carry on eating. My hunger pains are retreating happily, and I want to keep it that way.

"Well, my grandfather told me about it..." he replies, looking rather pleased with himself until he apparently realizes neither of us are impressed.

"You told me that outside of the police station. So what exactly do you know, and why do you think it concerns us or why we should even care?" I ask, as I finish the last delicious bite of my bagel.

"Because it's about you," he answers.

"In what way does it mention me, by name? Have you read it?" I ask as I sip my coffee and think about getting something else to eat, maybe something chocolaty.

"Well, I haven't actually seen it myself, but my grandfather said a vampire his great-great-grandfather used to know, has it."

"So this is helpful to me how?" I demand, feeling completely confused. "I'll be back in a second. Do you want anything?" I ask Victor.

"No, I'm fine, thanks, love."

"Where are you going?" Jesse demands in surprise.

I try not to stifle a laugh. Without answering, I walk to the counter bringing my empty plate, knife, and fork with me. Handing them to the waitress, I check out the counter and pick a slice of chocolate cake which looks so soft and delicious, I understand why it's called "Devil's Delight."

"Would you like cream with it?" the sales assistant asks me.

"Oh, yes, please." I pay and collect a fork and napkin and bring the plate of joy back to my table. Sitting down, I slide my fork into my cake, then dip it in cream before popping it into my mouth. Closing my eyes in a moment of sublime pleasure, I savor the rich flavors. A hint of dark velvety decadence with orange swirling through and rum?

"So what did your great whatever say, causing such a lasting impression on your whole family?" I demand.

"The one with Double Magick will lead us to our freedom in the fight against *The Protectors*."

"Say what?" I choke, leaning forwards I push my dessert away from me. "What the hell does that mean?"

"It means you need to find the vampire with the Prophecy," he answers, looking pleased he finally has my full undivided attention.

"And do you have any idea of where it is?" I growl in aggravation, as I glare at the self-satisfied look on his face. Smug bastard!

Chapter 3

"Well?" I demand. "Do you have any idea where it is, or are you just annoying me on purpose?"

"No…well, I don't know where it is…But my great-great-great-granddad told his son, my great-great granddad, he was in London when he met the vampire who was keeping it safe. I distinctly remember because it was 1868, and the Midnight Slasher Whitechapel murders were happening. They were in Whitechapel," he announces as a huge smirk spreads across his face.

"Anything else you were told we should know?" Victor demands, as he looks thoughtfully at Jesse.

"Umm, no, isn't that enough?" he huffs in annoyance before looking in puzzlement at my hands.

"Do you know the name of the vampire?" I ask quickly before he can ask about the tattoos. Feeling Victor glance at me, I let the fingers of my hand glide across his hand in supplication. Thankfully, he doesn't say anything.

"No, no, I don't remember it, if I was ever told it," he answers, as a frown flickers across his forehead.

"Well, if you think of anything else let us know."

Quick man he is, he realizes I want him to leave, pushes back his chair with a loud squeal, making everyone grit their teeth. He gives us a look of anger and indignation before storming off.

****

Pulling my dessert back toward me, I take another wonderful forkful before looking at Victor. "So, the Midnight Slasher? Did you know your sire was there then?" I ask as I wiggle in my seat with curiosity.

"Yes, so were Vincent and I. Vincent is my vampire brother," he informs me. His jaw tightens as a look of disgust and anger fills his beautiful eyes.

That look shocks me, and I hope it isn't aimed at me. Choosing to stay quiet, I carefully carry on eating my cake as I watch him out of my peripheral vision. The cake tastes like sawdust now instead of the chocolate heaven it had a moment a go.

"Vincent...Vincent." Giving a sigh of frustration, he looks at me, surprised to see me squirming in my seat as I destroy my cake. Placing his hand on top of mine, he stops my restless destruction. He traces a soothing pattern upon my hand.

"He was created within days of me. We'd grown up together and were good friends. But once he was created, he became power hungry, savage, and cruel to anyone who was unfortunate enough to be in his vicinity. When I was created, I was still in contact with my family and friends. Thinking back, this could have been one of the reasons my sire decided to create him. Company of a friend, through generations of life. Except..."

"Except what?" The words leave me on a whisper of a breath. I turn my palm around and capture his circling fingers in mine, linking our hands and giving a gentle squeeze.

"He murdered my entire family. Ripped them apart, so there was no way they could be saved. And then disappeared. For a century, we heard nothing of him. Every now and again, rumors of violent murders surfaced, and deep down I was sure they were his doing. A way of letting us know he was still out there."

I feel sadness and surprise over the torment caused by his friend and vampire brother.

"In the year 1868, we were in London. I was called there by my sire. We'd previously parted ways but met up every now and again when either of us needed assistance or just to catch up. As it happens, this time was because of the Prophecy. It was the first time he ever told me about it and the only time I saw it." By the look on his face, I realize his thoughts have gone back in time.

"Next thing I know, a cry of murder went up. The body of Penelope Adams was found. I'd heard of two other killings, and to this day I believe Joanne Tate was one of the Midnight Slasher's victims. But I believe the Slasher is actually Vincent."

"What? Are you seriously saying the Midnight Slasher is actually a vampire?" I demand. "But no blood was missing."

"Each victim was slashed across the face and torso. They were all displayed in lurid positions, as if mocking their profession. They believe Joanne Tate was moved because of the lack of blood. I don't. I think she was drained before being murdered. Vincent is demented and loves hurting those who are weaker than him.

"Granted as a vampire, it means all humans. The thing is, his mother was often drunk and would attack him for no reason. Quite often as a kid, he would stay at home to keep out of her way. He hated women drinking, as if drunken violent men are better.

"His dad had died when he was a baby, so he had no memories of a drunken father to go by.

"At first, we thought nothing of it. But as the Slasher murders continued, and the descriptions of the Midnight Slasher came about, we both believed it was Vincent and tried to find him. We even came close once. We managed to interrupt him killing Janice Peabody, though he disappeared before we could catch him.

"All the blood he drinks makes him faster. Obviously he didn't go far as, within an hour, he was killing again. One of the main reasons I think he went after those eight women is simply because of the last victim. Natasha Henderson."

"What? Why?"

"Natasha Henderson looked like his mother. I believe the other murders were torment killings. Hunting his prey in a circling fashion. Putting them on edge, never knowing if they were going to be the next victim. Until finally he killed her beyond recognition in the most brutal of murders."

"But she was the youngest. She wouldn't even have been the same age as his mother," I blurt out, as I rack my brain of what I knew about the Whitechapel murders.

"I know. But she looked enough like his mother would have when she was the same age. There would have only been about ten years' age difference between them. So the difference wasn't so great. His mother was fourteen when she married her husband, the same as mine," he informs me with a sad smile filled with heartbreak.

"Times have changed so much through the

centuries. Sometimes I forget just how young our parents were when they married, compared with today's standards where marrying so young is against the law."

Glancing at me, he gives me a teasing smile. "I'm glad times have changed, Candi. If you were married, we would never be sitting here today, for I couldn't stand the thought of another man having claim to your affections." With a chuckle of delight, he watches as I blush fiery red, before he carries on with his story.

"Since then, I've tried to keep an ear open for any sign of him. There have been some strange and horrific murders happening, and I wouldn't be surprised if he'd done them. Especially murders of prostitutes. There are plenty of unsolved cases where the killer disappeared afterwards.

"I also believe he returned to London in 1942." Seeing my clueless expression, he explains further.

"West London was terrorized once again. Eight prostitutes were murdered. I think he returned to his old hunting grounds. To be honest, there are probably hundreds more unsolved murders I've heard of over the centuries, and more I haven't, which could be connected to him. Not that I can prove any of it.

"Whenever I've gone to the vampire elders, they've been uninterested, as it's only humans he's after. I'm positive these victims are his," he finishes, rubbing his hands through his hair tiredly. "The worst of it is, the only reason he's alive in the first place is because of me," he grinds out in frustration through gritted teeth.

"Look, there's no point blaming yourself for his existence. You didn't change him, and he chose to be a sadistic bastard, not you or your sire. So blaming yourself is just a wasting energy. Come on, let's go to the hospital and see if Jasmine and Kheda are being released yet."

Standing up, I gather my plate of destroyed cake and our mugs. Heading toward the counter, I say thanks to the waitress and place the dirty dishes on the counter in front of her, leave, and head toward my car. A second later, Victor's strong hand links with mine, and I give his fingers a gentle squeeze.

Five minutes later, we arrive at the hospital. Victor grabs the bag of clothes I'd stored behind the backseat. We climb out, and I lock my car behind us before heading into the hospital.

Chapter 4

Entering the hospital, we climb the stairs to the second floor where Jasmine's and Kheda's rooms are. The smell of disinfectant and infected wounds assails my nose. I hadn't noticed it last night. Glancing at Victor, I notice his nose crinkling in distaste as his eyes widen in surprise. Huh, I'm not the only one. As we near Jasmine's room, we hear voices coming from inside. I peek my head around the door and spot Kheda sitting awkwardly on the edge of Jasmine's bed, trying to keep the hospital's paper gown from flashing his backside to everyone. Giving a wolf whistle, I laugh as he blushes and makes a further grab for his dignity.

"You're fine, Kheda, you're covered. I was only teasing you." I wickedly wiggle my eyebrows at him in mock lasciviousness making Jasmine laugh. Hearing a snort of laughter coming from behind me, I move to the side allowing Victor entrance into the room.

"Wicked girl," he whispers in my ear while gently caressing my jean-clad bum and legs as he passes me, causing shivers of desire and pleasure to course through me at his gentle caress. I move into the room after him closing the door behind us.

"How are you both feeling?" I ask as we walk closer to our friends.

"We brought gifts of your own clothes," grins Victor, wagging the bag in front of Kheda before snatching it out of his reach, making us all laugh, except Kheda, who lets out a string of curses as his paper gown gapes, flashing Jasmine. The wide eyes and huge grin plastered on her face says it is a very pleasing sight. Passing the bag to him, Victor gives him a wicked grin of unrepentant humor. "It's good to see you up and about."

Pausing from removing his clothes from the bag, he looks up and realizes we are genuinely pleased to see him. With a nod of appreciation, he quickly retrieves the rest of his clothes, freezes for a split second to stare into the bag, before, with a gulp, he passes it to Jasmine. Securing his hospital gown, he retreats from the room, a fiery red color staining his cheeks. Giving a slight inclination of his head, he gently closes the door behind him.

Curiously, I glance toward Jasmine who's looking in the bag, scarlet rising in her cheeks. She looks up at me with a smile curving her lips. "Red underwear on top, really, Candi?" she mutters in mortification even as she reaches in to touch the offending items.

"Oh, whoops, total accident as it happens, them being on top, not you having them in the bag," I explain as mirth bubbles inside me. "I only remembered after I'd packed your stuff Kheda had clothing I could grab for him. I just put them all in the same bag for convenience. Anyway, be grateful they're pretty. It'd be a lot worse if they were granny-basher panties. Now, that would be embarrassing, comfort or not." I openly laugh at the horror flitting across Jasmine's face.

"Granny bashers?" Victor enquires looking between Jasmine and I for an explanation.

"Yeah, really ugly big panties which are seriously

comfortable. No girl likes to admit she has them, but…" With an expressive shrug, I trail off. "Are you and Kheda getting released today do you know?" I ask, smoothly changing the subject.

"Apparently they'd prefer us to stay for one more night for observation reasons, but Kheda and I both agree we want to go."

"We'll take both of you home once you've been checked over today if that's the case. We'll tell the doctors you won't be alone; someone will be with both of you at all times, in case—I don't know—you have an accident or something. It smells wrong out there," I add, looking over my shoulder toward the closed door.

"It's the main reason we don't want to stay," Jasmine quietly admits, glancing about the place as if expecting someone to overhear, even though she is talking so quietly I have to strain to hear what she's saying.

"We'll wait outside while you get dressed." Turning to Victor, I ask him, "Can you go and make sure Kheda gets dressed and come back here with him please?"

"Sure, no problem."

"I'll wait outside and hopefully spot a doctor who can sign your release forms, and then we can go." Turning, we head outside to give Jasmine privacy. Victor squeezes my hand before walking off, heading toward Kheda's room.

I enjoy the view of his ass walking away from me and let out a sigh of appreciation. Apparently, it's louder than I thought as he turns and gives me a wink, a cheeky smirk, and laughs at me as heat rushes into my face. With a shake of my head and a silly grin on my face, I turn away to see if I can see anyone coming.

After a couple of minutes, I spot a member of staff farther down the hallway moving in and out of the rooms without stopping long enough to check on any patients. A frown creases my forehead as I watch this puzzling behavior, until the staff member seems to sense I'm watching. I watch the person glance in my direction, turn swiftly around, and move quickly back down the corridor.

"Sorry, excuse me, please," I call out as I move to follow after the swiftly retreating staff member, until I come to a screeching stop as I realize I hadn't seen the person's face. Not because I was too far away to see it, but because there was no face to see. That's when I see the individual disappear. One minute the faceless person is gliding away from me, and the next he/she is gone. With a shudder, I move back toward Jasmine's room, keeping a wary look out, just in case anything else strange happens. A few minutes later, she pops her head out the door. Noticing my unease, she furrows her brow, and with a simple "What's up?" breaks my concentration and worry.

"Nothing. I think...I just saw the most bizarre thing," I admit, then proceed to tell her what I'd seen.

"You saw Death?" Jasmine demands with a trace of awe in her voice as her eyes widen and her eyebrows shoot up.

"Death? Nah, seriously? Really? Huh." I give her a thoughtful look, before looking back down the corridor. Could I have seen Death? And if so, did I frighten him off? Can Death even be frightened?

A few minutes later, a sexy vampire and werewolf enter the corridor heading toward us. Seeing our worried expressions, they give us concerned looks.

"Are you both okay? Has anything happened?" demands Victor as he reaches out to me.

"I think Candi saw Death," Jasmine answers.

"Death? Are you serious?" demands Kheda, regarding us through narrowed eyes before looking around the empty corridor, as if he's trying to figure out if we have either gone crazy or are pulling some kind of weird prank.

I quickly tell them what I'd seen. We all turn to look at the rooms, as if to see if anything else will happen. I ask everyone if they have everything, receiving grunts for a reply in the affirmative. We go in search for a doctor who can release Jasmine and Kheda.

****

We eventually find three doctors congregating around the reception desk.

"It's completely mysterious. I have no idea what's going on, but they're dropping like flies. Oh, can we help you?" demands the doctor as he glances up to see the four of us nearing the counter.

"We'd like to be released," Kheda answers, pointing to Jasmine and himself so there's no confusion about who he's talking about.

"Well, I don't know…"

"Maybe it's for the best," interrupts another doctor, with a raised eyebrow at his collogue. "Especially after what you were just saying," he finishes on a mutter.

"Ah, yes, probably would be for the best. But if you feel dizzy, nauseous, or have headaches, come straight in. Just for safety, though going by your test results and blood work, you're both fine," he instructs, while checking their charts. They quickly sign the forms they're handed, and we leave.

Going by everyone's expression, we're all dying of curiosity, wondering what the doctors were talking about. I'm guessing it has something to do with the faceless person I'd seen and the smell of death and decay reeking through the corridors. We hurry outside before any of the doctors change their minds. Looking at Jasmine, I give her a relieved smile.

"Whew, that was a close call. Do you guys want to go anywhere in particular or back to my place?" I enquire as I belt up and put my car into reverse.

"For now, yours will be good. I could do with a shower to get the smell of the hospital off me." Jasmine sighs as she gives herself a delicate sniff, wrinkling her nose in distaste.

"Same here, if it's okay?" agrees Kheda.

"No problem," I reply. The slight scent of the cave and the hospital waft from them. My nose twitches, and I wind my window down to let air circulate. The others do likewise, as I drive toward the exit and turn left, go over the bridge, and turn right onto the road leading home.

Before long, I pull up into my parking spot, and we all clamber out, heading for the front door. I smile at the carpenter who's fixing the front porch. This time I get a disgruntled look from him, as he takes in our small group. I unlock the door and allow everyone in before me.

"You're either very brave or very stupid," a voice behind me says.

Turning back, I glance at the carpenter who's stood up to talk to me. He's younger than I'd thought, maybe thirty-five, with short brown hair and coal black eyes, full lips and a crooked nose, which by the looks of it has been broken more than once. His six-foot two-inch body is lean and compact underneath his jeans and shirt, which don't hide his obvious strength.

Before, I'd thought him to be older, shorter, and nowhere near as muscled. I now realize my mistake, though why the deception I have no idea.

"Why hide your true form behind the older façade?" I demand.

A smirk spreads across his handsome features as he looks me up and down. "No ordinary witch, so what exactly are you then, I wonder?" he quizzes me as he reaches out a long finger toward my jaw.

Feeling uneasy, I slap his finger away before it can reach its destination. As I look at him, I realize I have no idea what exactly he is.

"I'm Fey," smirks the man before me, "and you are quite delightful."

"Why the…"

"Candi, are you all right?" Victor enquires from directly behind me, slipping his arms around my waist, pulling me back against his hard body.

With a feeling of relief, I lean into him.

"Yes, I'm fine, thanks. I was just wondering why…"

"Dante, my name is Dante, dear Candi," he informs me with a triumphant look on his handsome face. "I'll see you soon." Turning, he walks away. With a slight rustle of movement, the other workers, whom I now assume are also Fey, join him, before they all disappear.

"What was that about?" demands Kheda coming up behind us.

"Apparently Dante is Fey, and probably the others

as well, though I have no idea what exactly it means," I add in confusion, as I look at where they'd disappeared.

"Crap," mutters Victor, before pulling me inside and closing the front door behind us.

"Do you know him?" I ask curiously, as I turn around to look at him.

"No, not him in particular, but it's never good to attract the attentions of the Fey. They're…"

"Irritating, dangerous, and unpredictable," growls Kheda, his big body practically vibrating in agitation.

"Wow, what's affected you so strongly, Kheda? And who's annoying, dangerous, and unpredictable?" laughs Jasmine, as she descends the stairs. Dressed in black jeans and a red t-shirt, her long wet hair flows loosely around her shoulders and down her back. She's painted her toenails a bright red, and I notice Kheda can't seem to look away from them.

"The Fey apparently," I reply, as I try to stifle a laugh as Jasmine freezes, leaving her body suspended midstep. She quickly puts her foot down before she falls down the stairs.

"Are you serious?" She looks at each of us in turn, her voice barely above a whisper. "The Fey? They're real?"

"It seems so, though I'm unsure as to why their sudden interest in us," I admit.

"I'd say the interest has a lot to do with the recent goings on. They've probably heard about the murders and the pub explosion, and the fact it all started when you moved back to town," grunts Kheda, as he drags his gaze up Jasmine's body before smiling at her. "Feel better?"

"Yes, much better thanks, you?"

"Yeah, though I would be happier if the Fey weren't butting in," he huffs, as he glances again at the front door.

"Are they really so bad?" I ask in surprise, leaning my head back onto Victor's muscular chest and enjoying the comfort being in his arms brings me.

"They can be," he admits. The reverberations of his voice rumble through my back, soothing me and making me want to purr. A gentle laugh escapes him, as if he knows the effect his speaking is having on me and delights in it. Then again maybe he does. Hugging me closer for just a second before pulling away, he lets out a regretful noise. "We need to decide what our next plan is."

With a silent groan, I nod in agreement. It's time we tried to get ahead of the situation. This blundering about in the dark is getting old, fast.

"Okay, how about we put the furniture back into the sitting room first? At least we can have a comfortable place to sit and make our plans." Feeling happy I've come up with a plan.

It's hard to believe even with removing all my furniture, there still hadn't been enough space to display all of the crime scene photos. Never mind the fact that, last night, Jasmine and Kheda had almost been killed in the same cave of horrors.

"Sure, at least it's something productive. Jasmine and Kheda, why don't you two get something to eat, while Candi and I get started on the sitting room?"

"Won't it be easier with our help?" Kheda enquires in surprise.

"Not necessarily, and anyway, the two of you should have something to eat first. I'm sure whatever

you were served in the hospital probably wasn't great."
I smile at them.

"Try disgusting," Jasmine mutters with a delicate
grimace of distaste.

With a snort of laughter, I grasp Victor's hand and
drag him toward the pile of boxes to be moved first.
The two of us start moving them as quickly as possible.
Neither of us want Jasmine and Kheda to move them.
They have been through a big enough ordeal yesterday
and already look tired and slightly pale. Once we've put
the boxes into corners of the sitting room, we move the
sofa and the rest of the furniture back into the room.

I observe Kheda and Jasmine flash us guilty looks
every now and again, but with a quick shake of my
head and a grin, they eventually relax and rest. This
alone tells us just how truly exhausted they are. An
hour later, we're finally done. In relief, I collapse on the
sofa with a happy groan. A minute later, Jasmine comes
in holding two steaming mugs of coffee, one for her
and one for me.

"Oh, you angel, I could kiss you, if only I had the
energy to do so," I murmur in gratification.

With a wave of her hand and a gentle smile, she
brushes my thanks aside. "I should be the one thanking
you. Giving you a coffee is hardly adequate." She
laughs as she sits opposite me and curls her feet
underneath her. Kheda enters and passes Victor a mug.
By the look of surprise on his face, I'm guessing it's not
coffee but blood.

"Thank you." Accepting the mug, he gives Kheda a
grateful smile.

Clapping a hand on Victor's shoulder before sitting
on the sofa, Kheda groans in exhaustion. "I hadn't

realized just how tired I was, until sitting down and eating lunch."

"Same here," agrees Jasmine, letting loose a jaw-breaking yawn and setting the rest of us off.

"I'm tempted to go for a nap." I laugh as I smother my yawn. "Actually, it would probably do us all the world of good to go for one. It's been a long night and a busy couple of days. With a fresh mind, we might come up with a decent plan for our next move, whatever it is." I take a fortifying sip of my coffee, before leaning my head against the back of the sofa.

Victor sits beside me, so close we're touching from our shoulders to our feet. I instantly feel calmer, and yet, every particle of my being becomes hyperaware and extra sensitive, and for a brief second, I hate the effect he has on me of how my body betrays me so easily around him. Until I realize what I really fear is the thought of opening myself up to being hurt.

Looking inside myself, I can almost see my self-preservation trying to force close the doors to my emotions; with an inward shake of my head, I push them open wider. It might not be the perfect time to become emotionally entangled with someone, but if he can admit how he feels and accept it, why can't I?

With a secret smile curving my lips, I twitch enough so I can rest my head on his shoulder without putting any distance between our bodies. A gentle rumble of a chuckle surfaces from him. He drapes a muscular arm around me bringing me even closer to his body. He brushes the briefest of kisses across my forehead and rests his head on mine; just like that, I'm completely at peace.

Chapter 5

Reluctant to move from the warmth and security of Victor's embrace, I rest my empty mug on my leg. I notice Jasmine nodding off, her mug leaning at a precarious angle.

"Jasmine. Jasmine," I repeat louder.

"Wha…what's up?" she replies sleepily, rubbing her hand over her face.

"Go to bed. You're exhausted."

"No, I'm okay…Actually, never mind, I do need sleep badly." Uncurling her legs, she slowly gets up, stretches carefully so as not to spill her now cold coffee, and shuffles into the kitchen to get rid of it, before heading upstairs with a tired groan.

I'm tempted to go up as well, but I don't want to move.

"I think I'm going to head up too," murmurs Kheda, around his hand, as he tries to smother a yawn. "I'll see you guys later."

"Sleep well, Kheda," Victor replies.

"See you later," I add around a huge yawn of my own.

"Come on, Candi, let's head up too. You'll feel better after resting, and so shall I to be honest." He slowly disentangles himself from me, stands up, reaches for me, and gently pulls me to my feet. We pass Kheda in the hallway as we head for the kitchen and he exits it. With a tired smile, we nod our acknowledgments, too exhausted for anything else. Putting our mugs in the sink to sort out later, I allow myself to be led upstairs.

By the time we reach my room, I'm practically asleep standing up. Every bone in my body feels extra heavy. I try removing my top, but my arms don't cooperate. With a weary sigh, I sit on the edge of the bed.

"Here let me." Smiling tenderly at me, Victor brushes my fingers aside. Leaving me in my bra and knickers, he puts me into bed and covers me with the blanket.

A second later I feel the bed dip, the blankets shift, and myself being drawn and tucked around a rock-hard body. A light kiss brushes across the top of my head, and with a contented smile, I fall asleep, secure in his warm embrace.

****

I slowly awake to the soothingly circular patterns being traced across my back. Victor's fingers barely skim my skin, yet his butterfly caress brings heat and desire rushing through my system at the speed of a freight train out of control. In languid motions, I return his touch, tracing my fingers along the ridges and valleys of his powerful chest.

I give his pectorals an open-mouthed kiss before sucking gently on his pebbled nipple. His indrawn breath echoes loudly through the room, his penis jumping to attention between us, brushing against my stomach and twitching in acknowledgment of his rising desire.

I reach between us and grasp him, giving a gentle

squeeze and a quick stroke. His fingers wrap around my hair a split second before he jerks my head back; his lips claim mine in a passionate kiss which leaves me reeling. Hooking my thigh around his waist, he dislodges my hand from him, moves my panties to the side, and enters my body in one swift thrust, impaling me before withdrawing and thrusting into me again.

Our tongues mimic our bodies' languid motions as they entwine and withdraw from each other. Our hands squeezing, stroke and caress each other in a mating dance of leisure and discovery. His taste explodes along my tongue, hot desert and spices, and something uniquely him.

Opening my eyes, I drink in his beautiful face. Passion and restraint are etched across it. As if feeling me watching him, his eyes open, flashing blazing blue fire, while only a hint of his beautiful silvery-green color remains.

As our gazes lock, he thrusts into me harder, and I writhe against him, rocking myself and impaling myself on him. My magick stirs as our pace increases, causing sparks of gentle heat to enter him. Pushing me onto my back, he thrusts into me faster, and for just a second I think I hear the thud of his heartbeat.

All coherent thinking leaves me with our increased pace as I get caught up in our mating dance, until I shatter in a powerful orgasm, my body convulsing, my vagina clenching around his penis, until with a final thrust, he roars his completion a split second afterwards. My body shivers and pulsates around him, milking every last drop from him. Sweat coats our bodies, and he collapses on top of me, gently panting, before rolling off me and pulling me on top of him, his hands stroking my back as he gives me the gentlest, emotion-filled kiss I've ever had.

"I'm falling in love with you," I admit, once we've stopped kissing long enough for me to catch my breath.

"Good, because I'm already in love with you," he replies, with a satisfied smile flickering across his face. "I've never known anyone like you, and I can't get enough of you."

I trace the contours of his beautiful face. "That's how I feel about you too. I'm not sure I like it because it makes me feel vulnerable. You could so easily hurt me, but denying how I feel about you isn't making my feelings disappear.

"And to be honest I don't want them to. I like how alive I feel around you. You make me feel powerful and desirable, special and protected. As if I can do anything and yet stay secure in the knowledge you will be with me if I need your help. And even if I don't."

With a slight snort of laughter, I shake my head. "I think I'm more than falling in love with you. I believe that train left a long time ago, I just didn't realize it. I am in love with you."

On this last declaration I give him a searing kiss. Slowly, I untangle myself from his warmth. Seeing his quizzical expression, I mutter a need for the bathroom.

Collecting a long cardigan, I draw it around me, exit my bedroom, and hurry into the bathroom. The moment I've closed the door, I burst into unexpected tears. In confusion, I shudder and cry. Collapsing onto the ground, I hug my legs tightly into myself, crying into my knees.

****

The door behind me opens silently, pushing me out

of the way, and then closes; instinctively my body tenses as I've never felt this vulnerable, sobbing this way, huddled on the bathroom floor. Unsure of why I'm even crying.

Victor's warmth surrounds me as he sits behind me. Taking me into his arms, he says nothing just embraces me. His legs encircle me as his arms drag me back into the hardness of his body, holding me securely to him. My thin cardigan and underwear the only barrier between us. His embrace is purely one of comfort. Bit by bit, my muscles release their tension, and my sobs turn into gentle hiccups and the occasional sniffle.

Still he remains quiet. With his chin resting on my shoulder and his front plastered to my back, I feel his warmth seeping into every part of me. Slowly, I become aware of the gentle rise and fall of his breathing. I find comfort on a level beyond my understanding, and I wonder if he knows I need to feel him breathing. For as a vampire, he doesn't need to.

I suddenly become conscious of Victor's scent surrounding me, warming me. His scent is intoxicating to me, like a drug, spice and desert heat. I'm wondering if I'm the only one affected, when I feel Victor's nose dip to the base of my neck where it connects to my shoulder, inhaling my scent. A groan of what sounds like agony rattles from his powerful body, just before his tongue snakes out and tastes me.

Licking a warm, wet path from my shoulder to just below my ear. A shudder of desire ripples through me, and I offer my neck to him. A moment later, his lips connect with my skin, gently kissing and sucking it before his fangs descend and slide into me. My blood rushes hot and fast to the sharp fangs, an eager offering to him, and with a moan my head lolls to the side resting on my opposite shoulder.

"Why were you upset?" Victor's voice resonates through my head, and with a start I realize he's talking to me telepathically.

"I don't know," I admit. "I think, I think it might have to do with admitting how I feel about you. As if now I've finally admitted it…"

"You're opening yourself up to getting hurt. But Candi, you can hurt me just as much, if not more."

I feel the truth in his statement. He sounds as vulnerable as I am, which leaves me feeling more confused than ever. "I don't understand. How I can hurt you more?" I reply out loud.

Extracting his fangs from my neck, he places a fleeting kiss on the spot before turning me to face him.

"Because, I haven't loved anyone in almost two hundred years, other than my family. Allowing you close. Giving you the power to do what you wish with me…giving you the opportunity to break my heart is bad enough. But if anything happened to you, I don't think I would be able to recover. I don't think I would want to go on," he admits, staring intently in my eyes so I can see the truth of his statement.

I also feel it, resonating throughout my body. As if it's a pledge, not just a statement. Reaching out to him, I reverently trace my fingers along the strong contours of his beautiful face, through his hair, and pull his face to mine so I can kiss him. Our kiss is slow and sweet, filled with an unspoken promise to cherish one another.

Pulling back from him I let out a sigh. "We have to go to London."

"What?" A frown furrows Victor's forehead as emotions shift lightning fast across his face. Puzzlement at the abrupt change of conversation, curiosity of why London, and finally his beautiful eyes narrow as his lips thin out into a straight line.

I'm surprised his full lips can flatten out so much, and wonder what on earth he's thinking for him to have this reaction. I decide to put him out of his misery.

"I don't know what conclusion you've come to, but we must go to London to search for the Prophecy. I've just remembered the scroll we found in the plaque. It said to go to where you saw it first. Earlier you told me you'd only seen the book of Prophecy once before, in London. So we gotta go to London," I say, waving my hands in front of me, as if showing my train of thought.

Chapter 6

Giving an amazing likeness to a fish out of water, he opens and closes his mouth, repeatedly. I've never seen him look so flabbergasted

With a snicker, I place a finger under his chin, and with a gentle push, his teeth snap together.

"Now I want to know what reason you thought I wanted to go to London for. And I want to know now," I carry on as I see him squirming, looking like he's trying to come up with some reason.

"To see Vincent."

"Say what? Vincent? Your childhood friend who killed your family? The Midnight Slasher Vincent?" Seeing the sheepish look on his face, I realize this is exactly who he'd thought I was wanting to go to London for.

"Are you out of your ever-loving mind? I don't even know him or want to meet him. I mean, come off it! Hold on a second. Why is he in London, and more importantly, why the hell would you think I was heading to meet him?" I demand, as my hands curl into fists. I refrain myself from strangling the annoying man. Mind you, could I really strangle him? He is after all already dead.

"Okay, do you remember when you first saw me in the woods?" he hastily asks, as he warily looks at my curled fists and my furious expression. At my grunt of acknowledgement, he carries on, "Well, I'd just found out Vincent was back in London."

I stare at him blankly. To be honest I have no idea where he's going, and I know I have a big question mark scrawled across my forehead. I can feel it.

Apparently, he catches on to my lack of knowledge. In a hesitant voice, he states, "I thought you knew."

"Knew what? Seriously, am I being really stupid here, or is this conversation just getting weirder by the second? Victor, I've never met Vincent or heard of him until you mentioned him. Well, obviously I've heard of The Midnight Slasher…" Waving my hands in irritated frustration. "What exactly did you believe my wanting to go to London was for?"

"Jamison informed me he was back in London and waiting for someone. So when you said you needed to go to London…"

"You assumed to meet him? Even though, when you told me about him earlier, it was pretty obvious I'd never heard of him?"

"I didn't say it was a logical conclusion," Victor mutters as heat tinges his cheeks.

"But Victor, I said we need to go to London. If I was going to meet him, why on God's green earth would I bring you along?" Letting out a huff, I look at him and shake my head. "You're damn lucky you're so cute otherwise…ahhhhhhh." Rubbing my hands over my face, I suddenly feel exhausted.

"Help me up, please. I need to go pee and my panties are giving me a wedgie." I mutter the last part but going by his amused look he obviously hears me.

He rises smoothly to his feet. His beautiful naked

body towering over me, one large strong hand reaches for me. I lick my lips, as a bolt of raw lust shoots through my system, leaving me gasping and quivering in anticipation.

My scent rises, and I detect the second he realizes I'm aroused. His fangs descend, and blue fire bleeds into his eyes, as his penis lengthens, becoming hard and thick. Twitching and standing proudly erect. I take his hand to leverage myself to my knees.

I release my hand from his before he can pull me completely to my feet; I grasp his penis firmly in my hand and give it a quick stroke. Leaning forward, I kiss and then slowly twirl my tongue around the tip as if it's a lollipop. Gently I suck on it and hear him groan in pleasure. His hand tangles into my hair as I slowly twirl my tongue around his width and suck as much of him into my mouth as I can before retreating.

My left hand cups his balls, gently squeezing and rolling them. My right hand holds onto the base and strokes the length of him. My lips and tongue move up his shaft. With a wicked grin, I glance up at him before getting back to sucking, licking, and lightly scraping my teeth along his length.

I increase the tempo, until with an animalistic groan, he shudders and shouts his release. With a final lick and a kiss, I release him and climb to my feet.

I watch him watching me through his blue fire vision, his powerful chest expanding and falling, his lips slightly parted, and his fangs elongated. He looks magnificent. Something primal in me awakens and the word "mine" reverberates throughout me as if I'm claiming him.

"You're mine," he growls, pulling me flush against

him.

I wonder what just happened to make us both become territorial. But as I drag his head down to mine I don't care why; I just want to claim him.

"And you're mine," I purr back before slanting my mouth across his. Our teeth clash and our tongues invade each other's in a kiss more of claiming and branding than of passion.

****

After kicking him out, I finally answer my body's need. Returning to my bedroom, I find Victor dressed and making the bed. I throw on some clothes, grab a note book and pen, and head downstairs. To be honest, I feel a bit weird. I've never felt so emotional toward someone before and especially not so quickly.

The fierce claiming kiss and the need for both of us to state our claim is bizarre and a little scary. But the howling need inside me to mark him, so anyone looking at him will know he's mine, terrifies me.

"I have a need to brand you," I blurt out. "It's clawing inside me, this uncontrollable demand I mark you, to show everyone you're mine." I feel the heat rushing to my cheeks in mortification at having admitted this internal calling, as if my wolf is howling her cravings to possess him.

"If it helps, you're not the only one." Giving me a wry smile, he takes a hold of my hand and gives it a reassuring squeeze. "My blood is calling for yours, a deep-seated need to be bound to you, for eternity. I knew I wanted you from the first time I saw you. What I didn't know is I need you with every particle of my being. You're my soul mate."

The word starts to bounce around inside me,

feeling like a siren's call on a gentle breeze. The truth of his words calm my inner wolf. And with a satisfied huff, she settles down, as if his admitting what she already knew is calming.

"Soul mates." Giving a slight huff of a snort laugh, I look at him. "Well, that explains the clawing need to claim you as mine." I laugh. "And why I felt so jealous when Sally touched you, even though you were unconscious. I wanted to tear her head off," I admit with a growl rumbling up from deep inside of me.

"Well, as you ripped her throat out, I do believe you solved the problem nicely," the cheeky sod teases me.

His expression at this declaration is one of such male satisfaction, I feel like pointing out it was self-preservation, not claiming, which caused me to kill Sally. Instead, I roll my eyes and leave our bedroom. I come to an abrupt halt. I can't believe I'm thinking of my bedroom, as ours. It's all happening so quickly. The sooner we go to London, the better. Maybe distance and neutral ground will help calm our territorial instincts.

"What's wrong, Candi?" he asks from directly behind me.

Without turning around, I shake my head. I'm acting erratically. With a tired sigh, I turn around to face him. I'm surprised how strained he looks. Tracing the angles of his face, I give him the barest of smiles.

"I need coffee and to come to terms about my feelings and just how intense they are," I admit. "Mainly coffee though." Reaching up, I give him a simple kiss, the barest brushing of my lips against his. I pull away before it deepens. Linking our hands, I lead him downstairs.

Entering the kitchen, I release his hand and rush to the coffeemaker. Thankfully Jasmine or Kheda had the foresight to clean and prepare it. I press the button to start heating the water, grab four clean mugs, and wait in anticipation for my first mug of energy.

I become aware of noises behind me. Turning in curiosity, I'm surprised to find Victor preparing what looks to be the makings of dinner. Before I can say anything, the percolator gurgles for my attention, and I eagerly turn back to it, pop a mug under it.

As the aroma of coffee fills the air, I watch in anticipation as my mug fills up. Once done, I change the pods and mug and press the button again. I remove the milk from the fridge and add some to my coffee before taking a sip. I feel the tension leave me, and I moan in pleasure as I move toward Victor.

"What you making?"

A small smile flits across his face before he answers me. "Lasagna. Feel better now you've had some coffee?"

"Getting there with every sip," I admit. "How do you know how to cook?"

"I trained to be a chef."

At this unexpected statement, I almost drop my coffee. "I'm serious, Candi." Victor laughs. "Is my coffee ready?"

"Huh? Yeah, hold on a sec." I quickly grab his mug, adding a splash of milk before handing it to him.

"What made you become a chef?" I demand, as I watch him put the dish into the oven and switch it on. "You don't preheat it?"

Turning to look at me, he leans against the counter behind him.

"My mum loved cooking. As a young man, I had no interest in it. Also back in those days, it was unnecessary for men to cook. It was the women's work. But I wanted to feel closer to my memories of her, so I learned. Now every time I do, I feel a happy connection to my past, as if for the length of time it takes to prepare a meal, my mother is with me. And no, I don't preheat the oven."

I watch the emotions of remembrance flit across his face. Love, fondness, sadness, pain, and eventually peace. Bittersweet emotions caused by making a meal.

Chapter 7

I'm on my second mug of coffee before I hear the sounds of movement from upstairs. I quickly make Kheda and Jasmine's coffees and bring them into the sitting room, to await their imminent arrival.

A few minutes later, their sleepy heads peek around the door. On shuffling feet, they enter the room and spy their salvation in the steaming depths of the dark liquid calling to them from the coffee table. I stifle a laugh but completely understand their reaction.

"What's cooking?" Kheda mumbles between sips of coffee.

"Lasagna. It'll be another forty-five minutes before it's ready though." A chuckle of amusement rumbles through Victor as he hears grunts of satisfaction at the idea of a delicious dinner and groans over the length of time to wait.

"Guys, we need to talk. We have to go to London," I interrupt, "and the sooner the better."

"London? Why?" Jasmine demands in confusion.

Quickly, I explain what Victor told me and remind everyone about the parchment. "So basically we need to search for the Prophecy in London."

"You're right; you need to go to London. I can't go though," Kheda informs us.

"I think I should stay behind too," Jasmine adds. Seeing my mug pause midway, she probably senses my surprise as she adds, "We called our sisters in arms. If they arrive to find us gone, they won't be impressed, and I wouldn't blame them. I'll stay but the two of you should go."

"It'll probably be easier with just the two of us," Victor agrees. "Especially with Vincent in London. If a group of us arrive searching for a document, it could hinder instead of help us."

"Okay, if you're all sure. I'll try and see how soon I can book flights…"

"No need, I'll sort it out," he interrupts. Satisfaction practically radiates from him as he rises to his feet. "I'll be back soon. When I return, dinner will be ready," he adds, before swiftly kissing me and leaving.

I stare in confusion at the others. "What just happened?" I blurt out.

"I have absolutely no idea," Jasmine admits.

"If dinner is ready when he returns, I hope he comes back soon as I'm starving." Kheda groans as his stomach lets out a grumble of discontent.

****

Forty-five minutes later, we're eating the best lasagna I've ever had the pleasure of eating, and Victor has informed me we're leaving for London first thing in the morning. I don't know if I should be in awe at the speed of his sorting out the flights and hotel or pissed off at the unexpectedness of just how quickly it's all happening. I know time is of the essence, but I haven't had time to take it all in. I feel like I've jumped on a train that is suddenly speeding along faster than I want, and I can't jump off. I'm not used to feeling so out of control, and I don't like it.

After dinner, Kheda insists on tidying up, and Jasmine insists on helping me pack. Victor advises I bring clothes I don't mind getting ruined and dark clothes for any surveillance or nighttime unethical searching. His words, not mine. I just hope we don't get caught or arrested.

An hour later, I've packed for London, so I start unpacking some of the boxes in the sitting room. The ones containing the TV and video player and a box containing films. As none of us have any inclination to do anything, we opt to take it easy and watch a couple of movies before going to bed.

The next morning, we leave for the airport. Kheda and Jasmine are in Kheda's car so they can see us off, and Victor and I are in mine. To be honest, I feel like I'm going on holiday, more excited about going away than thinking about what we're going to be doing once we arrive. Probably a good thing. I'll get battle ready once there. We park in the short term car park, grab our bags, and meet Jasmine and Kheda by the elevator. As a group, we head toward the airport entrance.

****

It's her. What is she doing here, and where is she going? Why is the vampire with her? Does he never leave her alone? I must calm down, I must think. Should I follow her and find out where she's going? I wonder if she knows just how beautiful she is. When I tell the council, she'll be no more. She'll be ashes in the wind.

****

I feel like I'm being watched so I casually glance around.

"Sisters, we're here."

49

With a start I look at Jasmine. "Did you hear them?"

"Yes."

Excited, we head over to where passengers are coming out of duty-free. A minute later, twin sisters Nancy and Selene Holden exit the gates. For a zombie, Nancy looks brilliant. To be honest, you would have never known if you hadn't been told. Both are five foot seven, have blond hair, and porcelain skin. Nancy had been killed in action and her sister Selene, a powerful necromancer, brought her back. For some unknown reason when Nancy woke up, her blue eyes had turned brown.

Vivian Dwight was just behind them. A petite five foot, she has short brown hair and emerald green eyes. She looks delicate and as if butter wouldn't melt in her mouth. She is in fact a lethal werewolf, with a short temper and a razor-sharp brain.

Felicity McCormack, Talia Thompson, and Jezebel O'Malley exit behind a group of tourists following Nancy, Selene, and Vivian. The three of them are striking and turn a lot of heads.

Felicity has mousy brown hair and turquoise eyes. Rosebud lips, large breasts, and an hourglass figure. At five foot six, she is stunning. She's also a witch with exceptional powers.

Talia, or T.T. as we all call her, is also a witch. At an impressive six foot, she has a lean body, pale blue eyes, high cheekbones, full lips, and her jet-black straight hair comes to the middle of her back in a luxurious sheet. Her caramel skin sets it all off, giving her an exotic look.

Jezebel, at five foot eight, has cocoa-brown hair,

golden eyes, and lily-white skin. She's a beautiful jaguar shifter, tough and stubborn as hell. You don't want to get on her bad side.

We rush over to them as they exit the gates.

"Oh my god, I'm so happy to see you all," I screech as I throw my arms around Nancy and Selene.

"It's so good to see you. How's Jas…"

"I'm here, and it's great to see you all too," interrupts Jasmine as she gives a beaming smile to the group.

"Jasmine, oh my god, you're okay," Vivian squeals as she practically throws Nancy out of the way so she can hug her.

"I'm fine, thanks, Viv. I'm glad you're all here."

"Who's the wolf? And is that a vampire? I thought they were just a myth," Selene asks me. Curiosity and just a hint of bewilderment laces her voice, as she nudges me in the side and nods toward Victor.

"I'm glad I'm not the only one who thought so." I laugh. "The wolf is Detective Kheda McKnight, and the vampire is Victor Harlow and my partner." I feel my cheeks heating up at admitting my relationship with him. I'm not embarrassed, it's just I've never been one to date. I've always kept things simple, uncomplicated, and unemotional. No chance of becoming attached or hurt.

"Say what?" gasps Nancy, turning to stare at Victor before giving me a big grin. "Nice, he's seriously hot."

"And I can hear you," he mutters as a blush heats his cheeks.

"Damn, I didn't know they could blush," laughs Vivian.

"How about we grab a coffee and catch up? Victor

and I have a flight to catch. We're going to London."

"Hold on. You're off to London, so why did you drag us here? I skipped bail to get here," demands Jezebel. A scowl of annoyance furrows her brow, her vision narrows, her lips thin out, and her hands curl into fists.

"Let's grab our coffees, and we'll explain everything. We do need you all here. And what do you mean, you skipped bail? What did you do?" I demand.

"It doesn't matter. I'll go back once this is sorted out. It is good to see you all. I've missed you and Jasmine."

We order our coffees, then find a quiet corner and catch everyone up on what's been happening. Sipping my coffee, I glance curiously around me and catch sight of a man quickly looking away. A frown of uncertainty furrows my brow. I recognize him from somewhere, but where? I look away as if he hasn't caught my attention and shift my body minutely, so I can see him from the corner of my vision.

He looks about thirty-five. Has short chocolate brown hair, tanned skin, and a broken nose. I can't see his eyes, but he has strong features, hard and determined looking. A distinctive scar slashes across his face from the corner of his eyebrow in a jagged cut down to his chin, making him look more ruggedly handsome and dangerous. He's an impressive-looking six foot five inches. His body is strong and muscular in a lean package. For some unexplained reason, he is watching Jezebel, though not in a friendly way.

"This is why we are heading to London now. We have to find the Prophecy. Jezebel, do you know the man to your five o'clock? He's been watching you."

"What? Oh damn. He is persistent. I'll give him that much," grumbles Jezebel.

"Who is he?"

"Well, you know I said I skipped bail to come here? Anyway he's a bail retrieval agent, otherwise known as a bounty hunter. And a damn good one too." Disgust laces her voice even though a gleam of excitement sparks in her, causing her to sit a little straighter and her nostrils to flare.

"You're right; you do need to go to London. We've hired two cars and will follow Kheda and Jasmine. If you need us, let us know, and we'll fly to London to help," agrees Vivian with a decisive nod of her head. "We'll also keep a watch on Jezebel's man, though he can't do anything here as he has no jurisdiction. Mind you, he doesn't look like the type to allow it to bother him."

"We best be going, Candi. It was nice to meet you all, and we'll see you when we get back." Standing up, Victor picks up our bags and rests his hand on my shoulder.

"I'll see you soon, and I'm so happy you all came. Be safe and keep an look out for, well, anything really," I add. Standing up, I link my hand with Victor's. It's only when I hear muttered exclamations of "bloody hell" I realize I've surprised everyone except Jasmine and Kheda by this simple contact.

I've never been one to show affection with a man before. Even something as simple as holding hands is completely abnormal for me. Or was, and yet holding hands with Victor causes me pleasure and contentment. Why on earth did it take me so long to open up and allow myself to be happy? With a quick smile of contentment and a warm fuzzy feeling in my stomach, I allow him to lead me to the departure lounge.

Entering customs, I mutter a concealment spell on the luggage containing my weapons and clothing.

Nothing to see,

Nothing to detect,

Ignore the metal,

Ignore the weapons.

Even the metal detectors won't detect them now. I calmly walk over to the customs scanning belt, place my bag in the tray supplied, with my shoes, belt, coat, and purse before walking through the metal detector. Quickly, I retrieve my stuff, once they've passed through the scanner. I put on my shoes, belt, and coat. A minute later, a sexy vampire joins me.

He quickly gets ready, and we enter duty-free. We wander around aimlessly, just wasting time until our flight is ready to board. Scanning through some books, I select a paperback I haven't read before and buy it. We grab a coffee each and queue up with everyone else for our flight. Ten minutes later, we're boarding the plane.

Chapter 8

An hour and a half later, we arrive in London. We quickly collect our luggage and hurry through customs. Victor is practically growling at the slowness of our fellow passengers by the time we exit the airport and collect the car he's hired for us. I'm trying to stifle my laughter. I sober up quickly when I remember Victor's vampiric brother is here or was a month ago.

"Are you okay?" I ask as I climb into the car he's hired. Butter-soft leather seats envelope me as I relax into the passenger seat. I turn to look at him and feel lust shoot through me; god, he's gorgeous.

"I'm good, just anxious to find the Prophecy." His head drops slightly, and I watch him take in a breath before admitting, "I'm also hoping we don't run into him. I have no idea what he would do, and it worries me."

Putting my hand over his for an instant, I give it a gentle squeeze. "Whatever happens, we'll deal with it together. Let's get to the hotel and then head straight to…where are we going?" I can't believe I've only just realized I have no idea where we're going to look for the Prophecy.

"The Black Rose Bar," he replies. A sigh whooshes from him, sounding like a deflated balloon. "It's where I was with my sire when he showed me the Prophecy."

"Oh," I grunt for lack of anything else to say. My

eloquence and lack of brain function doesn't surprise me. All I can think about is what he had told me happened next. A shiver ripples through me as a cry of "murder" reverberates around my head. Could Vincent really be the Midnight Slasher? Glancing at the vampire beside me, I hope he isn't. It must be bad enough believing his friend and vampire brother is a serial killer, but surely he must hope he's wrong. Hope somehow Vincent is innocent.

Silence descends on us. I stare out the passenger window, drinking in the sights. London is beautiful. The old buildings mixed in with the new blend together surprisingly well. Soon, we pull up at a town house in Durward Street.

Seeing my puzzled expression, he informs me, "Durward Street was called Buck's Row in 1868. The Black Rose Bar is a little further down the street. This is my London home." He nods toward the house we're outside of, before climbing out of the car. Victor has a house here? Oh my god, Buck's Row is where Penelope Adams died! On this final thought, I feel the blood leaving my face as I exit the car.

"Did you live here when she died?" My question barely manages to squeak past my suddenly dry throat.

"No. I bought it about sixty years ago, I think." Unlocking the car boot, he turns to me as I come up beside him. "Every time I came to London, I went to the Black Rose Bar and eventually decided to just buy a place I can stay at when here. It works out easier for me in the long run."

A breath escapes my body I didn't know I was holding. For some reason, I'd thought he was living here when the Whitechapel murders were happening and had a horrible thought of Vincent killing the women to frame him.

"Why do you keep coming back here?" I ask.

What would make someone keep coming back to the place of such a dark history? A history he had lived through and still reverberates around the streets of Whitechapel. A place of dark secrets which holds them within its grasp never letting them go. Where the ghosts of the past are living, haunting the area in their anger and fear. Whitechapel is literally cloaked in cloying evil.

Yet strangely, the people have brought a light back into the place, breaking through the oily darkness in patches and spurts. Seeing an oily shadow slide along the road coming in our direction, I reach into the boot, grab our bags, and encourage him to get the "damned door" open.

"What's wrong with you?"

"Can't you see it? Never mind. Just trust me when I say we need to get inside fast!"

Observing the shadow's progress, I barely take time to acknowledge Victor's surprise and confusion at my reaction.

I do notice him giving the general direction I'm watching a curious look as he hurries to the front door, runs his fingers down it to unlock it, and ushers me inside. I'm just grateful that though he apparently can't see the shadow, he trusts me enough not to ask questions and just react to my urgency. Mind you, we have been through a lot in the short time we've known each other.

Chapter 9

As the door closes firmly behind me, I'm positive I hear a squeal of anger from the other side. Seeing Victor's sudden stumble as he whips his head around toward the door so fast I'm surprised he doesn't give himself whiplash, I'm guessing he heard it too.

"What the bloody hell was that?" His voice sounds more like a harsh croak than his usual velvety tones. His eyes have gone so large and round in his head they look like beautiful golf balls. I notice blue fire leaking into them, reflecting his emotions.

"It was an oily shadow." Seeing the blank look on his face, I continue to explain, "Basically an oily shadow is the evil essence left behind of a soul; a dark spirit."

"What the fuck is a dark spirit?"

"A dark spirit is a spirit of great evil. Well, mainly they're spirits of great evil. People that committed crimes so horrific they have become a stain on the world after their demise, unwilling or unable to move on. Other times, they've been called back to Earth by a powerful witch to do their bidding."

Moving further down the hall, I arrive at the sitting room, where I drop our bags beside the leather sofa. Looking around, I take in the simple but comfortable furniture. "But if the witch or coven isn't powerful enough to hold the spirit, it can escape and look for a body to take over."

"What do you mean by mainly spirits of great evil?"

"Sometimes they were people who were sacrificed for magical means. Sadly, it's more common than you'd think or hope. If they were powerful enough and angry enough, they can lose themselves in their anger and pain, and then they become a dark spirit."

"Christ, how do you stop them? Wait, you can stop them, can't you?" he demands, glancing back toward the front door with a shudder.

"Sometimes. You have to know who the spirit was to do so. Where they were buried and then salt and burn their bones. Strangely enough, it's one thing the ghost stories got right, how to get rid of ghosts."

"Probably so non-magickal people can learn how to protect themselves," he mutters in reply.

Giving him a quick smile, I silently agree it was most likely the reason. It's not as if a witch could reveal herself to get rid of the troublesome spirit without putting her own life in jeopardy. After all, in parts of the world today, witch-hunts still happen. "So what's the plan for today then?" I ask, happy to change the subject, and at the same time genuinely curious about what the plan is.

"We'll head down to The Black Rose Bar. Sunny, the owner of the bar, is also the archive keeper. He'll allow us to search for any reference to the Prophecy. Though I have to admit, organizing is not his forte so…"

"So I shouldn't expect it to be easy?" I interrupt. I had hoped we would just find the Prophecy straight away without any hassles or searching.

"No, definitely not easy, though we can always hope." A chuckle escapes him, his beautiful eyes crinkling at the corners.

With a grunt of disgust, I shake my head at him. "You're lucky you're so damn cute, or I'd leave you to hunt for it on your own!"

Throwing his arms out dramatically, he extends his right leg, before sweeping into a lavish bow. "My lady fair, how you wound me with your cutting remarks. Wouldst thou really abandon me, to search yonder dusty volumes on my own?"

I can't help myself. I burst out laughing. I can feel my face turning bright red as I try to control myself. My side is beginning to ache, and my laughter is turning into a wheezy sound, like deflating bagpipes. Completely cringe-worthy. With a snuffle and a snort, I manage to get myself under control, until I look into his twinkling eyes, which sets me off again. Five minutes later, I'm taking deep breaths and refusing to look at him.

"Come on, wheezy, let's take our bags upstairs." Picking up our bags, he leaves the sitting room with a big grin on his face.

"You look like you're the cat who got all the cream," I call after him, shaking my head in amusement, before following him. My only answer is the sound of his rich laughter floating down the stairs and doing the tango with my nervous system. For just a second, I let it wash over me. I give myself a shake, and hastily climb the stairs.

Looking around the bedroom, I realize there are no personal items to be seen.

"Why do you have nothing personal here if you

live here?"

"Because this isn't my permanent home. I just use it as a base when I'm here."

Looking at him closely, I wonder if there is more to the reason than he's telling. Mind you, if there is, he'll tell me when he's ready.

With a slight shrug of his powerful shoulders, he admits, "I don't like staying here."

****

London. She's somewhere in London. Or at the very least, it's where she flew to. I must find her. I must protect her. Protect her? Of all the supernaturals, she's the last one who needs protecting. But when *The Protectors* find out she's alive, they'll need to know where she is. So I must follow her to London. But then what? I don't know where she was heading...Unless she's gone to Whitechapel.

Storming over to the check-in desk, I impatiently check my watch and wonder how long I'll have to wait before I can follow her. Glaring at the assistant, I growl my demand for a change of flight before shoving my boarding details at her. "I need to change my ticket for London."

I notice her suppressing a shudder as she accepts my pass. Then quickly types something.

"The next flight isn't until tomorrow at six a.m. Would you like me to go ahead and book you a seat?"

"Yes, unless there is another flight on a different airline leaving sooner?"

"Sorry, sir, this is the only one leaving from Cork Airport."

"Then book it!"

****

Twenty minutes later, we walk into The Black Rose Bar. Intricate black rose patterns are engraved on the oak wall paneling, bar, and tables. Glancing down at the floor, I notice them there too. Sconces in black and gold illuminate the bar in warmth. If a Victorian man or lady suddenly appeared, I wouldn't have been surprised.

Customers are scattered about the place. A group of wizened-looking old men glance up at us as if assessing our worth, before putting their heads together to discuss their findings. We cross over to the bar, where a huge muscular man is busily cleaning a glass.

Blimey, he must be at least six foot seven, and I'm positive his muscles have muscles. His dark hair is shaved closely to his head, flattering the planes and angles of his features, though I have a feeling it's not his intention. When he finally speaks, without looking up at us, I'm surprised how deep and gravelly his voice sounds.

"What can I get you?"

"Two pints of lager and two packets of pork scratchings," Victor answers, leaning casually against the bar counter.

"Victor, me old mate, how you been? And who's the bird?"

"Bird...?" I splutter before being hastily interrupted by Victor.

"I'm good, thanks," he answers, resting a placating hand on my arm. "Sunny, this is Candi. Candi, this is Sunny, owner of the Black Rose Bar and keeper of the archives."

Sunny looks me up and down, taking in every inch of me, as if testing my mettle. When I feel tendrils of power prodding against me, I give them a bitch slap of mental power. I do not appreciate the intrusion, something Sunny realizes quickly when he flies back several feet smashing into the back of the bar.

Bottles and glasses tremble, and some tip over and smash around him. His expression is comical, and I restrain myself from laughing at him. He reminds me of a floundering fish out of water, his jaws gaping and closing, his eyes bugging out of his head. It's Victor's quiet "Ah, crap" which keeps my mirth from escaping though.

Leaning over the bar at Sunny, I give him a baleful glare. "It is rude to prod at people to test their power," I growl. "Don't do it again." Then with a click of my fingers, I right the fallen bottles and glasses. Making everything as it was before Sunny had smashed into them.

"Holy shit," gasps the fallen man in surprise. "Shiiiiit. I've never seen anything or felt anything like you before. What do you need?"

"We need to look at the archives," Victor informs Sunny, smothering his surprise before it can properly form.

Hmmm, he's surprised Sunny is willing to help. Is it because of my telling him off or something else?

"The archives?" Sunny drawls before looking at me thoughtfully. I give him a bland look back and just watch him. "Okay. Sure, why not? Are you looking for anything in particular?"

I catch sight of myself in the mirror behind the bar. I'm surprised to see a faint violet shimmer staring back. I pull my power back tight inside of me and watch the color change back to normal. I see Sunny blink in confusion as if unsure if he'd seen anything. Giving him another bland look, I answer with a simple grunt. My eloquence holds no bounds.

"Okay. I'll get your order first before showing you the archives. It'll be thirsty work, and you won't be allowed in with liquids."

He quickly supplies us with two pints and two packets of pork scratchings. With a final curious look at me, he gives the bar a quick swipe with a wet cloth, before heading around the bar to collect empty glasses from the tables. I watch the old men give curious glances toward us, then start gossiping amongst themselves again.

Spotting a pool table, I head over and rack up, before breaking. I then quickly line up and shoot a couple of balls in the pockets, before passing the cue to Victor. With a startled look at me, he accepts, and we start playing. By the end of the game, I'm feeling pretty relaxed and by the looks of him, so is he. A pint and two games later, we're relaxed and ready to start hunting for information.

Collecting our empty glasses, we head to the bar and then follow Sunny out the back to the beer garden. He leads us away from the tables where a couple of customers are drinking and smoking. A loud grating laugh bursts from a woman in a red dress, making me wince. There's nothing friendly about the laugh, no joy or pleasure in it, only malice and coldness.

He takes us up a flight of concrete steps to a door. Instead of pushing on it, he presses on an intricate black rose built into the wall, before turning it to the right and releasing it. I watch in fascination as the black rose twirls around, unfolding its petals until it's blooming.

Then the door swings inward, and we follow him into a corridor.

Once I pass the threshold, it swings shut behind me with a thud of finality. Nothing creepy about that! Especially when sconces lining the walls suddenly flare into life, illuminating the way.

The smell of must and dust assails my senses. My nose twitches. A high-powered sneeze zooms out of it sounding like a demented rabbit on steroids. Completely humiliating, especially with both men laughing at me. I give them both a stink-eye glare. I'm just grateful nothing escaped with the sneeze.

We continue down the corridor, bypassing rooms on the left and right until we turn right at another corridor. How big is this place? The corridor suddenly descends. If I'd been wearing heels, I'd probably have fallen flat on my face. As it is, I manage to catch myself by grasping the wall and Victor's strong shoulder to steady myself.

The floor is at an almost thirty-five-degree descending angle toward the flat surface it was previously. With another sharp right turn, we come before a huge black iron door, again made with intricate black roses. Sunny grips two of the roses and turns them toward each other. Their petals unravel, and the door swings open.

As we step through, I realize we've entered a large empty room. The door shuts behind us, and slowly wood-paneled walls of deep mahogany with the usual rose design appear. Next, a large table in the same wood and design, with two sturdy desk chairs in black leather and wood placed in front of it. And lastly shelves of scrolls appear. This room is literally an archive with thousands of scrolls. I look around drinking in everything that is illuminated by the sconces which are still appearing. With every new sconce appearing, the larger the room grows, the more shelves and scrolls on them appear. I've never seen anything like it.

"You can stay here as long as you need to, and you can come back as often as you like," Sunny informs us. "At the back of this room is a door. It'll lead you onto the street. You can come and go through there.

"Only thing is, you can't take any of the scrolls away with you. Even if it's the one you're looking for. Here's a key." Passing Victor the key, he gives us a warning look before leaving. As the door opens, everything goes dark only to appear again after it closes behind him.

"Hmmm, now that is interesting magick," I mutter. Catching Victor looking at me, I flash him a small smile. "Just thinking out loud. We can use it as a warning system if need be. Why was he so insistent about not taking anything? We're after something that belonged to your sire that he wants you to have."

"True, but it won't be here. Only a clue to where we should look next will be here."

"Yeah, it makes no sense to me at all," I grumble, before looking around and wondering where the hell to start.

Chapter 10

Heading over to the first set of shelves, I'm relieved to notice they're dated. Noticing the date reads 563, I delve further into the archives to search for 1868. About halfway through, I find the section we're searching for.

"What's our timeline, do you reckon?"

"Probably from 1868-1870 at the very latest, but if we haven't found the information there, then we'll have to look further," Victor informs me as he scans the amount of scrolls in front of us. "Our best bet is to work together shelf by shelf. This way we won't miss anything, hopefully."

I grab the first scroll and turn around to take it to the table. Coming to a sudden stop, I'm dumbfounded to find the table and chairs directly behind us.

"Wha...okay, handy but creepy. I'm not sure if I should be impressed or just plain spooked," I admit to Victor. Seeing his expression of befuddlement and uncertainty, I'm guessing he's feeling similarly to me. As strange as it seems, my apprehension eases significantly enough for me to sit down. "What exactly are we looking for?"

"I'm not sure, but it's probably a cryptic message about Penelope Adams's murder. As it's when I saw the book of prophecies."

I carefully unroll the scroll and scan it for anything

to do with the murder. Finding nothing, I roll it back up and return it to its place, select the next scroll, and sit back down. Three hours later, I'm feeling stiff, hungry, and badly in the need for a bathroom.

"I need a break," I admit.

With a nod of agreement, he finishes scanning the scroll he's reading and puts it away. We gather our jackets and head out the back door. It closes with a slam of finality. Walking back to his house, we go inside to freshen up.

I hurry to the bathroom to wash the dust and grime off my hands and face. Next I grab my wallet and camera and then head downstairs to meet him and notice for the first time he looks worried.

"You okay?"

"Yeah, I'm fine. It's just I can almost feel how close we are to the answers, and we're looking for a clue we could easily miss." Rubbing his hands over his face and then through his hair, he gives me a look of uncertainty.

"Victor…"

"I'm not sure if we're on the right track, searching the right place. I…"

"Stop worrying. Look, if there is a clue in those scrolls we'll find it. If there isn't, we'll hopefully find out soon enough. Whatever the case though, there's no point doubting yourself or our search. The only thing we knew when coming to London is somewhere in Whitechapel there is a clue. So let's take time out. Get some food. Maybe sightsee a little. Then if there's time, we'll carry on searching today, if not, we'll get an early start tomorrow."

Grabbing his hand, I drag him to the front door.

Once he's run his fingers down the door to open it, he gestures for me to go first. I sense someone watching. I can't see anyone though. Shaking my head, I exit. Covertly glancing around, I think I see a shadow move in the alley, but I can't be sure. Turning to Victor, I quietly ask him if he can see anything in the alley.

"What alley?"

"What do you mean, what alley? The one right across…" I'm in midpoint as I turn back toward the alley, except there isn't one there. My hand drops like a lead weight to my side. I stare at the house which stands where a moment ago an alley was.

"What the flipping hell?" I mutter in confusion. Did I imagine it? Turning a fierce look on Victor, I growl out in pure frustration, "It was there! I saw it as plain as…"

"I believe you."

His simple words ease the tension building inside me. I release my breath in a puff of relief. With a final look back at where the alley should be, I turn away.

"Let's get some food. We can check it out later once it's dark." Closing the door behind him, he looks down at me, gives me a reassuring smile. I see curiosity in his glance before his gaze flicks up in the general direction I'd pointed to a moment ago.

With one last glance, we head off to find some food. Between one step and the next, something shifts. A faint luminous violet line appears before me. Like a single thread, it runs in the middle of the path.

"Do you see it?" I demand of Victor in a hushed voice.

"See what?"

I feel him looking at me. Looking at him, I incline

my head toward the path. "The luminous narrow line, right there." I point to it as if it will help. "I think we should follow it."

"I can't see it," he replies in an apologetic tone, "Lead the way though. Obviously, it's something visible only to you or at the very least, one of your magicks."

With a nod of agreement, I follow the thread. It runs along the path and with each step I take, it becomes brighter and thicker. Almost as if it was unsure if I'd follow. At the end of the street, the line arrows across the road to the left and around the corner.

I hurry after it only to be yanked back. A car horn blares, the driver hanging out the window shouting obscenities and gesturing madly as he passes me.

"Watch the road, dick-wad, before you crash," I holler back. Hearing a groan from beside me, I barely have time to glance his way before the car comes to a screeching halt.

Victor grabs my hand and drags me across the road. "Where to next, Candi?"

"This way, sorry about that." I hurry around the corner with my hand still firmly held in his larger one, as if he's reluctant to release mine. I hear a shout of, "Oy, you," but I ignore it and continue to follow the thread.

A rough hand suddenly grabs my shoulder dragging me around. A snarl curls my lips, and I glare at the driver who I'd almost walked in front of earlier.

"Let. Go!" I growl. A rumble rises from inside of me. Victor swings around to face the man. His fangs are descended, and blue fire blazes bright around his pupils. The man doesn't notice the vampire he's angered as he's already retreating. With a huff, I turn around to follow the trail and notice it's dimmed a bit. Once I start to follow, it brightens.

Eventually, we arrive at Highgate Cemetery just in time for it to close. My feet are killing me. I'm hot, bothered, and starving. I'm feeling rather peeved the bloody glowing line didn't let me know it would be easier to drive. The worse thing is, Victor looks completely unruffled. Not even a bead of sweat!

The annoying glowing line is pulsing through the closed gates, making me feel more aggravated than anything else. It's just five o'clock. Though it's getting dark now, it's still too early to try climbing over the wall to follow the insistent line.

"We have to get in there," I mutter to my companion so no one else can overhear me.

He gives me a sidelong look, then a sharp nod of his head in answer. "We'll come back later. Let's get something to eat and then go back for the car."

I must have had a look of dread on my face. Not surprising really as I want to groan my unhappiness at the thought of the walk back.

"We'll take the underground back, don't worry. I'm in no hurry to make the walk anytime soon if ever," he reassures me while placing a warm hand on my lower back, rubbing gentle circles.

His comforting hand quickly brings desire rushing through my body. Biting my lip, I try unsuccessfully to control my emotions. How can he possibly cause such an intense reaction with a simple touch? I can't help biting my lip at the sight of him when I finally look at him. His eyes are warm, almost like heated silver in a green fire. His lips parted slightly, nostrils flaring as he breathes in my scent. Liquid heat burns its way through my system, pooling between my legs. Suddenly, I find it very hard to breathe or think…

Next thing I know, I'm dragged away from the cemetery and rushed to the nearest underground station. A few minutes later, I'm trapped in a corner of the tube by Victor's muscular body. I lean slightly into him inhaling his scent like it's going out of fashion. He is intoxicating. Sensual. Divine. I let my hands run up his torso and wrap them around his neck before slowly bringing his head close to mine.

"Bank Underground Station," a disembodied voice announces.

We quickly disembark and hurry to the next station to catch the tube. Twenty-five minutes later, we're in a corner shop paying for some groceries. I've barely exited the building before I tear into a prepacked sandwich. On the walk to Victor's house, the only sounds I make are groans of happiness. Once devoured, I throw my empty packet into the nearest bin.

"Better?"

"Much." I flash him a grin, link hands with him, and lean slightly into him as we stand in front of his door. While he opens it, I do a cursory look around, concentrating on the invisible alley. Another thing we'll need to check out. Damn, this list is growing!

Once inside and the door closed securely behind us, we head for the kitchen to unload our purchases. Filling up the kettle, I switch it on to prepare some coffee.

"We need a plan of action," I blurt out.

Pausing in emptying his bag, he looks at me and gives a nod of agreement. "Yes, we do. Every time we look around, something new to investigate pops up."

I watch in bemusement as he abruptly leaves the kitchen, only to return a couple of minutes later with a pen and pad.

"Okay." Pen paused over the paper, he looks at me expectantly. "Graveyard and archives."

"Mystery alley…source of the dark spirit. Ummm, can't think of anything else for here."

"So far, it does cover it, I think. So tonight's priorities are the cemetery and the archives. If we have time, then the alley too. The cemetery and the alley will have to be after midnight."

"Agreed. Why don't we have a quick break and then go back to the archives. You have the key to the back door. Hopefully, we'll find a link to the cemetery."

An hour later, we re-enter the archives. Heading straight for the section we were working on, we continue our search.

A number of scrolls later, Victor pauses in his search. "Candi, look at this."

Leaning over him, I look at where his finger is resting on the scroll and start to read. Drawing in a harsh breath, I read it again. "Bloody hell!" I exclaim in disbelief. "Is this definitely true?"

"If it's written in here, then yes, it's true."

"Fucking hell! A supernatural massacre. How did I not hear of this? I mean, this is huge." I sit down on the nearest chair, shaking my head. I'm completely dumbfounded.

"I think it was a cleansing. With everything going on with the Midnight Slasher, it seems *The Protectors* came in and did a sweep, getting rid of hundreds of supernatural creatures in one swoop."

"Jesus, it explains why Whitechapel is such a hot spot, and the dark spirit…Christ, there could be more…" I feel drained suddenly. I rub my hands up the middle of my face, then outwards and down toward my chin again, creating a heart shape pattern. "What else does it say?" I ask, leaning forwards and resting my elbows on my knees and cupping my face in my palms.

"The massacre happened just before the Midnight Slasher's final murder. It caused a magical backlash. Apparently for three days and nights after, a vortex appeared…"

Straightening up in my seat, I turn eagerly to face Victor. "Did it create the alley?" I demand in excitement.

"I'm not…Hold on, the entrance was sealed up. There were rumors of people appearing suddenly before disappearing just as quickly."

"Blimey. I wonder when the rumors stopped or if they still continue?"

"Not sure, we'd have to search later documents to find out. Mind you, since you saw someone appear in an alley, the vortex must still be usable, just spelled."

"Hmmm, I wonder if it's a controlled vortex. Either witches or werewolves, since I saw it and you didn't. Or if it's simply a time factor. After all, when I looked again to point it out to you, it was gone." I feel a headache gathering in the middle of my forehead and rub gentle circles around it, trying to ease the tension.

Looking at him, I can't help a slight smile flickering across my lips. The concentration on his face is endearing. I've never seen him look so serious, confused, and intrigued before. His emotions are flickering across his face lightning fast, battling for the dominant position, until finally curiosity wins.

"We really do need to check it out," he mutters so quietly under his breath I almost don't catch it. "I think we should check out a few more documents, see if we can find out any other information about…Well, anything at this stage."

"Okay. Once done though, we go grab a drink and then go back to yours, have sex like bunnies, and get ready for a little late night adventure."

A burst of laughter escapes Victor, startling me out of my thoughts.

"Have sex like bunnies?"

"Yeah, quick and fast. We won't have a lot of time," I mutter back feeling the heat of my blush bloom from my toes to my hair roots. My headache intensifies from the heating of my skin, so not good. For a second, I feel queasy until my blush reduces, easing the pain.

"Sounds like a plan," he murmurs shooting me a smile so hot I feel my bones liquefy.

A shiver of desire ripples through me. My lungs feel restricted. My heartbeat accelerates. I feel out of control and want to pounce on him. Rip his clothes off and devour every last glorious inch of him. I hear a rumbling growl coming from me. What the hell?

"Candi, you okay?" Concern laces his voice. He reaches a hand out to touch me. No way can I let him touch me. I'm barely hanging onto my resolve as it is. Quickly shoving the chair I'm on backwards, I manage to tip it and me onto the floor. With a crash, I land painfully on the floor, and my breath exhales in a loud puff. My head bounces off the floor, and sanity returns. What the hell was that!

"Bloody hell, Candi, what's going on? You're beginning to scare me." Crouching down toward me, one hand extended to help me, yet unsure after my behavior if he should. He looks a mixture of baffled and worried. Kinda the way I'm feeling now I'm coming back to myself.

"I'm okay. Well, I should say I'm okay now," I admit, rubbing the back of my head gently from where it cracked on the floor. "I have no idea what just happened," I reluctantly admit.

"You weren't yourself, were you?"

"No." Shaking my head, I reach out tentatively to grasp Victor's hand so he can help me untangle myself from the chair and stand. When nothing strange happens and I don't attack him in a lust-driven rush, I breathe a sigh of genuine relief. I don't like feeling so uncontrolled. As if someone else was controlling my actions. It's weird and extremely unnerving.

"I'm not sure what happened," I admit. "It was as if cravings of intense lust had overwhelmed me, but they weren't mine."

"Could you have been possessed?"

I almost laugh at him as he looks around with a worried frown on his face. Was he expecting a lust shadow was going to wave at him? I stifle my laughter and think seriously about his question. Could I have been possessed?

"No, well…I'm positive I wasn't. Don't get me wrong," I interrupt him before he can say anything. "Something other than me was in charge, but it felt more like a memory of a lust-driven need instead of being taken over by something. Does it even make any sense?" Shaking my head at my own question, I glance down at the ground and see the dust covering me.

Bending to brush off my clothes, I spot the document Victor had been reading. A word catches my attention, epithumia. With a trembling finger, I point to it.

"What exactly happened during the massacre?" I demand as I stare in horror at one simple word which changes everything.

"What is it? What have you noticed that has spooked you so badly?"

"Epithumia means lust. Lust and a massacre is black magick of the worst kind. This is big as in epic disaster big. Fuck!" In agitation, I start pacing the aisles until he grabs hold of my shoulders and drags me to a stop.

"Breathe."

I take in great gulps of air. With each inhale and exhale, I feel calmer. My brain goes from panic station to clarity. Closing my eyes, I center myself. Once more feeling calm, I give him a grateful smile.

"Thank you." Our gazes lock. He searches mine for something. Whatever it is, he apparently finds it, as with a nod of his head he releases me.

"Okay, how about you read this document in case you spot something else I missed? I'll make notes of anything you find.

I sit down to peruse the document. Nothing else jumps out at me. I exchange it for the next document. Scanning it, I spot what I'm looking for.

"Victor, the bodies were cremated, and their ashes were taken to Highgate Cemetery. Jesus, they dumped them all in a single grave. It's all written here.

"The desecration of the unnamed was an

unfounded attack on the supernatural community. The brutal rapes, torture, and murders were excused as a cleansing for the crimes of one. An entity known as the Midnight Slasher. The Slasher has been proven to not have been amongst the masses. The nameless ones were further violated by being burnt to ashes and thrown into a mass grave in Highgate Cemetery. A marker of no name is the only telling of this darkest deed in supernatural history since the hunt for the Warrioress Daphmire Janna. What you seek holds the answers in the past."

My blood runs cold, and a shiver rakes through me. Such brutality noted down in a couple of sentences. A very simple description without describing anything at all, yet a clue imbedded in the words. Who was the Warrioress Daphmire Janna? Is it her past that holds the answers?

"A Daphmire Daphmires do exist?" exclaims Victor in surprise. His expression becomes thoughtful. I wonder if he's thinking the same thing I am.

"Who was she, I wonder, and did they ever find her?" I decide to ask instead of wondering what he's thinking. "Do you think it's your sire who wrote this?"

Looking at me, he gives a sharp nod. He copies the document, returns it to the shelf, and collects the next one. We both scan it for any information. Finding nothing else of interest, I return it.

"I don't think we'll find anything else which will help us here tonight," Victor informs me from behind, making me jump. "Sorry, I thought you heard me coming up behind you."

"No, I was miles away, and also thinking along a similar path as you. Everything is leading back to the cemetery and the alley."

"Let's go. Do you want to go back to mine and go through the notes, or go for a drink?"

"To be honest, a drink. We can always go through the notes if you feel a need to when we're getting changed. Though I doubt it's necessary."

Chapter 11

I chase condensation down my pint glass. Leaning back into the chair, I'm relieved to take a break from the searching. My mind is going crazy. So many answers lie in the past. A past we don't even know about. I feel like I'm following a trail of breadcrumbs. Only thing is great patches of the trail are missing. How can so much history, violent history, be buried? If it weren't for the archives, there would be no record. All those deaths would be unknown...

Taking a sip of my pint, I look at Victor and realize he's also deep in thought. What a pair we are. Glancing around the pub, I notice a couple of customers watching us. The pub is full and noisy; our quietness shouldn't have drawn any attention. Gently kicking him under the table to get his attention, I roll my eyes in the direction of the couple and quirk an eyebrow at him. Hoping he understands my silent question of "Do you know them?"

Picking up his glass, he looks above my head for a split second, takes a sip of his drink before looking back at me, and gives his head a tiny shake as he returns his drink to the table. For a minute, I'm confused how he knows by looking over my head, until I remember the mirror on the wall.

"So where do you fancy visiting tomorrow?" he enquires suddenly, startling me. "If you want, we could do some sightseeing and maybe go to the museum?"

"Sounds good. If we have an early start, we could miss the main rush," I helpfully add, noticing our watchers are listening to our conversation. I wonder who they are and what they want.

We have a discussion on everything touristy to see in London and what we want to view first. All the while, we drink and pay attention to the customers. Once finished, we get up and leave. Outside, we turn right instead of going left to his house. We take different roads until eventually we end up at the back of his house. If anyone tried to follow us, hopefully they didn't succeed.

Quickly, he runs his fingers down the back door to unlock it and ushers me inside before closing it behind him. In darkness, we exit the kitchen, pausing when we see the shadow of a person through the glass of the front door. Silently, we climb the stairs and change our clothes.

I put on my favorite hunting clothes. A plain sports bra, knickers, socks, vest top, cargo pants, and knee-high boots. Every item of my clothing is black as I don't want a bit of color to stop me from blending into the shadows. I add my knives in their different sheaths and my guns into their holsters before throwing on my jacket and add plasters and my phone to my pockets, and I'm ready to go.

Victor is also dressed all in black. His cargo pants hug his narrow hips and embrace his muscular legs. His t-shirt clings to his torso, and I want to tear it off him. He's wearing those comfortable trainer boots again and a black leather jacket. Damn, he looks delectable.

"Keep looking at me in such a way, Candi, and we

won't be going anywhere."

His velvety rich voice washes over me. My heartbeat kicks up a notch, and I feel heat traveling through my veins. God, I want him so badly.

"Do you know what you do to me when you look at me like that?" His words come out in a growl. Walking swiftly to stand in front of me, he grabs my hand and presses it to his erection.

My hand instinctively curls around him and gives his penis a quick stroke through his clothes. In fascination, I watch him throw his head back and listen to a moan of pleasure ease out of his throat. His powerful chest rises and falls. His gaze locks with mine and shines with blue fire. His jaw parts slightly, and his fangs peek out. I give him another stroke, and a decadent growl ripples from him. Desire pools into liquid heat between my legs. My body is ready for him. Just a shame we don't have time to indulge.

As if reading my mind, he gently removes my hand and kisses my knuckles. "Later, I will take you. Possess you. Claim you. And make sure you know you're mine. And I am yours!" His words are as much a promise as a threat, and I don't care.

His right hand slips around the back of my head and drags me willingly to his descending mouth. Our breaths mingle as his fangs scrape across my bottom lip and our tongues entwine. Just as quick as our kiss starts, it's finished. With a promise of later, we leave the bedroom, descend the stairs, and I collect a container of salt from the kitchen before we leave.

Chapter 12

The darkness is like a cloak hiding us from everyone, allowing us to blend into the shadows. Silently, we creep around the wall surrounding Highgate Cemetery. Finding a section of the wall with a tree overshadowing the area, we opt to climb over. Using it as camouflage to keep us hidden. Before descending into the cemetery, I pause and sniff the area, letting my wolf dominate my senses. A couple of streets away something rustles. Otherwise, all is quiet.

I slip down the tree and land quietly beside Victor. He looks to me and, with a slight indication of his hand, lets me know I'm to lead. I take a quick glance around. I spot the glowing thread near the front entrance and start to creep toward it. As if it senses me, it suddenly vibrates, reminding me of an excited puppy, grows brighter, and swiftly moves away from the gate and toward the older graves.

I follow the bright thread deeper into the cemetery with Victor directly behind me. We pass crypts and a tree with headstones surrounding it becoming a part of the tree. Until we descend into the bowels of the cemetery. Darkness so black overshadows a single headstone, broken and forgotten hidden away amongst the many.

The luminous thread circles the stone, the only light in the deep dark. I walk slowly toward it to read the name on the headstone. A blank space where nothing was ever written is all I see. I remember the words from the document: a marker with no name. We've found it, found the forgotten ones, in a cemetery of many where no one remembers them. In the darkest of shadows, whether the night protects them or hides them, which I'm not sure.

Taking a deep breath, I center myself. Concentrating on the unmarked headstone, I slowly walk in a circle around it pouring salt as I go. Victor is standing quietly inside the circle I'm drawing, looking more like a statue of a warrior than a man. Once I finish the circle, I pass him the now-empty salt container before I move to stand in front of the headstone. Placing my left hand on the cool stone and my right over my heart, I lace my words with power,

"Forgotten ones, you are no more.

The past is meeting the present.

Knowledge hidden within your depths is needed now.

Let the truth come forth.

It is time."

My circle of salt turns violently green. Shades of purple bleed through it. Bursting flames roar high into the night sky and flicker over the headstone, disintegrating the shadows cloaking the area. A high-pitched whine escapes from the ground, erupting with a shriek of anguish. The spirits of the dead, hundreds of them, stand before me showing me their final moments on earth. Their rape and torture, so much pain and anguish. Until finally they die. I bear witness to it all as tears slide down my cheeks unchecked.

"Witness who feels, what you seek you shall find.

The clues are scattered in the past. Go to the Falls of Paradise, and search the Desecrated Ones' house. In the wall, you will find an answer to a question not yet asked. There is no more for you here. Follow your path, and you shall find the secrets of your past and the answers to your future."

Between one blink and the next, the spirits are gone, the flames die, and silence surrounds us.

I stand still, hardly breathing as I just stare at the spot where the ghosts had stood moments before. There is no darkness attached to them. No peace either, caught in limbo between pain and peace. I drag in oxygen to my deprived lungs. It's only then I notice the salt circle has sunk into the earth.

"Well, that's something you don't see every day," a cool voice states from the shadows of the crypts behind us. Whirling around in the direction the voice came from, I'm confused to see a tall dark-haired man leaning back against the nearest crypt. Arms folded across his chest, ankles crossed loosely in front. The awareness and strength coming from him belies his relaxed pose.

"Who are you?" I demand, I glance at Victor and am surprised how still he is. Not a muscle twitches in his face or body. Yet I know at a bone-deep level all is not right.

"I'm Vincent, love. My brother not tell you about me? Tsk, tsk, Victor, where are your manners?" I catch the underlying edge of anger in his voice. So this is the vampire who is Victor's oldest friend, who possibly is the Midnight Slasher. Something niggles in my brain. I glance from Vincent to the nameless grave behind me, then back again.

"You weren't the Midnight Slasher, were you?" I ask feeling puzzled at my certainty. At my question, both vampires give me startled looks. Victor looks stunned at my statement, yet a look of hope resides just under the surface of his expression. While Vincent...his expression is blank. I can't read anything from his face, but the sudden stillness and focus in his body tells me I'm walking a dangerous line.

"Now why would you say that?" His question holds an edge so sharp and pointed to it. If it were a real weapon, it would slice and do damage.

I look at him, my head cocked to the side and let my double magick see him. In that second, I know I'm right. I also know, for whatever reason he's letting everyone believe he is a mass murderer, it is a deadly secret. I blink, breaking my observations. Incline my head at him in acknowledgment. His startled gaze holds mine for a split second, enough time for me to see a burgeoning hope before it's ruthlessly squashed.

"Who are you? Or maybe I should ask, what are you?"

Ignoring his question, I ask one of my own. "What do you want?"

"Nothing, love. I came to see my brother. Heard he was in town. Been a long time since we were in the same place at the same time. Ay, Victor?"

As if breaking from a trance, he shakes himself and looks between Vincent and me. "How did you know where I was?"

"Some folks let me know."

By the way Vincent said the word "folks," I'm guessing they're not people he likes. I wonder if it was the watchers from the pub earlier.

"How did you know where we were?" I demand. We'd checked to be sure no one followed us.

"Well, love, I made sure I kept my distance. You are very sharp and cautious I must admit. You don't make things easy on a vampire to sneak around."

"You were a couple of streets behind us?" Thinking about the noise I'd heard before climbing down from the cemetery wall.

"You heard me? I did notice you didn't answer my question earlier. What are you?"

"She's none of your business, Vincent." The words come out on a growl reverberating in threat from Victor. I'm surprised, until I remember he believes Vincent's a serial killer. Now his brother being curious about what I am isn't helping the situation.

I move forward until I'm standing shoulder to shoulder with Victor, link fingers with him, and give them a gentle squeeze. I feel the tension ease from him as he squeezes my fingers back. His thumb rubs circles around the inside of my wrist. A gentle caress which ignites inside my blood.

"Well, now. Don't you too look all cozy. Good to see you, Victor, and you too, love. Though I'm still waiting on your name, even if you won't tell me what exactly you are." I notice his attention strays to the grave behind me and back to me again. What makes him so sure I'm not just a witch?

"Candi Reynolds, and I'm a witch hence the magick." My tone of voice has a note of exasperation in it. I jerk my thumb in the general direction of the grave behind me.

"Oh, I gathered that much, but no ordinary witch could call up those particular spirits. Many have tried.

So what makes you so special, love?"

"Bloody hell, will you stop calling me 'love'!" I explode. "Maybe the ghosts knew I meant them no harm. Maybe they had their own reasons. Whatever they are, hopefully I'll find them out. It doesn't mean I'm...What exactly do you think I am? I mean, you must have an idea, love, because you keep harping on like an old woman determined to gather gossip!"

Silence prevails after my outburst, until both vampires throw their heads back and roar with laughter.

"I like her. She's a feisty one you got for yourself, Victor." Shaking his head in amusement, Vincent pushes off from the crypt he'd been leaning against and strolls forward. His pace is languid, all power and control.

They even walk alike. Both walk like big panthers, powerful and deadly. I wonder if they realize just how similar they are to each other.

As he moves away from the crypt, I get a good look at him. He looks similar to Victor. Both are tall with dark hair and are muscular and gorgeous. Vincent's eyes are a naturally bright clear crystal blue. A shade which can be both as warm as a summer sky or ice cold as an arctic winter, depending on his mood. The coldness from earlier has gone, leaving amusement and a slight longing when he looks at Victor only to be quickly hidden.

He misses him. I wonder what led him on this path of needing others to believe he's a psychotic killer.

"You best go before someone realizes you're searching for answers most want kept hidden," he informs us with a slight smile curving his lips. "We'll meet again, soon, so don't be worrying about me." A disheartened chuckle escapes from him, unwanted, going by how quickly he clamps his mouth shut. Walking around us, he moves toward the grave, gives it a minute bow, and then walks off without a backward glance.

I turn back from observing Vincent to find Victor watching me.

"You okay?" I ask him as I search his expression.

"He's not…"

"Let's go home," I hastily interrupt him. God knows who might be listening in, and for whatever reason Vincent needs to keep the truth hidden, it has to be important.

Chapter 13

We don't check out the alley. I don't even think about it to be honest. My mind is whirling with what I've found out this evening. Unsure what it means. Except somewhere in Paradise Falls, there's a place that holds a clue. My mind flickers on Jasmine's house. The destruction willfully done to it. A gasp of surprise escapes from me as I realize how close we'd been to the answers; if only we knew.

"We have to go home," I whisper urgently to Victor.

With a nod of agreement, he flits us back to his house. Once more, we enter through the backdoor.

He has just closed it behind him when I pounce on him. My lips latch onto his as if superglued. My hands start getting busy dragging off his jacket and then his t-shirt, my mouth releasing his long enough to pull it over his head. My hands explore his beautiful chest, tracing lower until they latch onto his belt.

"Easy, Candi, easy." Easing me back, he locks gazes with me and searches for something. A sigh escapes him when he realizes it's just me being horny. Maybe he thought the lust entity, or whatever it was, was back.

"Victor," I growl, "I need you now!" On these words, I strip off my jacket, top, and bra. Before I can unbuckle my trousers, Victor's hands take over. Three minutes later, my legs are wrapped around his naked waist. My back presses against the kitchen wall, and he's thrusting into my welcoming body.

My body's need for release is building quickly. My arms wrap tightly around him, my muscles tensing, gripping him everywhere. I scream my release into his shoulder and sink my teeth into him, drinking the blood which escapes. I feel him shudder his completion into me, and in turn he sinks his fangs into my neck. As he drinks, my body vibrates, building up to another powerful climax. For a second, my vision blurs. I feel as if I'm half in this world and half in another. Everything around me looks gray, as if I've stepped into a shadow world. A world where supernaturals are presently being rounded up by masked cloaked figures!

"Ahhh." Startled, I try to jump back, forgetting I'm wrapped around Victor. I smack my head off the wall directly behind me. I'm not sure how he manages to keep his balance and not throw me on the ground. I'm still clinging to him like a monkey; my heart is pounding out of control. Not in a good way anymore though. Looking around, I'm relieved to see the shadow world has gone.

"Candi! Candi, answer me!"

The desperation in his voice penetrates my brain. With a shake of my head to clear it, I look at him. The concern and terror on his face is surprising. I stroke a trembling hand along his cheek.

"I'm okay," I try to reassure him. Seeing his doubt, I'm obviously not doing a good job of it. "I'm okay now," I amend with a bit more steadiness in my voice.

"What the hell happened?"

I try to unravel my legs from around his waist, until

one of his arms wraps around my waist in a steel band, the other grips my ass forcing me to still. His only relenting is to walk to the kitchen table, hook a foot around one of the chairs, pull it out, and sit down.

"What happened, Candi?" His gentle tone soothes me. Taking a deep breath, I explain what I saw.

"It was your house, but not as it is now. The furniture was new but not from this era. Going by the clothing, I think it was 1868. Victor, they were being collected, and their fear was intense. I've never seen anything like it before," I say with a shudder. "I felt so helpless, and I couldn't tell if it was even real or not."

"You saw death in the hospital. Maybe your powers are growing, evolving, so to speak." The thoughtful look on his face and tone of voice he uses makes me pause.

Could what I'd just saw really have happened? Could I change anything? Do something to help?

"There's nothing you can do to help them," he informs me. "No, I can't read your thoughts, but your expression says it's what you're wondering. You have to remember it has already happened."

"Okay, what if I could interact though?"

"Could you?"

"How would I know? I've never tried before. After all, one minute I'm having an intense orgasm, and the next I'm in 1868 and supernaturals are being rounded up by masked cloaked strangers." Shaking my head, I look at him and admit, "Trying to interact was not even in my thoughts. I wanted out. I was scared."

I feel shameful about my admission. I try to unravel myself from Victor, which he prevents by simply tightening his embrace.

"Let me up, Victor!"

"No. Not yet, Candi. You have nothing to feel ashamed over." Determination laces his voice. As if the force of what he's about to say can be drilled into my head. "I don't know anyone who wouldn't be afraid, not even counting the issue of being suddenly thrown back in time," he reassures me. Leaning forward, he kisses the tip of my nose, cheekbones, eyes, and finally my lips. A gentle no-passion I'm-there-for-you kiss.

Leaning away from him slightly, I give him a twist of my lips in an upward direction. As a smile, it's all I can manage for now. My emotions are calming down. My brain is beginning to register the truth in what he says. Though part of me wonders, can I interact with the shadow world, and if I did, what would be the consequences?

"I…"

"I'm taking you to bed now. We'll get some sleep and get an early flight home. We need rest. It's been a long day, a weird-as-hell day to be frank. All I know is the spirits told you to go home, and I'm inclined to do so. We can always come back another time…"

"Okay."

"Okay, that's it? No objections?"

"No." Laughter bubbles out of me. I've managed to leave him looking flabbergasted at my simple agreement. "I agree. Yes, there are things here to check out. Though they may be important, finding the Prophecy is our reason for being here and…I want to know what the spirits meant," I admit.

I climb off him, collect my clothes from the floor, and head upstairs. A second later, he follows me, his clothes bundled in his arms. We clean up and crawl into bed. Once more, I'm curled up in his embrace. His arms wrapped securely around me. I feel safe. Secure. And then nothing.

****

You must run, Janna. You know you're in danger. Protect yourself. Run!

"Never. I am a warrioress. I do not run! I fight! I conquer, and I will kill any who try and murder me or mine." Janna growls, flashing her canines at the man in front of her. "Vlasim, you know I can't abandon my mother. Why do you presume I will just because you ask?"

Shaking his head, he looks sorrowfully at the warrioress in front of him. "Janna, the council has ordered your death. They've wanted you dead from before you were born. Have tried to kill you and your mother numerous times. I don't know how either of you are still alive." Walking away, Vlasim gazes out the nearest window. "Janna, you are an anomaly. You shouldn't be alive. The council fears you, now more than ever."

"Why?" Janna growls in frustration. "I have been told this all my life, but never why."

"Vampires cannot have children. Yet you are a child of a vampire. Daphmire, they call you, child of a witch and vampire. An anomaly. A curse in their minds. It is the Prophecy they truly fear though."

"What Prophecy, Vlasim?"

"The one your mother predicted before you were born. You are the first but not the last. From you will begin a new linage. A Double Magick one will be born and from whom a Triple Magick one will come, and then there will be two. And *The Protectors* will be no

94

more."

"What the hell does that mean? Stop talking in bloody riddles!" Janna shouts shocking herself and Vlasim.

"It means *The Protectors* will hunt you and all related to you, until they stop this Prophecy."

"Vlasim, I am a warrioress. I will not have children. I will not…"

"You already have though."

"Yes, but surely they are safe. They must…"

"No, Janna. Your children were smuggled away. Separated from each other. For if one of them has a child, your line will continue. If both have children…"

****

I awake with a squeak. Holy cow. Janna! The Warrioress Daphmire Janna! I'm related to her? Fuck me sideways. Vlasim, could he be V?

"Wake up, Victor," I holler at him in agitation. I need to talk about this turn of events, badly! "Victor, wake up," I bellow, making him jerk awake.

"What's going on?" He pounces off the bed, fangs extended to fend off any threat. His body is in attack mode, a lethal naked warrior.

Oh my. Concentrate! Shaking my head to clear my thoughts, I quickly reassure him there is no threat. "Sorry, no one's here except us. I had a dream or a vision of the past…" I trail off, confused as to how to finish the sentence. What exactly was it I had?

"You had a what? There is no threat?" Straightening up, he rubs his hands over his face and hair making his hair stand up on end. "Okay, why did you wake me up?"

"Yeah, bear with me on this. I'm not sure how to

explain it. I think I had a vision of the past. The long, long gone past to be more exact."

"What? Okay, how about we get dressed and grab a coffee, then you can explain."

Letting out a relieved sigh, I dress and follow a now-clothed Victor downstairs. Ten minutes later, we're sipping coffee at the kitchen table, and I've just finished telling him about my dream.

"Holy shit!"

"That's all you got?" I demand, trying desperately not to laugh at the pure shock on his face. Silence greets my question. The complete silence in the kitchen becomes almost deafening in its intensity. I just start to fidget, when at last he speaks.

"I honestly don't know what to say. I've never heard of anything like what's happening to you happen before." He looks at me with a little smile playing at the corners of his lips. "You're truly unique, amazing. Mind you, I will have to work on your idea of a wakeup call."

A splutter of laughter erupts from me at this statement. I wish I could disagree with it. "Do you think it was your sire she was talking to?"

"Yes." I watch him stare into his mug, tapping a tuneless rhythm on the table with his fingers, while collecting his thoughts. After what feels like ages, he looks up at me and continues, "We know he wrote in the documents, since he mentioned Janna. We also know he was the keeper of the Prophecy. It makes sense he knew her. What I want to know is exactly how he knew her mother."

"Do you think he was her father?"

"Maybe. No, not really. I think he knows who her

father is though."

I look around the kitchen, pick up my mug, and wash it in the sink. I don't know what to think or do, for that matter. I feel confused. So much information or pieces of information are being thrown at us. Like puzzle pieces with parts missing and other parts from a different puzzle altogether.

"You okay?"

Warm hands turn me around to face him. An elegant finger lifts my chin, so we can look at each other. I can't help the smile which lifts the corners of my mouth, curling my lips ever so slightly. A soft gulp emits from Victor. His attention zeros in on my lips. I watch as blue fire bleeds through his silvery-green eyes and his pupils dilate. His fangs drop from his gums protruding over his bottom lip.

My lips feel dry; my tongue escapes to moisten them. The growl rumbling through his powerful body turns me on instantly. I lean forward to kiss him. Our faces a centimeter apart. I can almost taste him.

****

"Protect them at all costs! I will not allow my children and mother to suffer because of this group, these *Protectors*," Janna growls.

****

"What the fuck! Really?"

"Candi, speak to me. Where the hell did you go?" Worry laces Victor's voice. His brow furrows in concern. The look in his eyes is pure fear.

"I'm okay…"

"You were gone! It's not something I've ever seen. You were literally here one moment, then gone. Vanished!" The harshness in his voice surprises me.

97

I hear the fear, uncertainty, and awe in his tone. Though it's the helplessness in his face that calls out to me. I'm about to reach out to him to reassure him I'm okay, when his words penetrate my brain. "You were literally here one moment, then gone. Vanished!"

"What the hell is going on? How is it possible I disappeared?"

"I don't know, and I like it even less. What happened?"

"Janna again. It was just a quick glimpse. She was in armor. She was yelling at someone to protect her children and mother at all costs. That's it."

"You're bearing witness to her story. The spirits called you 'witness who feels.' Maybe they meant it in more ways than we could have imagined. Maybe..." I watch as he starts to pace in apparent agitation. His walk is jerky and unlike his usual fluid gracefulness.

"Maybe what?"

Shaking his head, he turns to look at me. "I don't know. To be honest, I have no idea how to finish the sentence. I feel helpless to be completely honest, and I don't know how to handle it. I'm not used to caring enough to feel..."

"Feel what?" I barely whisper the words. I badly want to know the answer to my question.

He comes to a standstill in front of me, and practically spits the word at me. "Fear, I feel fear for you. Raw, helpless fear. I don't like it. I can barely handle it. The thought of you being in danger and I can't help you drives me crazy..."

"I understand if..."

"I will protect you," growls Victor interrupting me with his words and by slicing his right hand forcefully through the air. "You aren't making it any easier by disappearing. The only comfort I have is you are more than capable of taking care of yourself. I've never known anyone with such inner strength, never mind your magickal abilities.

"I care about you. I love you. And I need you to be safe. If anything happened to you—" Shaking his head, he turns slightly away from me, breathes deeply before turning back to me and admitting, "I don't know what I would do if anything happened to you."

My vision fills up and spill over with silent tears. My bottom lip trembles and emotion clogs my voice as I admit, "I love you too."

I've just barely got the words out before his lips cover mine in a gentle, emotion-filled kiss. A kiss filled with love, fear, and hope. I never knew a kiss could transfer so many emotions, yet I feel every single one of them and so many more.

Chapter 14

It doesn't take us long to pack and head to the airport. I spell my weapons once more and breeze through airport security, thankful I don't have another Janna episode as I'm starting to think of them. Blimey, trying to explain them would be…weird.

"Do you want a coffee?"

"Ooooh, yes, please." My mouth instantly waters at the thought of coffee. While he goes to get us some, I decide to ring Jasmine. Let her know we're coming back.

****

I can't believe I can't find her. If she hasn't gone to Whitechapel, then where the hell did she go? Pacing in agitation, the killer glowers balefully at The Black Rose Bar. He'd been watching the entrance for the last day. At one stage, he'd been positive he'd caught a sight of her red hair exiting from a different door. But it was such a quick flash he was unsure if he had seen her or just wished he had, either a possibility. He couldn't keep this up much longer. His watching was beginning to cause attention, attention he didn't need or want.

****

"Everything's fine. I'll explain when we arrive," I reassure her. "Yes, of course Victor's coming back with me. Why on earth would you think…" I snort a laugh bubbling out of me. "No, I didn't shag him into the ground; get your head out of the gutter!"

"What? Who didn't you shag into the ground?" the man in question asks with laughter in his eyes, passing me my coffee.

Ignoring his question, I carry on with my phone call. "Look, I was only ringing to let you know we're coming back today…Uh huh, never mind. We should arrive home at one o'clock. Can everyone meet up for then?" Taking a sip of coffee, I listen to Jasmine as I casually look around the airport. "I'll explain everything in person. Okay, thanks, we'll see you all then."

Hanging up, I switch off my phone and put it in my pocket. We pick up our carryon bags and walk toward our departure gate. I feel on edge, expectant. Waiting for something to happen, anything and everything. I don't know what, just something. Maybe it's because we're on our way to get some answers. Now we have a starting point to begin our search from.

Our flight is called; I throw my empty coffee cup into the nearest bin. I hand over my ticket and passport to the stewardess. Once stamped, I retrieve them and follow the line of passengers waiting to board the plane.

Finally, we've boarded. I store my bag, and belt myself into my seat. I watch the steward give the safety directions and let my eyes rest for a second. I must have nodded off. Next thing I know, I'm being nudged awake; a familiar sexy voice is encouraging me to "wake up."

"I'm awake, mmmm," I drowsily reply, reaching a hand out to pat the hand rocking me.

"Candi, we're here. Come on, babe, wake up."

"Here? Mmm yes, yes, I'm…oh." My eyelids

spring open; I look into the amused gaze of my sexy lover.

I glance around, flush bright red when I realize we're the last on the plane, the stewardesses barely holding their polite smiles as they wait for us to leave.

"I'm so sorry," I mutter in mortification as I scramble out of my seat, collect my bag, and follow him off the plane. We go through customs, collect my car, place our bags in the boot, climb into my car, and belt up. I indicate I'm pulling out. Three minutes later, we're exiting the car park and on our way home. Thankfully, the trip is uneventful. I'm just pulling up to my house an hour later when…

****

The clash of swords rings in my ears. The screams of the dying echo and flow amongst the raging battle. I see Janna twirl around, her sword whistling and slicing through the bodies in her way. Her movements are fluid, strong, and sure. She reaches out for a falling body, bares her fangs, and sinks them into the strong neck of the fallen warrior. Drinking in his rich warm blood as his heartbeat slows. She thrusts him away, letting his large body fall backwards, toppling over, and crashing with finality, into the bloody ground.

****

"Fucking hell!"

I'm startled to find myself sitting on Victor's lap. The car is inches away from the porch. Jasmine, Kheda, and the others who'd apparently come outside to greet us are scattered. Astonishment written on their faces. Curses flying from them.

"Whoops," I mutter the understatement of the year.

"Really? 'Whoops' is what you come out with after

scaring the shit out of me and everyone else," growls a dangerous voice in my ear.

"Ehh, sorry? Look, it's not as if I…"

"I know, I know. It's just…" His sigh reverberates through his chest; his breath whispers soft flutters past my ear.

Climbing out of the car, I call out sorry to everyone as they pick themselves up off the ground.

"What the hell is going on? You were driving the friggin' car right up until you disappeared," demands Jezebel, fury and worry battling equal measures for supremacy in her voice and expression. Dusting down her leather trousers, she gives a disgusted snort when she notices her boots have a scratch.

"It's one of the things I need to tell you all about…"

"This has happened before?" demands Vivian.

"Yeah, just a couple of times. Granted, I wasn't driving at the time…" I trail off. "Look, let's get inside, and we'll explain everything that's happened, okay?" I don't wait for an answer. I collect my bag from the boot, pass Victor his, then close and lock the car. I head inside, glad to be back and hoping like crazy I have no more journeys to the past. Though admittedly the last one was kinda awesome. Janna was/is such a badass!

I've barely stepped inside before I'm being dragged into the sitting room, shoved into a chair, and ordered to talk.

I tell everyone what happened in London. About Janna fighting in the last vision. By the time I'm finished, I feel tired. Unsure of what's going on and more importantly how to stop the disappearing act the visions are resulting in.

"Where do you go? It sounds like you're viewing Janna, not being her."

"I am. It's like I'm standing right beside her. I'm able to see, smell, and hear everything. Though no one has sensed me there, it's a really weird feeling to be honest."

"Can you interact with anything?" inquires Jezebel, curiosity lacing her voice. She turns from her position at the window to face me. Clad in black leather low-riding pants, a leather corset shows off her toned midriff, giving Jezebel a fierce yet elegant look, especially with her five-inch-heeled ankle boots. I have no idea how she walks in them, let alone fights in them. She can also run in them, for miles! Her long dark hair is pulled off her face, and the curiosity in her voice is echoed in her glance, though a contemplative look is there too. What is she thinking?

"I've no idea to be honest. It happens so fast, trying to pick something up is the last thing on my mind."

"Maybe you should try next time. I'm curious to know if this is something you're only able to see or change," she admits, before turning back toward the window.

"To be honest, I'm curious too, though the problem there is if I can change anything, it could be dangerous…"

"You might change something you're not meant to," adds Kheda.

"Exactly, it could be something as simple as trying to pick up a glass and knocking it over by accident. Say the drink was meant to revive someone or kill them. They would either be dead or alive by my simple action. Then the ripple effect would happen."

"Bloodlines that should have ended or continued… Okay, maybe you shouldn't try interacting," agrees Jasmine with a worried look on her face.

"How much damage can she really do?" enquires Vivian curiously from where she's lounging on the sofa.

"Viv, were you not just listening?" demands Nancy in exasperation.

"Yes…"

"Well, there you go then. How would you like to not be alive? Knowing your luck, it'll be your bloodline which accidently gets wiped off the face of the earth," adds T.T. with a wicked grin on her face.

"Enough already, guys. I'll try not to touch anything if I can help it," I mutter in exasperation.

Felicity looks around at all of us, bursts out laughing. "Blimey, knowing your luck, Candi, you'll probably trip over your own feet and wipe out all of our bloodlines." Apparently finding this thought completely hilarious, she starts snorting in mirth. Trying to gain control of herself, she gasps in air before falling into further convulsions as the other girls join in.

"I'm not that bad." I huff, trying desperately not to remember my worst accident-prone moments.

"Sure you're not." Jezebel laughs. "Do you remember the time you fell down the stairs only to land on your hands and knees in front of…"

"All right," I hastily interrupt before she can continue. My poor cheeks are heating up at the memory. I try to ignore the curious looks on Victor's and Kheda's faces.

"You were saying?" enquires Victor while watching me.

"Ah, yeah it doesn't matter." Taking note of the furious glare I'm shooting her way, Jezebel hastily changes the subject. "So you said something about ruins and finding something in them?"

"Yes." I'm relieved at the change of subject, especially as it's a change we need to address. "I believe the ruins mentioned are Jasmine's house."

"Well, why don't we check it out now. We can grab torches and search." T.T. looks around at all of us. As no one objects, she nods her head, stands up from where she'd sprawled herself on the ground, and walks out of the sitting room.

One by one, everyone follows her out, collecting jackets and torches. I collect two spare torches and pass them to Victor and Kheda. The girls have brought their own with them. Like me, torches are part of their traveling kits along with weapons and hunting clothes.

Chapter 15

Three hours later, I'm covered in dust, peering at a barely visible infinity symbol in the wall of the upstairs bedroom. I reach out a finger to trace the symbol, unsure if I should, yet the temptation and certainty I need to do so drives me forward. A reverberation vibrates through me the moment I touch it. The wall shimmers before me as a purr of yes echoes in my head. A scene unravels as if I'm watching an old movie.

****

A man and woman rush into the room. Fear makes them hurry to the wall they had previously built in readiness for the box the woman now clutches to her chest. Placing the box containing the item they promised to keep hidden into the space, they cement and build a new wall, placing an infinity symbol on it. So those meant to find it, will.

They'd sent their daughter away days before due to the unrest amongst the neighboring witches. Being a shapeshifter on the border of the witches' woods has become too dangerous and unpredictable.

They'd sold their land and home to their closest neighbor, Mrs. Winters. A vision had told her they would not return, but their granddaughter would one day live there. A surprising but hopeful thought as their daughter had just turned twelve.

****

"Jasmine."

"Yes? What have you found?"

"Sorry, I hadn't realized I'd spoken out loud." I apologize. "Your grandparents owned this place," I inform her.

"What? My grandparents, how do you know?" I watch wonderment flitter across her expressive face as she looks at her home. "It must be why I felt drawn here from the very beginning," she murmurs in awe.

"From what I saw of the past, Mrs. Winters bought this place from your grandparents after warning them of the unrest going on with the witches toward the shapeshifters. She also told them you would return and live here. Your mum was only twelve at the time."

"Holy cow, wow, talk about a head fuck!" exclaims Jezebel, as she walks through the door.

"As eloquent as ever," snorts Nancy coming behind her.

Ignoring them both, I turn back to the wall and trace my fingers again over the infinity symbol. "Behind this is a box your grandparents were asked to hide. They managed to wall it up just before they left."

Covering the symbol with my palm, I gather a ball of power, releasing it in a pulsing wave. The wall beneath my hand disappears leaving behind a slim box with the same infinity symbol on it. *It must be why they put it on the wall.* Removing the box, I trace the symbol with my fingers. On silent hinges, it opens, revealing a single document. Retrieving it, I carefully place the box on the floor beside me. Opening it, I stare in confusion, then reread the letter.

Witness who feels, you must tread carefully.
The path the Warrioress Daphmire Janna has

taken you must follow. Do not change what you see as the consequences will be dire. The clues the Warrioress leaves in her past will lead you on your quest.

On the Remembrance Day of new beginnings under the full moon of the ball, you will find the one you follow. Only then your own path you shall take as all knowledge you seek will be found.

V.

"Well, that's helpful," I mutter in frustration.

"So you can interact with the past," Jezebel pipes up as she finishes reading over my shoulder.

"Really, that's all you come away with?" I demand trying to smother a slight smile before it can bloom.

"So who's V?" asks Nancy. "Going by the note, V thinks you should know," she adds.

"My sire." Walking silently into the room with Kheda on his heels, Victor looks at each of us in puzzlement. "What's going on?"

I hand him the letter, watching him as he reads it. Confusion flitters across his face before he shutters his expression. Glancing up, he looks directly at me. "Now why is my sire leaving cryptic messages for you?" Prowling toward me, he doesn't blink or smile. He's turned into a predator. I sense unease in the others rise as they warily watch the vampire in their midst.

"Well, he seems to know a lot that's going on," I inform him, staring him back without blinking. Matching him predator for predator, power crackles between us surrounding everyone like a living presence, snapping and twisting.

My gaze is drawn away from Victor's to the letter in his hands. I feel my eyebrows shoot up into my hairline as I stare at the pulsing letter turning red with a spell. Quickly, I snatch it away from him. As if a switch has been flicked, the predator in him retreats, and the power recedes.

"Blimey," gasps T.T. from behind Victor, "that was intense. What kind of spell was on it?"

"I think it was a hands-off one," mutters Kheda, glancing warily at the letter in my hand as if expecting it to pounce on him.

"I don't think you're far off the mark. It must have been spelled specifically for the one they wanted to open it. Though how it was managed, I have no idea," Nancy replies, looking thoughtfully at the letter. "Whoever did it was very precise and knew exactly what they were doing."

"It must have something to do with the eternity symbol." I add thoughtfully, "Whoever could open the box triggered the spell and was allowed to touch the letter. Anyone else..." I trail off looking at Victor. "Maybe it's just you who'll have a reaction. Does anyone else want to try?"

"Eh, no, thanks for the offer, but I think one of us turning into a predator is enough." Nancy hastily declines, shooting him an apologetic look.

I place the letter back into its box. Close the lid and stare blankly at it.

"What's on your mind?" Kneeling in front of me, Victor places a hand on my shoulder. He looks a mixture of embarrassed, apologetic, and curious all rolled into one.

Giving him a gentle smile, I admit, "I thought we'd find out more. Something helpful you know?"

"Yeah, so did I," he admits. "The spirits said you'd find the answers you were looking for. Instead we just got more riddles." Looking away from me, he looks at the others in the room. "Does anyone have any idea of what to do next?"

****

Staring into the mirror, Janna glares at the man behind her. Why can life never be simple? "Why have you returned, Hector? Why do you insist on not leaving me in peace?" Letting her head sag forward in an attempt to control her emotions, she doesn't sense him approaching until he reaches for her. Turning her quickly around to face him and dragging her into his iron-clad embrace.

"Janna, you know why I keep returning. You are mine, body, mind, and soul. As I am yours." His deep voice rumbles from his massive chest, growling in her ears.

"I can't do this right now. I have to get ready to travel to Kerry. I have a meeting..." His lips clamp over hers in a brutal punishing kiss, effectively stopping her protests. His arms tighten around her, plastering her even more to his rock-hard body. He lifts his head; his hazel eyes soften as they stare into hers.

"Then I shall go with you. No more of this separation, wife. Where you go, so shall I, be damned to this blasted war and the politics which go with it."

"You know it's not so simple, and I'm not your wife." Janna chides him gently, petting his chest in supplication.

"Only in name, but where it counts, in our hearts, you are my wife!"

"In our hearts, yes, I am. Though it matters little in this case. You are not coming with me. Now please, I must get ready to move out." Disentangling herself

from his embrace, Janna moves to the side, steps around him, and starts strapping on her weapons. After a few minutes of silence, she turns around to find herself alone.

****

"I'm serious, you have gotta stop disappearing. It's seriously creepy," exclaims Jasmine.

"Not as if I'm doing it on purpose," I mutter, "though I did find out we have to go to Kerry. Sadly, though, it's all I found out. Well, except Janna was madly in love with a man called Hector, and he was in love with her too."

"Okay, being in love with someone is nothing unusual."

"I know. The thing is…well, he reminded me of Vlasim. Not him, more of a younger version of him." I trail off, hoping like crazy I'm wrong. Remembering how Victor had told me on our first date his sire's brother had been mercilessly tortured.

"Jesus," he mutters under his breath.

Going by the expression on his face and his muttered expletive, I'm guessing he's come to the same conclusion as me, and I bet he's hoping he's wrong.

"Oooh, road trip, well, a short road trip, I should say," pipes up Jezebel, effectively breaking the silence which had descended on us. "Sooo, any idea where exactly we should go?"

"Yeah, no, not a clue," I reply before collecting the box and standing.

"How about we go back and get cleaned up? Have some dinner, preferably out," Vivian chimes in. "Tomorrow we can book a house or two in Kerry. Hopefully, you'll have another vision or whatever it is,

Candi, and know where we're to go."

"Nice," I mutter, "I'm a walking, talking, clueless compass."

"True, but we still love you," the girls all sing song at me, before starting a chorus of Jinx, making me snort out a laugh.

"Okay. Okay. Let's go."

Chapter 16

After we eat at the campus diner, we head back to mine. Once there, we opt to play some cards. Jezebel has just won the third game in a row when she suddenly looks at my arms.

"I have to ask, when did you get those tattoos on your arms? Don't get me wrong. They're beautiful. I just didn't peg you for something quite so elaborate."

"You're right. I wouldn't have picked anything like these," I reply to her confusion. "I had a dream and they appeared."

"If you didn't want to tell me, all you had to do was say so."

"She's being serious," Jasmine interrupts. Nodding toward Victor, she adds, "He saw it happen."

"Christ, really?" demands Felicity, leaning forwards to grab my arms.

"Hey, no peeking at my cards," I burst out as I see her try and peek at them. "You always were a cheeky sod. Glad to know nothing has changed there," I add, hiding my cards under my butt from her while showing my arms, so everyone can see the beautiful black lace and rose design covering my hands and arms before flipping my hands over so they can see the images of my two magicks in my palms.

"Wow, you dreamed these on so cool," mutters Selena, tracing my palms.

"It hurt like a bitch in hell," I reply. "It was like they were being burnt on, so not fun."

"Okay, that doesn't sound fun. Here's the thing though—would you get them done if you knew how beautiful they would look?" Selena inquires, arching her eyebrow at me as if it has the power to draw the information out of me.

"I have no idea, Selena. The option one way or another has been taken out of my hands. So wondering if I would get it done, I honestly couldn't say."

Nodding her head in a bouncing motion from side to side, Selena gives me a grunt of acknowledgement. "Fair enough. Not something you can answer since they're on."

Thankfully, the conversation soon changes to general catch-up, and we carry on playing cards.

"Jezebel, I've just remembered the man in the airport. Who is he, and what did you mean you're on bail?" I suddenly demand. How I forgot I have no idea.

"Ah, yes, the divinely gorgeous Cedrix O'Laughlan, retrieval agent and complete badass extraordinaire. He's hunting my fine ass because I jumped bail to come rescue you. You're welcome, by the way" Jezebel grins, cheekily throwing in a wink for the hell of it.

"What the hell did you do?" demands Vivian, outrage written clearly across her face and tightening her lips into a straight line.

"Well, I defended myself is what I did." Picking up the cards, she shuffles them with an expertise I envy. "Some guy decides he wants a piece of my fine booty, tries to take what's not offered, and I taught him a lesson he'll never forget." Dealing the cards out, she mutters, "If he wakes up, he'll never forget," making us all pause mid-pickup of our cards.

"If he wakes up?" enquires Kheda.

"Okay, my lesson might have gotten slightly out of hand. Hence getting arrested and released on bail. The guy's in a coma." A flash of guilt and sorrow flickers lightning fast across her face before determination settles in. "I'm not happy he's in a coma, but the next person he decided to try and force might not have been able to protect herself.

"It's the only thing getting me through this mess," she admits. She's sitting on the floor with one leg curled around her so her butt is on it. The other leg she's leaning into with her arms wrapped around it, and her head resting on her knee.

She looks lost, unsure and worried. Something she's never looked before.

"I don't get it; you were defending yourself from an attacker. Why were you arrested?" demands Felicity as anger vibrates in her voice and body. Anger reflected in each of our faces except for Kheda's. His expression looks thoughtful.

"Who is he?" he asks. His voice is calm and controlled with a hint of curiosity underlying it.

"Clever man," mutters Jezebel before huffing out a breath and looking at him. "Apparently he's the mayor's son. Though it shouldn't make the slightest bit of difference. The mayor is baying for blood though, my blood."

"Yet you were released on bail?"

"Because it was self-defense and the cameras prove it!"

"He was caught on camera trying to attack you?" I

gasp in surprise, astonished at the stupidity of some people.

"Yes, a weird coincidence happened." Mirth flashes across her face, and a bubble of laughter erupts from her. "The police were on a stakeout, recording the comings and goings of an illegal underground fight club." Shaking her head, she stifles a grin before continuing, "When dumb ass decides he wants a piece of me, I protect myself, he gets a trip to the hospital, and the rest is history."

"You're not telling us something," declares Kheda. A small smile quirks the corner of his lips.

"It was caught on camera with vital evidence which can't be erased. Especially since a known drug dealer the cops were after exited the premises during my attack." A smirk flitters across her mouth before she continues. "If the evidence disappears, then their case against the drug dealer will also be gone."

"You are one jammy devil." I laugh, shaking my head at the craziness of the situation.

"Blimey, if it wasn't for the fact they need the evidence…" Vivian trails off.

"Trust me, I'm glad they do need it. The mayor is fuming and trying to add pressure. Though the judge who granted me bail looked like she was about to throw him in contempt of court." Shaking her head at the memory, she looks around at all of us, gives a slight grin, and informs us in no uncertain terms the conversation is over.

"What about your retrieval agent, and what is one when they're about?" T.T. asks; curiosity reverberates in her voice and creases her brow.

"One, he's not mine. Two, a retrieval agent is

otherwise known as a bounty hunter. Basically they bring back anyone who skips bail."

T.T.'s lips form into an O shape in surprise. I can almost hear the silent "oh" coming out of it and try unsuccessfully to smother my laughter.

After a further change of conversation where we all catch up on what's been going on in each of our lives, we all head off to our beds.

Due to lack of space, I go to Victor's house with him. Jasmine and Kheda have been sleeping together in her room, while Nancy and Selena slept on the air mattress in my office, and Vivian slept on the single bed. Leaving Felicity, Talia, and Jezebel all in my bed.

We decide to walk to his. I need the exercise and the fresh air. Twenty minutes later, he's running his fingers down his door, the imprint mechanism unlocks, and the door swings open. Once we've both entered, it swings shut, locking us in. Taking my hand, he leads me upstairs to his room.

Not a word passes between us. The silence feels intense, filled with unspoken need and desires. I want him, badly. I need to feel his skin on mine. His arms wrapped around me holding me tight, keeping me safe.

Safe? Where did that word come from? I'm surprised to even think it let alone feel it. I've always been secure in the knowledge I can protect myself. *With everything going on, it's obvious I'm not in control. I'm at the mercy of an unknown past unraveling before me. Is it so surprising I don't feel safe anymore?*

Chapter 17

Leading me into his room, he closes the door behind me, before bringing me carefully into his embrace. Slowly, he traces the contours of my face with his eyes and hands as if to memorize them forever.

Without saying a word, he undresses me. Bringing me to his bed, he lays me down, brushing his fingers along my sides around my waist, hips, and ass. Squeezing, fondling, and exploring every inch of me with his hands and lips.

His mouth suckles my breasts as his fingers explore between my legs. His thumb plays with my nub as his fingers push inside me. My breathing becomes erratic until I'm panting and wriggling beneath him, trying to pull his hand away.

Lifting his head so he can look me in the eyes, he secures my wrists above my head with one hand, while the other carries on its tormenting exploration. "I need to give you this, Candi." Voice gruff with emotion and need, he leans down to kiss me.

His tongue thrusts into my mouth, tangling with mine. His kiss is like a heated brand of ownership, and I can't get enough. Slowly, his lips break away from mine to follow a path over my face, neck, shoulders, breasts, and stomach until he reaches his destination. His tongue replaces his fingers. Circling and delving into me, he retreats to blow gently before repeating, nibbling, sucking, and thrusting into me.

My body bows and thrashes. My legs wrap around his shoulders, dragging him even closer. My moans start slowly before eventually I howl my release as it shudders through me. Pure blinding white light explodes behind my eyelids as my orgasm erupts through me. Still he keeps going bringing me on the verge again.

At last he takes pity on me. He crawls slowly up my body until he enters me in one hard quick thrust. His hips swivel and slam into me. My legs are thrown over his shoulders making each push forward deeper and more intense.

Our lips once more fuse together, our tongues mimicking our body's actions. I thrust my hips to meet and collide with his; our pace becomes faster and more erratic. My body becomes slick with sweat. I try once more to release my wrists from his firm grip. I want to touch him badly. His grip is as unrelenting as his pace, and I can't help but love it, revel in it, and beg for more. I feel my climax coming at a frighteningly fast pace…

****

"Really? You have got to be fucking kidding me! Seriously, of all the fucking times to make me vanish?" Hearing a noise, I stop my ranting, pick myself up from where I'm sprawled naked on the ground, and cover myself as best as I can, one hand in front of my lady parts while the other tries to cover my breasts.

Breezing into her tent, Janna turns toward Vlasim who follows her inside. "We'll go to the waterfall tomorrow. What you need to leave behind will be safe there. Vlasim, what is it you're up to?"

"Securing the way for the future."

"How is leaving trinkets securing the future? Are you deliberately talking in riddles?" demands Janna in frustration as she glares at the vampire in front of her. "Whose future is it you're securing?"

"Yours, mine, everyone's."

"Everyone's? And how are you going to achieve that, pray do tell me?" Janna enquires, shaking her head at the absurdity of the conversation.

"With the help of 'the witness who feels,' " Vlasim replies to Janna while watching me. A wicked look of appreciation blazes from the look he sends me. "The cave behind Torc Waterfall is the perfect place to conceal what I need to leave behind. Guaranteed access."

"Holy cow, can you see me?" I demand while trying to cover myself even more. A nod of acknowledgment is my only reply. Well, except for the lecherous grin and wink!

****

I stare around Victor's room, spot him pacing the floor in all his naked glory.

"I'm back." My brain is obviously working overtime if it's all it can come out with.

"So I see."

"About seeing, apparently Vlasim can too. See me that is." I release my breasts to wave a hand up and down my body. Just in case he didn't guess my meaning.

"What? He saw you naked? Are you sure?" Striding to me, he grasps hold of my shoulders, drags me closer to his body, wrapping me in his heat and embrace while glaring around the room.

I get poked in the stomach by his penis as if

demanding my attention and wanting to return to where it'd been before I'd disappeared.

"Very serious. I did find out where to go in Kerry as in exactly where to go. We could go for a day trip instead of booking somewhere to stay," I add as an afterthought.

"He didn't try to touch you, did he?" demands Victor. It takes me a while to figure out who he is on about.

"What? No, why would you think that?" I wave my hand in the air dismissively, the answer isn't important. I decide to get back to where we'd been before I'd vanished.

"Now, where were we," I murmur, hopefully in a seductive voice, but I don't think I pull it off.

"You're okay though? Nothing bad happened?"

"Well, it depends on your definition of okay. I was this close to having another spectacular orgasm. When nothing..." I hold up my hand. My thumb and index finger are a centimeter width apart, showing him just how close I'd been to having an orgasm.

"That's not what I meant." A smile breaks through his worried expression for a split second. It's enough though.

"It's all I can think about," I mutter back. My eyelids half close, a slight smile curves my lips upwards, and a purr reverberates through me as I think just how close I'd been.

"Damn" is all I hear before his lips slant across mine in a scorching kiss.

An hour later, I fall asleep curled up and satisfied in his embrace.

Chapter 18

I slowly wake up, have a full body stretch which feels amazing, and climb out of bed. It's only then I realize I'm alone. Shaking my head, I decide to opt for a shower before doing anything else, like search for my sexy lover.

Thirty minutes later, I'm dressed and descending the stairs when I get the delicious whiff of coffee. My mouth instantly waters anticipating the first taste. I hurry and almost trip, catching my balance by grabbing the banister; I would have been okay if it weren't for the pathetic squeak of surprise which escaped.

Victor rushes out of his kitchen to find me gripping the banister in an awkward hug. Victor shakes his head at me, a smile flickers across his face before a speculative look takes its place and he insists on knowing the rest of the story of my unconventional landing the girls were on about yesterday.

"Don't know what you're talking about," I inform him, dragging my dignity around me like a protective cloak as I lift my head into the air and head down the stairs like a queen. I would have pulled it off too except my head apparently was a little too far up in the air and I miss the next step and I let out another mortifying squeal. *Kill me now!* I land upside down in Victor's very strong arms, my view of the stairs is uninteresting, so I promptly ask to be put down.

"Is it wise for me to let you loose on the world?" rumbles a chocolate velvet voice from behind me.

"What are you trying to say?" I demand, pulling my torso up so I can look the sexy sod in the eye as I give him a haughty glare. Apparently, I don't pull it off as he only chuckles at me. He does, though, shift his hold on me to allow my legs to face the floor before letting me down.

"I'm saying, maybe it's best if I keep you where I can keep a close watch on you. Make sure nothing happens to you, say like falling down the stairs and hurting yourself."

"Love to take you up on such an ever so kind offer," I mock, "but I have a waterfall to check out. You can come if you like though," I tease as I move around him in search for the coffee I almost hurt myself to get ahold of.

I catch him shaking his head at me out of the corner of my vision and the slight upward curve of his sensual lips. I'm assuming he doesn't know I can see him. Seeing him smile makes me catch my breath. Such a simple action shouldn't have such an instantaneous effect. So not fair. My poor heart shouldn't speed at this pace. *Well, unless I'm being chased by werewolves or murderers or…Never mind, don't go there; I might just tempt fate,* I mentally chide myself. Spying the coffee, I rush to it as if seeing an old friend back from the dead. I pour myself a mug and add milk. Curl my fingers around the mug and feel its heat…

"Are you going to drink it or just stare at it as if you're in love?" he chuckles from behind me, startling me out of my reverie.

Flushing slightly, I look at him from the corner of

my eye, take a gulp, letting the warmth and caffeine invade my body.

"Any chance you've talked to the others today?" I ask, thinking of last night and finding out about the cave. My mind shies away from being caught naked. A groan escapes me, startling both of us.

"What's wrong?"

"Everything," I admit. "How much longer will this disappearing thing carry on for? It's driving me crazy. I almost crashed the car, never mind last night!" I exclaim, waving my hand toward upstairs as if to remind him.

"I don't know. Is there a spell you could do to keep your body here?"

"I'm not sure. Though the idea of my body being left behind while my spirit goes off is disturbing." Thinking about it, I begin to wonder. "Maybe there's a spell to see things when it suits me. So it'll at least be safer." *And to make sure I don't get caught naked or in the middle of sex again.* I mentally add.

I quickly finish up my coffee, grab my jacket, and follow him out the door. We jog back to mine. Once there, we enter and my house greets me by wrapping warmth around me. *Welcome home* filters through my head. I place a hand on the wall giving it a gentle caress. I carry on walking, poking my head into the sitting room. Finding no one there, I continue on to the kitchen.

Upon entering, I'm greeted with "Mornings" from everyone. The table is filled with food. At the sight, my stomach yowls, and I promptly go and fill it up. As we're eating, I update everyone on what happened last night. Well, minus the being naked and what I was doing before vanishing. Going by the looks the girls shoot me, I'm guessing they have an idea there's more to the story I'm leaving out.

"Anyway," I continue, "I found out there is something hidden behind the waterfall."

"So we're off to Torc Waterfall, cool." Selena nods her head as she leans back in her chair before continuing, "I think we should still stay overnight there. Not at the waterfall, but in Kerry itself. I think we should scout out the area during the day and go back after dark to search."

Everyone agrees and heads off to pack an overnight bag. Kheda books us a couple of cottages near Killarney National Park. Close enough to the entrance to the trail so we can walk from the cottages, though granted, it'll still be a good walk as they're a couple miles away. So hopefully whatever was left won't be heavy or big and awkward.

I quickly throw some clothes into a bag. Once done, I search through some spell books trying to find anything to help me control the visions or visits. What the hell do I call them?

"How can I find something which I don't know what to call?" I mutter in exasperation.

"Have you tried astral projection?" asks Felicity coming up behind me.

"Astral…no, never even thought of it," I admit as I quickly search the indexes for astral projection. On my third book, I find a short passage dedicated to it.

Astral projection is when you leave your body and send your spirit on a journey. This can be dangerous if you leave your body unprotected without a ward as spirits or other entities may try to invade it. If this happens, your spirit will die.

"Lovely," I mutter, "and so not helpful. I'm about to close the book when I spy a tiny footnote at the end of the page.

It has been said some astral projectors may bring their bodies with them. For those who can, control and a safe destination are vital. Advice would be to practice in a safe and secure place with a clear destination in mind.

"Now, that is more like it. Felicity, do you think there is a way of stopping it?"

"Stopping yourself from disappearing...hmmm, maybe once you've gained control. Though I'm not sure it would be wise."

"Why not?"

"If you think about it, you're being sent back to view something important. Basically to learn something to help you."

"Yes..."

"Think of it this way. You're being sent back in time to learn something you need to know. Either by seeing it happen or hearing a conversation. You should definitely learn to astral project yourself, so you can go and return when it suits you. First, you'll need to know where and when though.

"So you would still have to go when called initially. Otherwise, you won't have any idea when or where you need to go to."

"Makes sense," pipes up Jezebel from the doorway. She prowls into the room before stretching out on the bed looking exactly like what she is, a beautiful deadly predator.

I give a nod of agreement. "You're right, it does

make sense. Okay, but I'll need help."

"We're all here for you. Just let us know when and where you want us."

I feel relief wash through me. At last, something can be done to gain some form of control over this bizarre situation. A breeze flits through the open bedroom window as a laugh echoes in the wind. *"I give you nothing you can't handle,"* Hecate whispers through the wind.

"You know voices in the wind creep me out," huffs Jezebel before standing up and stalking out the room. Her long cocoa brown hair swings from side to side.

I notice Felicity smothering a laugh and give her a wink and a grin.

Ten minutes later, we're loading up the car when Dante turns up. He looks around at us all in surprise. "Going somewhere, dear Candi?"

"Yes, not that it's any of your business. What do you want?"

"Hmmm. what a loaded question, let's see. I'd like hot chocolate cake smothered in chocolate sauce. I'd also like hot passionate sweaty sex. You up for it?" Dante asks, giving me a lascivious smirk and a wink.

I can't help it. I burst out laughing, shaking my head at him. "Seriously, what can I help you with, Dante."

"Ah, Candi, you are definitely unique." He sighs, shaking his head in a mock woebegone fashion. "You're right, though. I'm not here to proposition you in a fun way. I am here to offer my assistance though."

Pausing in dumping my bag in my car boot, I turn to look him directly in the face. I sense no ill will coming from him. No deception, just honesty. Looking at the girls, I see them checking him out too. Going by their barely noticeable nods, they can't sense any deception either.

"We're listening."

A crooked half smile, a barely there lift of one side of his lips, is all the answer he gives me, until he spies Selena. Suddenly, everything changes. His swift indrawn breath and his sudden stillness is our first clue. Next thing I know, he's standing in front of her almost touching her, inhaling her scent.

"Necromancer, I've been dreaming of you. I didn't know for sure if you were real."

I watch in stunned silence as he reaches out to trace her jawline. His fingers never reach their destination. Selena grips his fingers in her hand, blocking them from reaching her face. Well, until the electrical current sparks between them. Literally sparks.

"What the hell," yelps Selena, releasing his fingers she jumps backwards.

A wicked grin is her only answer before he grabs her by the shoulders and gives her a kiss. "Destiny is coming," is his only reply once he releases her. He walks off as if he didn't just cause confusion and a silly grin to spread across Selena's face.

I'm half tempted to call after him and ask what he wanted. I manage to refrain from doing so, mainly so I can grin at Selena as she touches her lips with the hand that had grabbed his.

"You all right?" I ask, my grin getting bigger as I see her bemused and slightly dazed expression.

"Hmm; yes, good, good. What?"

I can't help but crack up. I've never seen my normally cool and collected friend so frazzled before.

Shaking her head, Nancy laughs at her twin sister. "I think I like him. Anyone who can scramble you up so quickly has to be good for you."

On these simple words, I stop laughing. Grins are wiped off my friend's faces, and a thoughtful silence falls upon us.

Nancy's right. Dante is having the same effect on Selena as Kheda has on Jasmine and Victor on me. An image of the bounty hunter or retrieval agent flashes before me and the effect seeing him has on Jezebel. *Could he be meant for her? Is destiny sending us our other halves our soul mates, and if so, why now?*

We finish loading up, call out to Victor and Kheda we're ready to go, and then pile into the cars. Kheda is driving with Jasmine in the passenger seat and T.T. in the back. Jezebel is driving the car she hired with Vivian in the passenger seat and Nancy and Selena in the back. I'm driving mine with Victor next to me and Felicity behind me. I select a CD, pop it into the player, turn on the engine, and drive off.

Chapter 19

Two hours and thirteen minutes later, we pull up at the cottages. We would have arrived earlier except we stopped at a supermarket to buy food and necessities. Once the cars are unloaded, we decide to time our trek to the park and continue on to the top of the waterfall.

It takes fifteen minutes to get to the park and another thirty minutes to get to the top of the waterfall. The pounding of the water is deafening. I can't see a way to get behind the water to the cave. Other walkers are coming up and taking photos of the surrounding scenery.

Pulling out my own camera, I also take photos. I'll be able to sell them to a nature magazine. I might as well earn some money while searching.

Five minutes later, I've come to the realization I can't find the blooming entrance. I notice the frustrated expressions on my friend's faces and guess they've come to a similar conclusion. We'll be going in blind tonight, a simple fact I'm not at all impressed with. Something which sadly can't be changed due to there being too many witnesses.

We follow the trail around to the end, coming back to the car park from the opposite direction. By this time, I'm hot, bothered, and in desperate need of a shower. Putting it frankly, I stink. So does everyone else, which makes me feel a little better.

An hour and a half later, I'm washed, dried, and have my hands curled around a hot mug of coffee. Drinking it, I decide to see if I can astral project myself to the waterfall. Placing the empty mug down, I let my eyes slide close and breathe deeply. Inhaling and exhaling, I picture the very top of the waterfall. I hear the thunder of the water and smell the scents of the trees, mud, and water. I open my eyes, and I'm still sitting in the same spot in the sitting room.

Shaking my head in frustration, I try again. This time I focus my will on being there. When I peek through my lashes, it's into the startled face of a kid just before he starts screaming.

"Mummy," screams the kid in the shrillest voice I've ever had the misfortune to hear. I'm surprised my ears aren't bleeding. I know they're not because I actually check. A second later the kid's mother comes around the corner. The boy runs to her babbling about me just appearing.

Poor kid gets told off for lying, making noise, and disturbing me. Going by the five-minute lecture I hear his mother give him, I glean he didn't want to go on the walk in the first place. I'm betting he won't be in a hurry to go on another anytime soon. Especially as his mum drags him back down the path, lecturing all the way. Poor kid. I feel bad, I really do. Mind you my ears feel worse. Not only are they ringing from the kid's high-pitched screech, they're also ringing from the mother's rant too.

Looking around, I'm pleased to note there's no one around. I make my way slowly and carefully down the side of the mountain, grasping shrubs, grass, and rock to help prevent me from slipping. I almost slip down the side of the mountain when I accidently grasp hold of some stinging nettle. Damn, it bloody hurt!

Once I finish swearing like crazy, I heal my hand and move out of the way. I almost grab the nettles with my other hand, realize it just in time, and move it out of the way.

Twenty minutes later, my jeans have rips in them and I'm positive I have mud on my face. At the very least, I'm determined it's only mud, though it does smell funky. I want to cry, mainly from the smell, and celebrate the fact I've reached the entrance to the waterfall. Sticking my hands in the freezing water, I wash my face as best as I can.

Looking around, I realize the cave is bigger, a lot bigger than I believed. Calling a flame, I realize the cave has a series of tunnels and wonder if the mountain is filled with them. I mentally make a list of things we'll need to take with us. I concentrate and picture myself back in the cottage sitting room. Third try lucky, I open my eyes to the bemused expressions of those around me.

"What is that on your face?" Jezebel demands, curling her nose slightly. I notice with amusement her vision is watering. Her sense of smell is exceptional; something I'm guessing she's wishing wasn't the case.

"Where have you been?" demands Jasmine. "We've been worried sick. Kheda and Victor have gone out looking for you," she fumes, before phoning Kheda to let him know I'm back.

"I tried astral projection and made it to the waterfall." I tell them what happened.

"Oh, the poor kid." Nancy laughs, shaking her head at me. "You know you probably scarred him for life."

"How?" I demand in bemusement.

"First, you pop up out of nowhere. Then when he tells the truth, he gets into trouble for it. How would he not be scarred for life?"

I grumble for a bit about how it's not my fault and what about my hearing after his screeching. Though truth be told, I hope he'll be okay. If he never knew magick existed, it wouldn't be the best introduction to it, I silently admit.

"I'm going to grab a shower as I can't stand this smell any longer." I abruptly change the conversation, even if it is the truth.

****

Giving up trying to spot the witch, I leave the building where I'd been spying on the pub. I walk down the road in hopes I'll find her. Though I'm beginning to come to the conclusion she either never came to Whitechapel or she's already gone.

Anger simmers inside me, boiling at the thought she has escaped me. Seeing an alley, I enter it in an attempt to gain control of myself. What I don't expect is to be transported into the Otherworld.

"Holy shit." In horror, I realize the alley I've entered is in fact a portal. And worse of all, the fucking thing has closed. Looking wearily around me, I notice everything is shadowed, gray, and creepy as hell.

I feel fear, an emotion I haven't felt in more years than I can remember, slide inside me. Chilling me from the inside out. Screams of terror and anguish echo off the walls of the street. A woman in Victorian dress dashes past where I'm hiding, her skirts bunched up in her hands so she can run faster. Her shoes tapping along the cobbled road are a beacon of sound in the foggy street. An evil laugh, a scream, and a flash of a blade are all I hear and see before the thud of a body lands on the road.

I want nothing more than to get out of this hell I've stepped into. Cowering in my corner, I fall backwards. I've never been so grateful to land on my ass before. Finding myself in the alley I'd walked through, I pick myself up and run back onto the street. Relief courses through me. I dash onto the road and narrowly miss stepping into the vicious maw of the voracious dark spirit. A scream escapes me before I can contain it, and I run as fast as I can. Only stopping at the room I rented long enough to collect my stuff and flee to the airport. I have no idea where I'm going. Anywhere out of England will do.

Chapter 20

The clock strikes midnight. Silently, we leave the cottages. All of us dressed from head to toe in black. Armed with torches, weapons, and of course plasters. Just in case one of us gets injured. No way in hell can we leave behind our blood. After all, too many spells require blood, and it's not always practical to use up energy to heal when a simple plaster is efficient.

Silently, we head off down the road, keeping to the trees as much as possible. The darkness is like a blanket, wrapping us up in its embrace. We arrive at our destination only to realize we're up shit creek without a paddle. It was hard enough climbing behind the waterfall in the daytime, never mind in the darkness of night.

"Candi," whispers Jezebel making me jump, "any chance you can get both you and I behind the waterfall?"

"What? No idea. Why?"

"If you can get us behind there, we can try and find another entrance. Logically, there has to be one. If there is, I should be able to sniff it out."

"If I accidently fuck this up, it's not my fault. Don't complain if you land on your ass."

"Agreed. Now how do you want to do this?" she demands with a nod of her head toward the waterfall.

"I don't," I mutter. "Okay, how about we wrap our

arms around each other tightly and give it a go; unless you want to tie yourself to me?" I contemplate. "It could work, I guess."

"Ugh, no, we'll try holding onto each other first."

"So what about us?" demands Victor. "Are we to just wait here or search for an entrance?"

"Give us twenty minutes," I decide, thinking it's a reasonable amount of time for everyone. "That should be time to get there and a chance to have a look. If not split into two groups, and everyone, keep in contact." Looking at Jezebel, I open my arms. "Okay, let's try this out. Fingers crossed it'll work."

A grunt of agreement is her only reply before she steps into my embrace, wraps her arms so tightly around me I almost pass out. Strangely enough, this action reminds me of something.

"Victor, can you make it across there?" I ask. After all, he can fly!

"I should be able to. Though, it's the not knowing where the entrance is which could be a problem."

"How about once I'm over there, I call out to you. Would that help?"

"Yes. I'd be able to follow the sound of your voice. Once I'm there, I can come back and bring everyone over, two at a time. Though we still will need to find another entrance as it would use up a lot of my power," he adds.

"No, get yourself over there. We'll wait for the required twenty minutes to see if you've found another entrance. If not, we'll start looking," informs Selena, looking around at everyone. The others give nods of agreement, then crouch down or sit, keeping a look out on the surrounding area.

I wrap my arms tightly around my friend. I don't want to drop her. She'd never let me hear the end of it if I did. I concentrate on the thought of both of us safely inside the cave.

"Are we doing this or what?" demands Jezebel.

My eyes pop open, and I realize we haven't moved at all. Squeezing them closed, I push the image of us inside the cave to the forefront of my mind. Suddenly, the thunder of the water is deafening. I open my eyes and grin at the look on Jezebel's face.

"Holy cow, you did it."

"Yep, I'm totally awesome." Disentangling ourselves from each other, I go to the edge of the cave.

"Wait, let me transform before you call him over." Quickly going to a corner, she strips, folds her clothes, and puts them neatly in her backpack before transforming into a large black jaguar.

Her midnight fur gleams. I collect her backpack and sling it over my shoulders, give her a quick scratch behind her ears, for which I get my ass slapped by her tail and a chuff of laughter for my trouble. Going back to the cave's entrance, I holler through the curtain of water.

"We're here. Hello, we ma…"

"So I see," replies Victor a second later as he steps through the water while shaking his head and letting the water droplets fly. He curls a hand around my waist leading me away from the edge, but pauses when he sees the large cat behind me.

"Is that…"

"Of course it is. How many jaguars do you know just strolling around Irish caves?" I tease. In answer, he pinches my bum making me jump. Looking around, I realize this will take longer to search than I'd initially thought.

Stepping out of his way, I call flames to me, which erupt in fiery glory in my palms lighting up the area all around us. Victor searches behind me while Jezebel, her nose twitching and her tail swishing behind her, paces forward. I see nothing to show another entrance.

We descend deeper into the narrow cave. Jagged rocks try catching our clothes. The path dips and turns, and I hope like crazy we won't need to retreat quickly. Jezebel lets out a deep yowl of excitement, bounds forward, her tail whipping behind her and slapping my legs. It bloody hurts. Letting out a wince, I hurry after her. It's the shrubs sticking through the walls I notice first. A moment later, the slight breeze almost blows the flames into my face.

Putting my flames out, I hurry to the entrance and try shoving it. Victor puts his muscle into it, while Jezebel watches us before opting to wash her paws, cheeky sod. After a few unsuccessful minutes, we try pressing the rock around the entrance. I find a knot in the stone, push it, and a door swings silently open.

Poking my head out, I realize we're near where we started, just slightly below where we'd left the others. Creeping out, I sneak around and spot them, whistle a low tune to catch their attention, and wave them to me.

A few minutes later, they've all piled into the rather cramped space. I check the outside of the cave wall and spot where the opening is on the other side before entering the cave again. Silently, the door closes behind me.

"So how do we find what was left for you?" demands Nancy. "Can you magick your way into the past? After all, you know where," she adds.

"Will anyone else be able to see it? After all, the other one was visible only to you," enquires Kheda in a very practical way, making everyone groan in realization.

"Look, no offense, but if I can't help find the hidden area, then I'm getting out of here," Vivian pipes up, pushing her way through everyone to the closed door. "It's too squishy in here," she adds as if in apology.

Finding the knot, I open the door again and watch everyone pile out.

"We'll hang around and keep a look out. Make sure no one comes unexpectedly, though I think we're probably the only ones out here at this hour of the night," Jasmine informs me, giving my shoulder a slight squeeze of reassurance.

Feeling a tug, I look down to see Jezebel pulling gently on her bag. Taking the backpack off my back, I offer it to her. She grasps it between her teeth, before loping off into the nearby trees to change.

I have a slight feeling of abandonment, which is both absurd and daft, until I turn around and see Victor. He's leaning against the back wall. A slight smile curls his lips, and his arms are crossed in a casual way, which emphasizes his muscular arms.

I can't help the feelings of lust rising inside of me. I quickly quench it by thinking of spiders. I then realize what a stupid thing to think of when I'm in a bloody cave. *Ugh, will I ever learn?* A shudder ripples through me. Shaking my head, I try to banish the thought of giant spiders descending from the cave roof and landing on me.

"What you thinking about?"

"Spiders," I admit, feeling mortified when I see his eyebrows shoot into his hairline. I just know he won't leave it at that.

"Spiders, hmmm, what were you thinking of before you decided to think about them?" he teases. Bastard, he knows exactly what I was thinking about. The laughter in his eyes and huge wicked grin prove it a split second later.

"So how do you want to do this then?"

"We're not having sex in here!" I blurt out, making him burst out laughing. Too late, I realize he was talking about searching, not my libido. I hear the girls trying to smother their laughter from the cave entrance. Feeling a fiery blush rush through me, I quickly inhale deep breaths to calm myself down and gain some form of control.

"I think I know what to do," I mutter under my breath, surprised I hadn't thought of it before. "I need you to stand way, way back," I instruct him. "You'll need to stand further back or maybe go outside just to be safe."

Taking my words as an order, he exits the cave but leaves the door open to watch me. I see the others surround him, all watching curiously what I'm about to do.

Calming my breathing, I step into the middle of the area. Breathe deeply in and out, centering myself.

Calling my fire to me, I bring the flames higher, twirling my arms and body around in a dance. The flames swish and roar becoming a living breathing entity.

"Flames so bright,

I feel your might,
Show me what's hidden,
Show me the way.
Secrets to find,
Secrets to uncover,
It is my right,
I command thee.
I command thee."

On my final words, I blast the fire from my hands. With a howl of power, it rushes from me, burning a fiery path further into the cave and down a path we hadn't been. I follow it, leaving the others behind.

A few minutes later, I see the flames curling and caressing the wall. The symbol of eternity is etched into it, glowing brightly. I fire a pulse of power at the wall and watch as it crumbles and the flames die out.

Walking forwards, I kneel down in front of the broken rock, sift through it until I find a box with the same symbol engraved on it. I check to make sure there is nothing else to be found, then stand and turn around. Wide eyes greet me which scares the shit out of me. I hadn't heard any of them follow me.

Letting out a really embarrassing squeal, I promptly curse the lot of them as I try and gain control of my runaway heart. Taking deep breaths, I finally feel like my heart isn't going to leap from my chest.

"Okay, what the hell was that?" demands Felicity.

I give her a rather blank look trying to figure out what exactly she means.

"The whole fire dancing, chanting, everything!" she exclaims in apparent frustration. She's got such a grip on her hair, I'm genuinely worried she'll rip it out.

"I've, umm, gotten in touch with my power lately,"

I lamely explain, silently groaning at my inadequate explanation. I remind myself of a five-year-old trying to explain how I can do something most kids the same age can't do. Actually that's being rude to a five-year-old. I'm sure they'd explain it much better.

"How about we head back to the cottages and find out what's in this?" I show the others the box in my hands. Everyone retreats out the way we came until we're all outside. We quickly realize we're one short.

"Where's Jezebel?" Looking at the blank faces around me, I become concerned. "When's the last time anyone saw her?"

"Well, umm, I think when she went off to get changed," admits T.T., looking at the others who give silent nods of agreement.

"Ah crap!" I mutter in disgust while hoping like crazy nothing has happened to her.

Chapter 21

I slip the box into Nancy's backpack and sling it over my shoulder. When Victor tries to take it from me, he gets zapped for his trouble. Apparently, the box is territorial. Once done, we start searching for Jezebel, but we can't find any sign of her. Wherever she disappeared off to, she was obviously dressed. In her jaguar form, she would have dropped her bag. Twenty minutes into our search for her, my phone rings. Answering, I'm relieved to hear the cool tones of my missing friend on the other side.

"Hey, I'll be back later. I have something to sort out. I'll meet you back at the cottage in a couple of hours."

"Are you okay? You don't need us to come get you, do you? We will, if you tell us where to go."

"Candi, honestly, I'm fine. I'll see you later. I promise. Don't wait up though; I will be a couple of hours." On that cryptic comment, she hangs up.

Turning to the others, I give a shrug. "She's fine, says not to wait up. She'll see us later."

"Are you kidding me?" demands Selena. "She's fine, so why couldn't she have said something before fecking off?"

"At least she rang," soothes Nancy before turning and heading back toward the car park.

We all follow her, walking down the hill in silence

before starting the jog back to the cottages. By the time we reach them, I'm exhausted. Looking at the others, I'm pretty sure I'm not the only one.

We troop into the kitchen, grab drinks of water, and gulp them down. Victor removes some blood from the fridge and thirstily drinks it. A slight flush tinges his cheekbones. I wonder if he'll ever get used to freely drinking in front of so many different supernaturals.

Opening the backpack, I remove the box and trace the symbol on it. Pushing my fingers into it, the lid pops open. Inside is another scroll. Removing it, I open and read it. My eyebrows shoot up into my hairline, and I can't help the little "Oh" of surprise escaping me while reading the note. Finally, I look at the others.

"Apparently, we need to go to a New Year's ball in Transylvania!"

"What? Hold on a sec, didn't the other one say something about your birthday?" demands Jasmine in confusion.

"Maybe, I had thought it's what it meant. Reading this now…" I trail off, thinking about the two scrolls. "It never actually said anything about my birthday. It was new beginnings. You can't get a bigger new beginning than a New Year."

"Well, crap," states Felicity in exasperation. "The New Year is just under three weeks away. Can we even get a flight out there, never mind getting tickets for the ball?"

"The New Year's ball is free for all supernaturals," Victor informs us quietly. "Getting the flights should be easy enough. There's one thing though. We have to travel through the Carpathian Mountains the traditional way, not by car. We'll need to hire horses and carriages."

"Are you being serious?" inquires Kheda. Curiosity laces his voice, while the glass he was about to take a sip from is raised halfway to his mouth, slightly tilted as if frozen in surprise.

Jasmine gives him a gentle nudge and nod toward the glass, while trying to smother her laughter at his reaction. It's not often we get to see him so befuddled. I almost laugh, smother it in a cough, and refuse to look at anyone.

"What exactly does it say?" Kheda asks, scratching his head with his free hand, while his other hand puts his glass carefully on the counter.

"It says,
Witness who feels,

This is the last time I'll leave notes for you. On the stroke of midnight when the past year leaves and the birth of the New Year begins, in the ballroom of the Dragon named Dracula you must be. Find the final clue in the moonlit garden. Your answers will be realized.

V"

"Oh."

"That's all you got? Oh? So insightful and helpful. Thank you, Kheda, for your valuable insight," I tease him before erupting into the laughter I'd held back.

Shaking my head, I let out a groan at a sudden thought. "Will we have to wear ball gowns, and where in hell will we find one at this late date?"

"Yes, everyone will have to dress accordingly. We can get them in Bucharest," my knowledgeable vampire informs us.

Looking at him, I have to admit I can't wait to see him dressed up in his finery. *Maybe this could be fun.*

146

"How about we sort out the tickets later, as in after we get some sleep? I don't know about anyone else, but personally I'm exhausted." Giving a cracking yawn as if to prove her statement, T.T. mutters goodnight and heads off to her bed. One by one, we all slip away to get some sleep.

Once in our room, I undress and crawl into bed. Every single bone in my body cries out from exhaustion. The bed dips, blankets shift, and strong arms wrap around me, pulling me into his embrace. I inhale the scent of his skin. A purr of contentment rises.

"Shhh, get some sleep."

"Drink from me," I sleepily reply, the words coming out in barely a whisper.

"Are you sure?"

"Always," I reassure him. A second later, his fangs slip gently into my neck; I feel the sensual pull of his sucking the blood from me. *Sleep, Candi. We have a long couple of weeks ahead of us,* his voice whispers in my head. His teeth retract, a gentle kiss replaces the spot his fangs had been a moment ago, and I drift off to sleep.

Chapter 22

Slowly I wake up. Rolling over so I'm facing my sleeping vampire, I kiss him awake. His eyes open and blue fire bleeds into them as his fangs descend and his penis rises. I grasp hold of him, stroke him firmly, slipping my tongue between his lips as I increase the pace of my hand on his manhood. His fingers delve between us. Like a heat-seeking missile, they zoom in on my hooded lady, rubbing and slipping inside of me.

Our breathing quickly becomes heated. Removing his hand from me, I push him onto his back, straddle him, and slide onto him. His hands grasp my hips, thrusting me up and down on him. Sitting up, he latches his lips around first one breast, then the other.

He pierces both nipples, causing delicious tremors to shoot through my body. As I fall and rise on top of him, our pace increases in a tempo as old as time. A keening cry sounds in my ears, and I'm surprised when I realize it's coming from me.

My orgasm builds at a furious pace inside of me before erupting, making me shudder at the force of it. It's only when the taste of his blood hits my tongue I realize I've bit him. I feel his release shudder through him, the sink of his fangs into my neck, and a deep rumbling moan of completion. I collapse against his heaving chest, kiss the bite mark on his neck, letting a trembling smile escape.

"Morning," I whisper in his ear.

"Good morning, my beauty. I feel you're well today," he rumbles back while cupping and massaging my ass.

I give a laughing snort for a reply and wiggle my ass, making him groan. Clenching my inner muscles around his firming erection. "You seem very well today too," I reply.

Hearing a noise from downstairs, we stop before we can commence with round two. With a groan of dissatisfaction, I climb off him, throw on some clothes, and head to the bathroom down the hall.

Once washed and dressed, I descend the stairs, following the voices into the kitchen. I come to a startled stop when I see the man from the airport who had watched Jezebel. Relaxing in one of the chairs, drinking coffee as if it is the most natural thing in the world.

"What the hell is going on?" I demand while glaring at him. I feel a little of my tension ease from me when I spot Jezebel, who's clearly unharmed and completely unflustered.

"Well, you remember at the airport I mentioned he was a retrieval agent and a persistent one too?" Jezebel asks before carrying on. "He followed us here and got a little surprise when he found me transforming back into my human form in the trees."

A deep rumbling laugh escapes from the man in question. "A little surprise is not quite how I'd call it. Try almost a heart attack." His voice is a gravelly warm rumble which catches all the females in the room's attention.

Looking at him, I'm curious as to why he's

surprised. I can sense the magick in him, so it's not as if he's a human facing his first supernatural. I catch Jezebel shaking her head at me. I narrow my vision at her.

"What the hell is going on?" I demand. I have a sick feeling in my stomach he honestly doesn't know or didn't know about the supernatural community before last night.

The next words uttered convince me I'm right.

"Cedrix was adopted. He apparently never knew about…"

"The supernatural community," I interrupt with a barely audible groan. "Oh good god," I mutter before looking at him again. "You're taking this rather well, aren't you?"

"To be honest, granted I wasn't expecting to see a shapeshifter, but I'm not completely surprised. I've always believed in certain things which lean toward the supernatural," Cedrix admits before taking a sip of his coffee. "I know there aren't any gods or goddesses…"

"Actually, there are," I interrupt him.

His coffee mug slips from his fingers, smashing on the edge of the table. Without thinking, I wave my hand, the pieces of the broken mug reattach, and the spilt coffee returns to the mug. Safely on the table though.

This time Cedrix leaps backwards, toppling his chair with a crash. Points at the mug and swears a lot.

"Wow, chill out. It's just magick," I sooth or try to at least. I don't think it comes across that way, what with his swearing increasing and calling me an evil witch bitch. I've no idea what is with his reaction, but now I'm mad, and there are growls and curses coming from everyone else. Also, I hear Victor coming downstairs which won't help at all.

"Enough!" I roar. Power pulses from me, and flickers of lightning curl around my fingers just waiting to let loose.

Everything goes quiet. It's as if all have been frozen in their spot. Reining in my power, I take a deep calming breath and let it out.

My gaze settles on Cedrix, and a feeling of anger surfaces. A growl escapes me; my wolf wants to take a nip out of his ass. I feel her peeking out. His gasp of surprise gives her satisfaction, going by her happy chuff of contentment.

"Do not swear at me again," I growl. "I don't appreciate it in the slightest."

"What's going on?" demands a mouthwateringly sexy voice from behind me.

"Nothing now. This is Cedrix, the bounty hunter who is after Jezebel. Apparently, witches freak him out."

"Really? How come when he's…?"

"He was adopted," Jezebel quickly blurts out.

"Okay, what is my being adopted got to do with anything? And how can you be so at ease with a witch around?"

"What happened to your birth parents," I ask instead.

"They were murdered. The killer was never caught."

"A really brutal murder, as in almost sacrificial gone demented?" I ask quietly.

"How did you know? Are you part of that witch cult? What exactly is going on? You all obviously know something about my past which I don't. I want to know now!" Fury laces his voice. The scowl on his face is seriously fierce. I bet he's damned good at his job.

I look to Jezebel; she can have the honors of telling him. A huff is her only reply before moving to the table and sitting down.

"Okay. Damn, I don't know how to tell you this... Right, so you know I am a shifter. Well, so was my biological father. My mother was human though."

"Okay, what has this got to do with anything?"

"My parents were of different supernatural species. My mum was a witch, my father a werewolf, and no I'm not a part of a cult as you call them," I interrupt, receiving a relieved look from Jezebel. I pour a mug of coffee and join them at the table.

"There's a rule enforced through a group called *The Protectors*. You can't have a relationship with another from a different species. My parents obviously did." Taking a deep breath, I continue, "They were hunted down and murdered. I found their bodies."

"Jesus, wait, what does it have to do with me?" Confusion laces his voice, though his face shows no emotion at all.

"You have magick inside of you. I can sense it. Your parents must have been supernaturals."

"I don't have any magick. Trust me, if I could wave my hand and fix broken things, I'd know."

"Have you ever known something was about to happen?" I ask. Taking a sip of my drink, I watch him over the rim of my mug. "Or sensed you need to be somewhere? It doesn't make sense, you follow your intuition, and then something happens."

He opens his mouth to reply, closes it, and exhales

through his nose. Opens it again as if determined to dismiss my question, only to have a "Yes" escape.

"It's your magick at work. You're untrained, so you haven't developed it further. Every time you use your instinct and intuition, you make those areas stronger."

"So wait, you're saying I'm a witch?"

I look at him, my head slightly tilted to the side, just watching him. I lean an elbow on the table and rest my chin on my fist. After a short while, I answer him. "You have magick inside you. You can train and develop it or carry on as you are. The choice is yours. As for saying you're a witch, you are what you are. Putting a label on it won't make the foggiest bit of difference. If it helps, yes. You are a witch."

"Are you all supernaturals?"

"Yes."

"What, witches and shapeshifters?"

"No."

"Well, what else is there?" Frustration and anger lace his voice. The glare he sends me could peel paint.

Yowsers, he's got one vicious dirty look on him. I must admit, I'm impressed by it. Looking at everyone, I get nods of agreement to tell him what they are.

"Okay, Victor here is a vampire. Kheda is a werewolf. Jezebel, as you know, is a jaguar shapeshifter. Talia is a witch. Felicity is also a witch. Vivian is a werewolf. Selena is a necromancer, and Nancy is a zombie. She was previously a necromancer too, though, and finally Jasmine is an Alsatian shapeshifter." With each introduction, I point out who I'm talking about just to make it easier, and each person gives a nod or raises their hand in acknowledgment.

"Okay, it's slightly mind-blowing. Wait, you said Nancy, was it? Was a necromancer before becoming a zombie? How is she not one anymore?"

"This is when it gets slightly complicated. In the majority of cases, you can only ever be one form of supernatural. When Nancy was changed into a zombie, she lost her necromancer powers." Taking a breath, I explain further, "It's like when children of mixed parentage are born, they either have one or the other of their parent's abilities. Or none at all."

"You said in majority of cases. There's an exception or at least a minority?"

"Exception, and you're looking at her. I have two different types of magick. I inherited both of my parent's abilities."

"So you're a witch and a werewolf? Correct? If you're an exception, then how is it possible? Or how do you know there aren't more supernaturals with more than one magick?"

"There's a Prophecy written about me. It's what has *The Protectors* on their murdering spree."

"Wait, they're the ones who killed my parents. Are you saying it's because of you?"

The air crackles with tension; anger vibrates like a living breathing being in the room. A growl reverberates loudly, a harsh warning that blood will be spilled. Taking a calming breath, I hush my wolf.

"My parents were also murdered. Thousands have been slaughtered in this war with *The Protectors*. Fear and hatred drives them. Their need for control is legendary," I growl, barely keeping my temper in control.

A warm hand rests on my shoulder, soothing in its

warmth and silent support. I place my right hand over his. Grateful for Victor's silent support.

"No," Nancy informs him in the coldest voice I've ever heard come from her. "It's not because of Candi your parents were murdered. It's because of the sadistic murderous group of ass-wipes, *The Protectors*!"

"Okay, fair enough. What exactly does this Prophecy say for them to be so scared?"

"We don't know. We're still hunting for it," I reply, once more feeling under control of my emotions.

"I want to help."

I had just taken a gulp of my coffee. At these words, I splutter, spraying Cedrix and Jezebel with cooling liquid. Heat rushes through me burning my cheeks in mortification as they wipe their faces with napkins passed to them.

"Oh my god, I'm so sorry," I apologize.

"Ugh, gross," mutters Jezebel before glaring at the girls who are beginning to snicker. "It's not funny," she growls at them until her lips twitch.

"I suppose I deserved that." Cedrix grimaces; amusement lights his pale ice blue eyes and a smile curls his mouth.

I notice with amusement how Jezebel watches his lips. A look of longing flickers across her face for a split second before being ruthlessly wiped off. Damn, the girl has serious control over her emotions.

Looking at the two of them, I wonder if he's exactly what she needs.

"You want to help us find the Prophecy?"

"Yes, especially if it means stopping this group from killing more innocent people."

"Okay. We're going to book flights to Romania,

you coming?"

"Romania? When...I wasn't gone that long last night," splutters Jezebel.

A snort of amusement escapes Vivian. "You missed shit loads. Candi has gained some seriously bad ass powers since we last saw her."

"Really, like what?"

"Romania, are you coming? Oh, and it's a ball we're off to," I add as an afterthought.

"A ball, really? Oh my god, I've always wanted to go to a ball."

I look at my friend and can't help bursting out laughing. She is literally wiggling and bouncing on her seat in excitement. I've never seen her like this.

"Wherever she's going"—pointing toward my bouncing friend—"I'm going," he replies. I notice how he watches her. There's an intensity and curiosity in his gaze. Well, also determination too.

I wonder if he realizes it can't be just his job making him chase her around the world. After all, he doesn't have the ability to drag her back to America with him.

"Okay, so let's get these tickets booked. Find outfits for the ball and go to Dracula's castle."

"I'm sorry, go to whose castle?" demands Cedrix in puzzlement, as if unsure he's heard right.

"The ball is at Dracula's, Vlad the Impaler's castle," I repeat. Standing up, I wash my mug and hunt down some food. "We best get packing as we have to hand the keys back in an hour. Blimey, time's gone really fast. Where are you staying?"

"What, oh, you change conversations quickly. Are you always like this?"

I think about it for a second giving everyone else time to say "Yes" in unison. *Huh, charming. Mind you...*

"So where are you staying?"

"Around the corner; the cottage nearest the road. Perfect position for seeing you all coming and going without you noticing me."

"Damn, you are good, aren't you?" I get no verbal reply, just a smirk, as he crosses his arms over his rather powerful-looking chest. I can't help but notice the way his biceps bulge and the way a certain lady is practically drooling over them.

I also catch the glower Victor sends him. A tingle of something warm and fuzzy flickers through me. When he catches me looking at him, he gives me a devastating smile. Liquid heat travels straight to my center, pooling there in anticipation. I hear a few sighs from some of the girls, and a possessive streak rushes over me, taking me aback. I've never thought of myself as possessive, yet where he's concerned, I can't deny it. I am.

Chapter 23

Once packed, cars loaded, and keys handed in, we head back to Paradise Falls. This time, though, Jezebel is returning with Cedrix, and Felicity is driving the rental.

On arriving back, I'm surprised and not in a good way, to see Officer Nina standing impatiently on my doorstep.

"Oh, good god, there are more of you," she growls in irritation, glaring at everyone as we exit the cars.

"Nice to see you too, Nina. Why are you here?"

"No need to be snippy."

"You're on my property being rude. I can be snippy if I want to," I growl at her.

"Actually, it's the vampire I came to see. I had an idea he'd be with you," she sneers. Turning to Victor, she gives him a look of disgust before informing him his bar has been declared safe to do whatever he pleases with.

"Thank you."

Wariness flashes across her face before she gives the slightest of inclinations of her head in acknowledgement. I notice her glancing at Jasmine and Kheda, and a slight smile barely noticeable flashes across her face before being hidden once more.

"I'm glad you two are looking all right. There's some strange stuff going on at the hospital.

"Death," I mutter without thinking.

"What did you say?"

"Ugh…"

"If you know something, I need to know. Please."

"I don't…"

"Please, my little sister is in the hospital." Her words barely travel to me. The emotion behind those words, though, slaps me in the face, desperation, pain, helplessness.

"Come inside," I instruct. Retrieving my bag from the boot, I ascend the stairs, unlock the door, and walk inside. Warmth encircles me in a welcoming embrace. Placing my palm against the wall, I whisper hello before entering the sitting room.

I hear a startled exclamation of "Bleeding Hell" from Nina before she enters the sitting room with a wide-eyed nervous look. I wonder if she's going to bolt and assume she's never been to a house like mine, in other words, practically alive.

"Right, what do you know about what's going on at the hospital then?" she demands while looking nervously around.

I tell her what I saw when I was outside Jasmine's room. Of how I'd thought it was a doctor doing their rounds until I realized there was no face. "It's all I know or saw. To be honest, it creeped me the hell out," I admit.

"Let me get this right. You saw a faceless person visiting rooms. When said person notices you watching it, realizing you could see it, it hurried off?"

"Yes."

"Well, that's fucked up!"

"Definitely," I agree. A small smile escapes from

me at her eloquent yet straightforward words.

"You didn't chase after him/her/it, what the hell…"

"No. I didn't, and I have no idea what sex the person was. To be honest, I was a little rattled at seeing no face."

"Fair enough. Completely understandable giving the description. Did anyone else see…?"

"No. I was on my own at the time."

She leans back in the chair she's sitting in and scrutinizes me. A frown forms across her brow. She continues to stare intently at me. With a slight nod of her head as if she's come to a decision, she finally speaks.

"What you've told me is completely crazy. Yet I believe you. I also think I might be going slightly crazy for doing so. Since you've arrived back in town, the shit has really hit the fan. All the weirdness has come crawling out of the woodwork."

I'm about to interrupt when she places a hand up in the air in the universal sign for "Stop" before continuing, "Don't get me wrong. I know it's not your fault. It's just highly annoying I can't throw your ass in jail and have everything smooth out into a controllable situation.

"Obviously I can't do this, and I doubt it would make the slightest bit of difference for the better if I did."

She takes a much needed pause. I could have said something but am too surprised she's talked so long for me to do so. Also what the hell can I say to such a speech?

"If you need my help, you can call on me." Looking around at everyone, she gives a nod in their direction. "That goes for all of you. I don't know what exactly you're up to, though I have a feeling it's a fight for the better good of all supernaturals. A fight I want in on."

She stands and leaves without another word.

Chapter 24

It's only when the front door has closed behind her, I realize there's no sign of Victor and assume he's gone to check out his pub. Not knowing what to think about the turn of events unraveling before me, I decide to change and go for a run.

I grab my bag, climb the stairs, and change into my running gear. Collecting my camera, keys, and phone, I finally head out.

I start off at a light jog to loosen up my muscles. I head into the woods and decide to go to the cliffs. The ground is firm beneath my trainers, the air crisp. Winter is settling in. I'm slightly surprised how lucky we've been weather-wise for how late in the season it is.

I increase my pace, my feet pounding out a rhythm. Between one step and the next, I transform into my wolf and let her free. Everything smells sharper. The frostiness of the air, the moss on the trees, and the decomposing leaves. I sniff out a squirrel which chatters and tries to scratch my nose for disturbing its sleep. Just for that, I pretend to take a nip out of its butt. My wolf is such a tease at times.

I leave the squirrel and carry on with my play. Bouncing between the trees and disturbing the sleeping creatures. I arrive at the cliffs and return to my human form, inhaling deeply.

The waves crash below me. The gunmetal sky

reflects in the water, their colors blending with one another. A gull cries somewhere. I can't see it, though it sounds close. Removing my camera from my pocket, I take pictures, capturing the gull in a sideways maneuver as it flies overhead.

Putting my camera away, I take out my phone and text my grandmother. The years she raised me after my mum's murder and her teaching me witchcraft and the love and kindness she's shown me are pushing through my anger and hurt over her betrayal. I still can't get over the fact she was going to sacrifice me for my magick. But, at the end of the day, I love her. *Are you okay?* A simple text, a text loaded with so many questions. I don't expect a reply. Good thing as I don't receive one.

Chapter 25

By the time I've returned to my house, Victor is just turning up. He stops me before I go inside.

"I've just checked out the pub. I've made a call to get the builders in. I had to remove the enchanted objects, so they don't get ruined or stolen. Which is why I went straight away."

"What enchanted items?"

"The bar counter and the species eye-chart. They're enchanted against, well, everything to be honest."

"Oh" is all I can say, until what it means filters into my brain. "Hold on a sec. It means blood magick. Going by their age, that's a lot of…"

"They're steeped in it. My sire passed them on to me. All I know is the witch who owned them was extremely powerful…"

"Janna's mother, the witch, she was Janna's mother."

We stare at each other for a bit. To be perfectly honest, I think my brain has gone on pause and is just beginning to go into…

"What the fuck!" exclaims Victor, who apparently went into the same thought mode.

"Do you get the feeling of being led by the nose down a merry path?"

Dragging me into his embrace, he kisses me on the

forehead before replying, "Dragged down a path by the nose, yes. On a merry path, not so much; more of a pot-holed crater of a road."

A snort escapes me when I laugh, and I can't help cringing. Shaking my head, I look at him and wonder, *if his sire hadn't given him Janna's mother's support beam and plaque, would we have met? Everything from so long ago seems to have brought us together. Led us to here and now.*

He looks at me and traces my features with his fingers. A slight smile plays across his mouth. Barely there, it still has the power to make my heart flutter eagerly.

"I wonder if my sire had given the items to Vincent, would he be standing here right now instead of me?" he asks. Uncertainty flashes across his face for a split second before steely resolve replaces it. "No point with what-if's. I'm just grateful I'm standing here, because you're mine and I'm yours. End of discussion."

His lips descend on mine in a fierce heated kiss. His tongue pushes between my lips, past my teeth to tangle with mine. His fangs graze my bottom lip, nip, and suckle it. I wrap my arms around his neck and plaster my body to his.

He bends slightly, grasps my thighs, and lifts me into his embrace. My legs circle his narrow waist, tighten around him making him groan. I purr in satisfaction at the effect I have on him because he has the same effect on me.

"I need you now." He lifts his head long enough to pant the words out, I have just enough time to nod my head before he flits into the woods. Far enough away from everyone, I'm released long enough to unbutton my trousers and pull one leg out while he unbuckles his trousers and releases his manhood.

Then I'm back in his arms, and he's thrusting into me. His strokes powerful and forceful push me further into the tree supporting me. My body writhes and meets his with thrusts of my own. I can't get enough of him, and I don't care anymore.

My fingers are clawing at him, dragging him impossibly closer. Small growls are escaping from me between my panting. Our orgasms rocket through us, both of us biting into each other's necks at the same time. Shudders wrack my body, sending spasms of ecstasy rippling through me.

A contented sigh puffs out of me. I give his neck a quick lick and a kiss. "Damn, I can't get enough of you."

A rumble of laughter vibrates through him. "Good because I can't get enough of you either," he admits before slowly thrusting his already erect penis in me again.

This time we take our time. Kissing and stroking each other. I run my hands through his hair giving it a gentle tug before slanting my mouth over his once more. Our lips mimic our bodies' languid movements.

I rise and fall on him, enjoying every slow withdrawal just so I can impale myself on him once more. Our pace increases, becoming more frantic than before, as once more we race to reach our mutual release together.

This time, after a couple of minutes to gain control of our breathing, he slides out of me. I unwrap my legs from his waist and unsteadily stand up. I'm glad the tree is behind me as it helps to support my shaky limbs.

Victor bless him goes down on one knee, while I place my hands on his shoulders, as he redresses the lower part of my half naked body. He places a gentle kiss between my legs, whispers "mine" before covering me up. I honestly don't know if he knows I heard him.

"If you're claiming my body as yours, I'm claiming your body as mine," I inform him, as I stare down at him. His only reply is a wicked grin and a wink. I'll take it as agreement.

Once he's put himself back in his trousers, we slowly make our way back to my house. We have plans to put in action. Flights to book, ball-gowns and tuxedos to buy. Never mind booking carriages and traveling through the Carpathian Mountains, during winter!

We get back to mine to find out the flights have been booked. We need to leave for Dublin airport now. Our flight leaves tonight. I quickly shower, dress, repack my bag with warmer clothes and grab my passport, camera, and a couple of books to read.

Once done, I head downstairs where everyone is loading up the cars again. I presume Victor, Kheda, and Cedrix went off to get whatever they needed as they're just pulling up into my drive in Cedrix's rental car.

Once everyone has loaded up the cars, we divide ourselves between them and head off.

Chapter 26

We make the final check-in with fifteen minutes to spare. Which means we have two hours to wait before boarding the plane. We grab some dinner, then head through customs. With only a short time before departing, we decide to wait in the departure lounge where we can relax, rather than hurrying back from somewhere farther away.

We spell our weapons so we pass through security checks without any issues. When it's time to board, we grab our stuff, get our passports and boarding passes checked, and follow the line.

Once seated and the stewards point out the safety exits and procedures, I close my eyes and fall asleep. We're flying over Bucharest when I wake up. I stare out the window entranced to see the tininess of everything below me, watching as buildings, cars, and people become full-sized as we descend and finally land.

"Welcome to Bucharest. We've arrived on time; thank you for flying with us. We hope you have a pleasant trip."

On these words, the whole plane comes alive with people wanting to disembark as quickly as possible. We join in, collect our bags, and exit the plane. Exiting the airport, we jump into a minivan taxi which can hold all of us and head to the hotel we'll be staying at for the next couple of days while sorting out our attire for the ball.

I take in everything I can see, which isn't much as it's dark out. I notice the others are trying not to nod off. We're all exhausted, which is not surprising since it is three-thirty in the morning. An hour later, we arrive at our hotel.

I look up and notice it's called Strigoi. *Strigoi, hmm, I wonder if it's a supernatural hotel. It'd make sense as Strigoi represents all supernaturals in Romanian folklore. I must ask Victor about it later.*

I practically roll out of the taxi as my limbs are too tired to support me. After collecting our bags, as one we shuffle into the hotel.

The scent of jasmine, lilac, and lavender greets us. I notice the beautiful flowers are scattered about the reception area, mixed together in a stunning bouquet. The floor is made of black marble with white swirls.

The armchairs and sofas scattered about the sumptuous waiting area are made from mahogany and blood-red leather. The drapes look as if they're made from black velvet with red velvet blood drops mixed in.

Mahogany and gold make up the counter, coffee tables, and bookcases. A crystal chandelier finishes off the room. Well, apart from the double-wide grand staircase. The banister is made of what looks like white marble with black swirls, supported on delicate twisted gold stems. The steps are made of the same black marble with white swirls. It is exquisite. I've honestly never seen anything like this place before.

I stop gaping long enough to catch up with the others at the reception desk. We sign for our keys, are informed where our rooms are, and shuffle off to climb the great mountain, otherwise known as the staircase.

I refrain from laughing, mainly because I believe my amusement is even too tired to come out. We all look like death barely warmed up. By the time we've climbed up the elegant staircase, I can honestly admit I hate the bloody thing. My foot has slipped three times on the marble floor. Beauty does not make something practical.

Our rooms are all on the same floor, which I'm surprised at until I'm informed they were booked that way specifically. I'm so grateful when I'm in my room and spy the large double bed. I actually cry from relief. I'd be embarrassed except I just don't care.

Ten minutes later my teeth are brushed, I've thrown off my clothes, and have crawled naked under the sheets. My eyelids drift shut as I feel my lover's arms circle me and pull me against him. A fleeting kiss across the top of my head, and that's all I remember. Sleep claims me like a welcoming friend.

Chapter 27

By the time we've all slept, awoken, dressed, and arrived downstairs, it's already lunchtime. We quickly grab something to eat before heading out to the recommended boutiques to find appropriate clothing for the ball.

At the first one, the three guys as well as Felicity, Jezebel, Nancy, and Vivian are lucky to find their attire. I can't help feel a twinge of envy they're done. Going by the looks on T.T.'s, Selena's, and Jasmine's faces, I'm not the only one.

The second shop finds me staring at a dress in awe. I tentatively walk over to it, almost afraid it'll disappear if I move too quickly. My hand rises up of its own accord. The tip of my index finger lightly brushes the bustier. I draw in a sharp breath. Daringly, I move forward, and this time I touch it with both hands.

"Would madame like to try it on?"

I start guiltily, turning to face the smiling sales lady. I nod my head, my gaze already turning back to the stunning creation behind me. "It's beautiful," I reverently whisper.

"It is, though not everyone can wear it. You though, yes, I can see you wearing it easily. Strange, the designer has never made anything like it before," admits the lady before carrying on.

"Sandra, the designer, told me she couldn't help

herself. As if she was compelled. The genius of the artist" A tinkling laugh escapes the woman, surprising me. It sounds almost like delicate bells ringing.

"Come, bring the dress, and follow me."

I take the dress and follow the woman into the backrooms to change. Quickly, I strip down to my underwear and try on the captivating dress.

Looking in the mirror, I barely recognize myself.

The heart shaped black leather bodice with gold lacings molds against my torso like a second skin. Starting just under my breasts, the lacings crisscross around to the back, where they tie up closing the bodice. The skirt is made of the softest black leather with golden amber lace covering it.

The dress is unusual, yet in a strange way quite exotic for a ball gown. Long butter-soft black leather gloves with intricate gold in a web-like design complete it. I take a step toward the mirror, pausing in wonder when the skirt parts, flashing one long leg at me before sliding back into place.

I walk again, fascinated by the flash of my leg and the glide of the dress instantly covering my limbs.

"Oh my," I whisper in awe. Looking up, I catch a glimpse of something crumpled on the ground. Turning back, I walk over and pick up skintight trousers made from the same soft leather and shade as the dress. I slip them on, realizing they are a part of the outfit.

On the sides of the trousers, pouches have been added to hold weapons close to the body. Once more. I move closer to the mirror. This time, I see no flash or slide of my leg coming forward. The trousers blend perfectly.

"My god, you're designed to conceal weapons and

to fight," I whisper in awe.

I look down thoughtfully at the skirt. *I wonder...*

Removing it, I look carefully around the waist. With a blink of surprise, I notice it has a concealed hook and clasp. Swishing it around so it's inside out, I let out a little scoff. *It's not possible, is it?*

Slipping the skirt around my shoulders, I secure the clasp and look at myself in the mirror. A little gasp of surprise escapes me. The skirt is now most definitely a cloak. Covering my top completely, it drapes elegantly around my body. Not a bit of the beautiful golden lace shows.

This is a dress designed for camouflage. A dress designed to be seen and hidden, blending in with the shadows if need be. It is a masterpiece of subterfuge.

Quickly, I remove it and dress once more in my own clothes. Gathering up the dress, I leave the changing room, pay for it, and wait for the others to finish with their purchases. I hug the bag to me as if terrified it will be taken from me. Strange how giddy I feel. I notice then how the other girls who have bought their dresses are also hugging their bags to them, as if the prize inside is priceless.

Excitement and wonder flickering across their faces. I can't wait to see everyone's outfits.

Eventually, we're back at the hotel, and all of us girls cram into Selena's bedroom.

"You are not..."

"I can't wait..."

"You have to..."

Everyone's talking over each other; voices blend into one another until it sounds like one babbling voice unable to finish a sentence.

I remove my outfit slowly and carefully. Lovingly, I caress it. The others pause in their excitement to stare at me before also removing their purchases from their bags.

Our outfits are all on display. Each is beautiful and vibrant with an understated twist. One by one, we take turns in modeling our gowns. When it's my turn, I show how mine becomes a completely different outfit altogether.

"Wow! I mean, wow!" Selena says in complete surprise.

"You said the saleswoman said the dressmaker felt compelled to make it. It's not her usual style?" asks Jezebel in a thoughtful tone of voice, catching everyone's attention.

"Yes. What are you thinking?"

"Maybe she was. Would it honestly be all so surprising with everything else that's gone on?"

I think about it for a second before agreeing. With everything that's transpired, one more unusual thing happening shouldn't be unexpected.

Later that evening, we go out exploring the town. Eat dinner and go to a bar for a couple of drinks before heading back to the hotel to sleep. We have an early start tomorrow. Seeing how everyone has managed to get what we needed on the first day, we'd all agreed to give ourselves an extra day traveling.

Chapter 28

Early the next morning, we check out of the hotel. Upon exiting the building, I'm surprised at how much snow has fallen during the night. Four sets of horses and coaches await us by the curb. We load our luggage into the third carriage and climb into the other three.

This way everyone will be more comfortable and our luggage will be safe and dry. Victor, Nancy, Selena, and I climb into the first carriage. I notice Jasmine, Kheda, Vivian, and Felicity climb into the fourth carriage. Leaving Jezebel, Cedrix, and Talia in the second one. *Cedrix sure isn't letting Jezebel out of his sight for long.*

With a snap of the reins, our driver sets us off slowly through the streets of Bucharest. I can't help feeling like I've gone back in time.

"Rest while you can. The journey will be long and tiring. Also if the snow keeps up like this, we might need to dig ourselves a path through it," Victor informs us.

On this warning, I pull out my phone and send a text, passing on the warning so everyone will know.

"Could we not have got the train to Brasov and the carriage the rest of the way?" I quietly ask.

"No, the only traveling allowed on this trip is by plane to Bucharest. The rest of the journey has to be done traditionally. Some rules are best not broken."

"Okay, just wondering. I suppose it's also keeping the old traditions alive," I muse. Glancing outside the window, I have to admit it might make the journey longer, but it sure is pretty.

Five hours later, I've dozed off and on and have a crick in my neck. Thoughts of it being pretty have flown out of my head. I'm restless and badly need to run.

"Victor, I need..."

"Shhh," he warns me flicking a quick glance toward the driver. "We'll be stopping soon for a couple of hours' rest before carrying on. Isn't that right, sir?"

"Yes, th..." The coachman stops speaking abruptly midword. He must have realized Victor hadn't spoken very loud, and by rights he shouldn't have heard us.

I feel Selena and Nancy tensing up beside me. I'd presumed they were asleep, they'd been so quiet.

"Can we stop here for a moment, please? I need the ladies room." Spying a tavern off the side of the road, I decide it's best to warn the others without drawing too much attention they're being spied upon.

The coachman grumbles and mutters while reining in his horses. I get the feeling he's giving himself a verbal tongue-lashing for falling for Victor's test so easily.

I disembark and hurry toward the tavern. I only slip twice, which isn't too bad. Spying a door marked with a picture of a lady, I rush through it.

Ahh, sweet heaven, I was busting. Once finished, I wash up and wait for the others. Talia is the first to come through. So I update her on the news of being listened to by the coachmen. When she bursts out laughing, I stare at her in confusion.

"All he'd have heard was Jezebel trying to unsuccessfully ignore the gorgeous hunter Cedrix. We almost tipped over at one stage while she was swapping seats before he retrieved her and sat her next to him again.

"I swear I thought she was going to box his ears for him." Talia laughs, shaking her head in happy remembrance by the looks of her. "I've been highly entertained through the whole journey thanks to their antics."

"Ugh, well, that's good. I think," I reply, feeling completely baffled over this turn of events. *Blimey, where does he think she'll disappear to in a carriage?* "Will you pass on the information to the others? Actually, don't tell Cedrix and Jezebel. It'll be best to leave them to their…I have no idea what to call it, to be honest." With a slight wave of my hand, I head toward the door. "I best go, I'm glad your journey has been entertaining." I laugh before exiting the bathroom.

We opt to have lunch here, which also gives the horses time to rest. After eating, I slip off to nose around. Transforming into my wolf, I glide through the trees. Snow slips from the branches. I manage to avoid some just to be splattered by more.

A sneeze escapes me. Shaking my head, I let the extra snow fly off my snout. I bounce and run and play, feeling exhilarated. Hearing a voice, I crouch down, flattening my belly to the ground. My ears prick up, swiveling. I crawl forward, my white fur helping me blend into the snow. Once I'm in hearing distance of a couple of men, I stop and flatten myself into the ground.

"…traveling by coach, they must have money."

"How can you be sure they're not protected in some way? They're a large enough group. We'd be stupid to try and rob them!"

"Does it matter?" bemoans the first man. "We're desperate. If we don't get money soon, we'll lose this place."

"Robbing ain't the way to go. We'd probably get ourselves killed, and then the tavern will be lost for sure."

I debate on what to do.

Should I transform back into my human form and talk to them or warn the others? It sounds as if the second man has convinced the first to stop this plan. I wait for a moment longer, watching them. Soon they separate; one heads back to the tavern, the other toward a house a little farther back.

I crawl backwards until my bum hits something. Turning around, I realize it's Victor. My tongue lolls out of my jaw, and my tail bangs his leg in greeting.

He looks down at me, a little smile flickers across his lips. "Nice to see you too. It looks like we might need to be on our guard," he informs me with a narrow-eyed look toward the house and then back toward the tavern.

Transforming back, I nod in agreement. "We should leave now before they can gather more people to assist them."

We hurry back to the others to inform them we're leaving; a sudden thought enters my head. Turning to Victor, I'm interrupted before I can even ask.

"I saw you go off, watched you play until you heard something. I followed you and listened too."

How did I not hear him or sense him following me?

Strong fingers reach for my chin and push it up, closing my jaw with a snap. A smirk spreads across his handsome face. A second later his expression gentles. The fingers which had closed my jaw now stroke my face.

"God, you're beautiful," he whispers before closing the distance and slanting his lips across mine in a sensual kiss.

My arms creep around his neck pulling him closer. After a while, we pull slightly apart, just enough so each other's faces aren't a blur.

"I love you," I inform him while a feeling of uncertainty knots in my stomach. Fear of admitting my feelings and wondering if I should have kept them to myself.

A huge smile spreads across his face. "I love you too. Terrifying, isn't it?"

"What?"

"Saying it first and admitting it in general. Being in love. All of it, everything, and yet none of it."

"I have no idea how it made sense, but it does and yes." My stomach eases, and contentment replaces my uncertainty. I feel lighter, happy.

"Yes?"

"You're right…"

"Say it again!"

"What?"

"I'm right, say it again. I've never realized just how delicious those words are till you said it," the cheeky sod teases.

"Nope, you've had your lifetime quota. No more shall be said on the subject," I tease back. "Oh hell, we'd best hurry back to the others." I can't believe I got distracted in reaching the others to tell them we best leave now.

"You grab them. I'll inform the coachmen," he instructs me before soundly kissing me and hurrying off at a human rush.

I hurry into the tavern. Trying not to draw any unwanted attention, I tell everyone we need to leave right now, and explanations will be given later. Slowly, everyone exits the building. Some heading toward the toilets, others straight outside to stretch their legs. By the time we're all outside, the carriages are pulling up.

As we hurry into them, I have to stifle a laugh when I notice the firm grip Cedrix has on Jezebel's wrist. He practically throws her into the carriage before climbing in after her. I hear the sound of a fist thumping something solid and a quiet male curse before the door slams closed.

Talia catches my attention as she scrambles to open the carriage door and follow the couple inside. She's barely holding back her laughter and is apparently looking forward to the rest of the journey.

Five minutes later, we're all seated and heading off to Brasov. I hear a distant shout of frustration and presume our departure has been noticed.

The journey thankfully proves uneventful. By the time we arrive, I'm exhausted and my eyes feel raw. Groans of relief escape Nancy and Selena as they disembark, and I'm grateful to know I'm not the only one relieved to be finished with today's journey.

We unload and troop inside. I'm positive I hear my bones creak in protest at the change in position.

We book our rooms and drag ourselves off to locate them. After entering our room, I plop on the bed to sit for a second. By the time my upper body has tipped backwards onto the bed, I'm already asleep.

Chapter 29

I wake, and it's dark. The blankets are tucked around me. I let a hand drift under them and notice the absence of my clothes except for my bra and panties. I stick my head under just to make sure.

Yep, cartoon panties and a plain white bra; as my panties say, that's all, folks. *Damn, I'll have to invest in sets.* A snort quickly follows my train of thought. I have a couple of pretty sets. They'll do unless I need more.

Slowly, I climb out of bed. Looking around confirms I'm on my own. Victor's suitcase is in a corner next to mine. I find the clothes I'd been wearing earlier, folded neatly and placed on a chair.

A smile breaks out on my face. I can't believe he takes more care over my stuff than I do. I find the bathroom and freshen up, throw on my clothes again, and go in search of the others. I find them gathering downstairs in the bar.

It's not hard to guess who got some sleep and who didn't.

We relax and chat a while before grabbing some dinner. It's only when we're heading to a booth large enough to hold all of us I notice a large bruise on the side of Cedrix's face. I place a restraining hand on his arm, stopping him from following the others.

"Can I help you?" He looks down at my hand where it rests on his arm, in irritation, his gaze instantly returns to the retreating back of a certain jaguar shifter.

"I know you're keeping an eye on Jezebel. I understand you don't want her disappearing or anything. She won't. Unless you piss her off, then she'll feel cornered. Trapped, and things will get..."

"Why are you telling me this?"

"Because I don't want her getting hurt, and I have a feeling, if she hurts you because of feeling trapped, in the long run it'll hurt her," I answer truthfully.

His ice blue gaze searches mine for a second before giving me a nod. He indicates for me to go ahead before following. As I pass him, he whispers so quietly I almost don't hear him, "Thanks."

"You're welcome," I reply as I walk away. I sense the falter in his step before he follows. *Ah, so he didn't expect me to hear him.*

Once we reach the table, I give everyone a big smile. "What's the plan for tonight and tomorrow?" I ask, completely ignoring the curious looks I'm receiving from everyone.

"We haven't made any," pipes up Talia with a raised eyebrow as she notices Cedrix sitting across from Jezebel instead of forcing himself next to her.

I almost burst out laughing when I notice him giving her a wink while Jezebel returns her usual glower.

He promptly ignores her; turning to Kheda, he asks him a question. Next thing Victor's called over and the three of them wander off to drink at the bar and chat, leaving the rest of us looking baffled.

Hmmm, he keeps that up and he might have Jezebel following him.

I try my hardest not to speak to her for a few

minutes. She looks like she might just rip anyone's head off who does. I take a sip of my pint. Glance up and decide the silence has gone on for long enough.

"I don't know about anyone else," I say loud enough to catch their attention without being completely obvious, "I really needed a nap."

Talia sends me a "really, you're going with that as an icebreaker" look.

While Selena looks relieved and joins in. "Same here. I hadn't realized I was so tired."

"Oh my god, you are such a horrendous icebreaker, Candi." Jezebel bursts out laughing.

"It was either a nap or talk about the wallpaper," I grumble, which gains more snickering for my efforts.

"Sorry, I don't know what's wrong with me."

"You like him," Talia informs her in a matter-of-fact voice, which gains complete silence worse than the last time.

I valiantly withhold my groan of frustration.

"Like him?" asks Jezebel in surprise. "Really? Oh. Oh my god, I like, like him!" she exclaims while looking at the table as if to find answers. "How did I not know this?"

"I think you did. You just refused to admit it," Vivian bluntly informs her before taking a sip of her drink.

"Really? Okay, if it's true, then how come I never admitted it to myself?" she demands, making us choke and gape at her. "What?"

"Are you serious, Miss Denial?" demands Nancy. "The words could have flashed neon in your face and smacked you over the head, and you'd still deny it!" she exclaims.

"I'm not that bad…"

"Are you serious? Okay, what about the time you refused to admit…"

"No point bringing up the past," she hastily interrupts, going slightly red. "I'll admit I might have a tiny problem about admitting certain things."

I burst out laughing, only to be silenced a second later.

"You can hardly talk so don't be laughing at me!"

"Okay, okay. Blimey, take a chill pill already," I mutter. "Yeah, I know I've had my moments." At the look the others give me, I hide a smile and admit, "I didn't say there weren't a lot of moments now, did I? Who here hasn't, though?"

Seeing their expressions go from smug and all-knowing to ah crap, I give my head a nod of acknowledgment. "Exactly we've all been there, done that, and got numerous t-shirts to prove it. So let's stop the bullshitting and get to the bones of the matter.

"How much do you like him and how long since you realized? I mean, when you arrived at the airport and saw him, it was so obvious!"

"Really?"

"Yes," the rest of us say in one voice.

"Wow, holy cow. I mean when I first saw him, I thought damn, then I realized he's out of my league big time…"

"Says who," demands Vivian in surprise.

"Well, me. Come on, look at him, he's gorgeous and I'm…"

"Stunning, beautiful, smart…"

"Damaged," interrupts Jezebel, "I'm damaged."

"Sweetie, it doesn't mean you don't deserve

185

happiness. Sometimes it means you deserve it more. We all do," Jasmine informs her quietly. "You have to take a chance, hun, or what's the point?"

"You really think so?"

"I know so. I'm going after my own happiness," she replies. Her gaze drifts toward the men, landing on Kheda. As if sensing her looking at him, he turns around and looks at her, a smile breaking across his face.

There's a lot of indrawn breath going on at the table from the looks the two of them share with each other.

"Wow, I want that," mutters Nancy. "Damn, you gotta take a chance for the opportunity at happiness," she declares in a firm no-nonsense voice.

"Agreed," everyone chimes in.

"But what if when I tell him about my past, he doesn't want me?" Jezebel's question is asked so quietly it takes me a second to register what it was she asked.

The emotion in her voice almost breaks my heart. She sounds like a little girl hurt and broken, wondering what she did wrong to make the adults hate her so much.

"Oh, sweetie, you're a survivor. You've been through so much already..." Her voice catching, Felicity reaches out to take Jezebel's hand, giving it a squeeze of reassurance.

"I know, I know. It's just if I have difficulty with my past, how can I expect someone to accept me?"

"Because you're worth accepting and being loved. We all are," Jasmine fiercely, almost angrily declares.

Silence descends on the table. No one knows what

to say. After all, everything worth saying was said. We drink up, get another round, and this time chat about the upcoming ball and seeing Dracula's castle. Normal stuff.

A couple of hours later, we start to head off toward our rooms. Well, us girls do, anyway. The boys are still chatting with one another at the bar.

I remove my toiletry bag and a baggy t-shirt that reaches half way down my calves from my suitcase. Enter the bathroom and prepare for bed. Once cleaned and changed, I bring my dirty clothes back into the bedroom, placing them in a plastic bag for laundry, which I leave tied up beside my suitcase.

I climb into bed, grab my book, and open it. I manage to read a chapter before I start drifting. When I realize I've read the same line five times, I give up and close the book, turn off the light, and drift off to sleep.

Chapter 30

I wake up bright and early wrapped in Victor's arms. I cuddle into him for just a moment before carefully extracting myself.

"Where you going?" he mumbles. Barely awake, he tries reaching for me to pull me back into his embrace.

"I need to go for a run. Go back to sleep," I whisper back. Quietly, I get myself ready. Put my room key in my pocket and head downstairs.

I think about asking for directions for the best place to run. At the last moment, though, I change my mind and head out the side door. I keep my breathing nice and even, inhaling the crisp air and smoke from fires.

My feet pounding along the path is the only sound for a while. Slowly, the birds make their morning calls. In the distance, a dog barks, and the sounds of the city awakening filter through.

I make my way back around to the hotel. I feel calm and peaceful. I badly needed this run. On returning to the hotel, I once more enter through the side door, take the stairs to the second floor where we're staying, and interrupt a man trying to force the door to my room.

"You don't want to do that," I calmly inform him, making him jump and drop his tools.

"Where did you come from?" he demands in

confusion. Looking wearily around, he bends over to retrieve his tools.

I stare at him. I don't move forward or even twitch. My stillness has the desired effect I want. The man becomes nervous and agitated, looking around wildly for something. The air changes and shifts. I sense his relief.

A moment later, an ox of a man comes pounding down the hallway. Lowering his head as if he's a bull and planning to barrel into me.

I gather power to me. With a subtle shift of my hands, I push the energy I've gathered out toward the men. The charging man suddenly slows as if he's trying to run through quicksand before stopping midrun. A look of fear and confusion flickers across his face. A whimper escapes from him when he realizes he can't move.

"What are you doing?" demands the first man looking at his friend. It's only when he tries to step away from the door he also becomes fearful.

This is the moment I choose to move. Walking with ease toward them, I watch with mild interest as they stare at me in horror before crying out "Strigoi" in fear. Stopping in front of the man who tried to run, I look him in the eyes and allow my wolf to peer out at him.

A squeal of terror escapes him. A second later, the hotel room doors along the corridor are flung open and my friends evacuate in various stages of undress.

"What the hell is going on?" demands Victor, upon halting his exit so he doesn't knock over the man directly in front of the door.

"Not sure," I calmly reply. "This man was trying to

break into our room," I inform him, pointing toward the man directly in front of Victor. A whimper escapes him when I turn my head to look and point at him. "This man came charging at me from around the corner.

"I have no idea who they are or what they want as I haven't had time to find out yet." I give them both a nasty smile, all teeth showing.

"She's a bit scary, isn't she?" I hear Cedrix ask Kheda, to which I hear a short laugh and a muttered "You have no idea" in reply.

"How about we bring them into your room and question them?" Jasmine asks around a huge yawn.

"Sure." With a little flick of my fingers, the men are moved as if on a conveyor into my room. Victor quickly steps back and out of the way before they collide with him.

"Fuck me!" gasps Cedrix. Bless him, he's getting a complete crash course in the supernatural.

From the frozen men, I hear whimpers as they're moved by air. From Jezebel, I hear an "I wish—" I look briefly at her to let her know I heard. And try not to laugh at the furious blush racing over her skin.

I'm good, though I don't say anything. As I turn to my room, I do catch sight of a certain male looking thoughtfully at my friend.

Did he hear her? If he did, things could become very interesting between them. I walk into my room and look at the two terrified men. Suddenly, I feel very tired.

A large warm hand lands on my shoulder, and a voice like chocolate velvet rumbles in my ear. "I'll take care of this. Go downstairs, and get some breakfast."

I'm just about to tell him no way, when I remember

the surprise on the face of the man trying to break into our rooms. *He wasn't expecting anyone to have left the room. Does it mean there's another member to their group keeping watch downstairs?* With a nod of my head, I collect my purse, exit the room, and am just about to close the door when the other two men in our group arrive. I leave them and join the girls.

"I'm going to get breakfast. Anyone wanting to join me?"

"Sure, why not. Are you leaving the questioning to…?"

"They're more than capable," I reply. Glancing at the door, I can't help a twinge of regret at not joining them. "I'll meet you downstairs in the dining room. I'm in desperate need of a coffee. Also, I have a feeling we're missing the brains behind those two."

I descend the stairs and enter the lobby area, startling the receptionist. Ignoring her, I carry on across the area to my destination. After entering the busy dining room, I pull out my phone and ring my room.

The moment the phone is answered, I quickly explain the receptionist's reaction at seeing me and then hang up before anything else can be said. I manage to squeeze into the line and grab myself a mug of coffee and some food before winding my way to one of the few empty tables. A few minutes later, the girls start piling in, grab some food, and join me.

"Very busy in here, isn't it?" asks Nancy while looking toward the lobby area.

A small smile flickers across my face. "Very. Rather interesting the receptionist finds us being here a surprise."

"Agreed, we'd better get back upstairs," adds

Felicity.

We quickly finish up, exit, and return to our rooms. Some of us take the stairs while the rest take the lifts. Covering all the angles we can.

Once upstairs, we hurry into my room only to find the men glaring furiously at the two terrified unwanted guests.

"Apparently, these men were informed of some tourists staying here. It seems they have a system of breaking into rooms early in the morning when everyone is asleep."

"They're petty thieves?"

"Well, yes, though not petty. They bind up and threaten one of the room's occupants and make the other empty out as much money as their banks will allow once opened," informs Kheda with a growl of anger.

"Well, you really picked the wrong room, didn't you? Your accomplice was rather surprised to see us earlier," I inform them.

"Accomplice?"

"Yes, the woman at the reception desk. I did ring and tell you she was surprised to see me downstairs."

Victor bares his fangs at the two men making them cringe. "You forgot to mention an accomplice."

"S-s-sorry," stutters the running man in fear.

"Does anyone have more questions for them?" I ask while wondering what to do with them.

"No, I believe it's all we'll get from them by normal means," replies Victor, making the two captives' eyes bulge even more than before.

"So shall we kill them, or what?" I ask while checking out my nails. Seeing everyone turn to look at me, I let my amusement show. "I'm messing. I say we let them go before any more unwanted visitors arrive."

Nods of agreement from my friends and looks of relief from the frozen men greet my statement. With a flick of my fingers, the men are able to move once more. The man in the running position falls flat on his face with a yelp of pain.

I crouch down beside him and whisper one word in his ear, "Run." Next thing, he's leapt up from the floor and is bolting out the door fleeing as quickly as he can, not even waiting to see if his partner in crime is with him.

I raise an eyebrow at his companion, who takes the hint and runs from the room. Shaking my head, I turn and address my companions.

"I believe we should all get ready and leave as soon as possible, as in we should all meet up outside within the next half hour."

Everyone quickly moves into action and heads for their rooms. I grab fresh clothes and head into the bathroom to get cleaned up in record-breaking time. I feel sweaty and gross. I badly need a shower.

Fifteen minutes later, I'm dressed and repacking my suitcase. Once done, I check the room to make sure we've forgotten nothing. I get an indulgent look from my sexy vampire before we exit and head toward the lifts where the others are gathering.

Six minutes later, we've checked out and are loading up the carriages, and once more climbing into the blasted things. I always thought carriages were romantic. Now I just find them a pain in my ass, literally.

Chapter 31

We start off on our final part of the journey to the castle. The snow is falling faster, and everything is covered by a thick sparkling white blanket. I'm just thinking how pretty it looks when the wheel of the carriage dips and slides, dragging the carriage off the road. Climbing out, we quickly realize we'll have to dig out.

I notice the horses whinnying at each other. I'm positive they're laughing at us. We remove the shovels strapped to the back of the carriages. I start clearing a path in front of the horses and am quickly joined by a couple of the girls.

The rest dig around the stuck wheels and in front of the next carriage. The horses stamp their feet and raise and lower their heads while the coachmen talk calmly to them. Rubbing their noses and soothing them.

Soon we're ready to help push the carriage while the coachman clicks his tongue, walks backwards, and encourages the horses forward. Three times we shove the carriage unsuccessfully. On the fourth time, I'm really tempted to use magick. Sadly, though, there are too many people around, mainly the four coachmen. No need to bring on another witch-hunt because of my impatience. The fifth time we try, the carriage lurches forwards and a couple of us face plant into the snow.

Picking myself up, I spit out the snow I managed to

shovel into my open mouth. Brush off the powdery substance from my clothes and troop with the others back into our carriages. Strangely enough, we're all grinning and looking more at ease. As if the purely human moment has taken a weight off our shoulders.

The rest of our journey proves to be uneventful. The scenery beautiful and silent. The only noise, the horse's hooves muffled by the snow underfoot. Picture perfect, it makes me feel as if we've been transported back in time.

Soon we catch glimpses of the castle soaring above us. I stick my head out the window, gazing in awe at the beautiful building. *It looks like a fairytale castle.*

"It's so beautiful."

"I know, not what most people expect for a place with such a brutal history," agrees Victor, smiling at me with a look of pleasure on his face. "Mind you, it's not our destination."

"Have you…" I quickly trail off remembering just in time we're being listened to. Then realize what he added. "Wait, it's not our destination?"

"Yes, I've been here before," he replies, giving me a slight nod to let me know he knew what I was really asking and his answer to the question. "And no, our destination is Poienari Castle."

I'm just looking back out the window when I realize what he's said. My head snaps around so fast I'm lucky I don't give myself whiplash. *Vlad Tepes is a vampire, holy cow!*

I feel Selena and Nancy looking at me curiously until they figure out what question must have been asked and answered. I almost giggle at their expressions which probably mimic mine from a minute ago.

I can see their silent question of "Really?" I give a slight nod of acknowledgment and excitedly look out the window again. This time their heads pop out the other one. I feel a gentle caress on my bum, look back to see an indulgent-looking vampire winking at me. I give him a big grin before continuing to stare at the beautiful castle.

I must admit I'm gutted we don't go and visit it; instead we carry on into the hills and through the Carpathian Mountains. We only stop for toilet breaks and a stretch of our legs before continuing on. Eventually, we arrive at our destination.

I can see the confusion on our coachman's face, realizing as a human he can only see ruins instead of a stunning castle before us. His curiosity becomes more evident when we disembark from the carriages to be greeted by men in livery.

They bow and help us out, inform us our luggage will be taken to our rooms, and indicate we should enter the castle. I thank our coachman and with a final look at him move forwards toward the giant doors.

I want to run inside and explore everywhere. Yet at the same time, I want to stay right here in the courtyard and stare at the magnificence of the building before me. A hand grasps me by the elbow. Looking up into silvery green eyes, I give a small smile and together we enter Poienari Castle.

Chapter 32

Tapestries line the walls of the entrance room. A grand staircase at the side of the room curves upwards to the floors above. I'm surprised it's at the side. I take a further step into the room only to come to a halting stop when I see a tall lean man come striding toward us.

His long jet-black hair is tied back from his face showing the perfection of his high cheekbones, large black eyes, and full lips. A five o'clock shadow graces his face enhancing his masculinity. Dressed in black leather, he is gorgeous and impressive. I inhale sharply realizing who he is. I begin to feel my jaw loosen, so quickly gain control of it.

"Victor, you made it," drawls Vlad Tepes of the House of Drăculeşti, Prince of Wallachia.

The only coherent thought running around my head like a hamster on speed is, *Is he still a prince of Wallachia?* I don't know how I manage not to ask the question. I'm grateful I don't. After all, I'll have plenty of opportunities to make a fool of myself. No need to get a head start.

"Yes, I am," Vlad informs me, looking directly at me.

"You are...oh god, did I ask that out loud?"

"No, I read minds. Also, your curiosity is like a living entity hard to ignore or resist."

At this comment, I just stare at him. My mind has

gone completely blank; I have no idea what to say. This gives me the second I need to put up an impenetrable block on my mind. My thoughts are my own. I hate the idea of someone prying in on my mental ramblings.

Victor quickly breaks the silence by introducing everyone.

Vlad greets each woman with a kiss on our knuckles making us blush in turn. What can I say? His epic love with his wife and her unfortunate end is legendary. It gives a girl a warm fuzzy feeling deep inside.

Our poor boys are ignored. I'd feel bad for them except, well, I'm slightly in awe at the moment. A scream shatters the quiet, startling us all. My mind tries to come up with scenarios, which I clamp down on, hard.

"My apologies, a guest is having…difficulties. Instead of talking, she apparently prefers to scream to get attention." A grimace of annoyance flashes across his face for a split second, quickly covered up by a smile. "Ah, sometimes I do miss the good old days." He chuckles, making me cough, before excusing himself and walking away.

We're brought to our chambers and instructed dinner will be served at six in the dining room. Since we have a couple of hours to spare, I opt to take a bath and relax. Quickly, I unpack and then enter the bathroom. The tub is built into the floor, deep and round, so you must step down into it. It's large enough to easily hold four people.

I fill the tub up with hot water and some of the oils left for use. Stripping, I climb in. A small moan of contentment escapes me as the warmth envelopes me.

My eyelids drift closed until I feel a warm palm drift up my leg. Opening my eyes, I look into Victor's beautiful ones.

Easing my legs open, he moves between them, leans in, and kisses me sweetly. Slowly we make love. Taking our time exploring each other's bodies, our mouths tasting and teasing each other's. My passion rises, and I'm just feeling on the verge of an orgasm.

"Candi, are you okay, sweetheart?" demands Victor from outside the tub, startling me. I look at him in confusion, noticing he's fully dressed.

In puzzlement, I look down as if trying to figure out what the hell happened.

"Weren't you just...did I fall asleep?" I ask in genuine confusion. "It felt so real though." I feel like a child who's had a fantastic treat whipped away from them. Utterly devastated.

Kneeling down, he looks at me with first worry then dawning realization. "You were having a certain fantasy?"

"I guess," I answer. A frown is etched into my forehead, bringing on a headache. Shaking my head, I look up at him. "It felt real, as if we were..." I trail off, stifling a groan at the memory of how bloody close I was to release.

"That good, hmmm?"

"Damn straight it was," I growl in annoyance. I stand up to exit the bath. Next thing I know, my hips are clamped between strong hands and brought to an eagerly awaiting mouth.

"Holy mother of god." I gasp as his tongue delves between my legs, slipping up into my entrance, suckling and lapping at me bringing me to completion in so short a time I should be embarrassed, except I'm too busy crying out in rapture. Next instant, his fangs slip into my femoral artery making me convulse and moan in ecstasy.

"Oh sweet Jesus," I cry out before collapsing over his shoulder, shuddering another release. He withdraws his fangs and licks the healed puncture wounds. Wraps his arms around the backs of my legs, stands, and carries me into the bedroom, placing me on the large canopy bed.

I lie there feeling like a limp noodle. Every muscle in my body has gone on vacation, leaving me useless. Well, until I notice him stripping, then I manage to raise myself up onto my elbows so I can watch easier. No point in straining my eyeballs after all.

Once naked, he walks toward me, grasps my ankles, pulling me closer to him until my bum is at the edge of the bed. Bringing my legs up, he places the back of my knees on his shoulders.

Running his hands down my legs until he reaches my ass, he grips it, raising my hips toward him. I reach for his manhood which is standing to attention, thrusting eagerly from his body. Circling him, I give him a pull closer, leading him into my body.

He enters me on one long hard thrust. My eyelids flutter, and I bite my lip. Through half-closed lids, I watch his body withdraw from mine only to come back quicker and harder with each thrust and withdrawal.

I flip myself over, so I'm now kneeling on the bed. I hear a grunt of approval as he caresses my ass. Reaching between my legs, I give his balls a quick fondle and gently scrape my nails along his length before thrusting back into him and grinding my bum against his pelvis bone.

Soon our pace increases, becomes faster, almost frantic, in our need. With each hard thrust, his balls slap my nub making me moan in ecstasy until I'm sent over the edge. I shudder and clench around him, pulling a growl from him as he in turn shudders and completes, roaring his satisfaction into the room.

Wrapping a strong arm around my middle, he yanks me up, sinks his teeth into my neck, and drinks. I in turn grasp his wrist, drag it to me, and bite into him. Drinking his blood, making him twitch inside me and harden once more, so we begin our dance all over again. Eventually we collapse on the bed.

Carefully, he rolls onto his side bringing me with him so our bodies are still attached. He places a kiss on my shoulder and tightens his embrace for a second in a hug. Slowly exhaustion takes over, and I fall asleep.

At some stage, Victor must have dragged the blankets across us while I slept. I'm guessing he did unless we had a visitor kind enough to do so. On that thought, I'm really hoping it was him.

It takes me a minute to remember where we are and another to realize someone knocking at the door is what woke me.

"Wha...? Just a second," I call out, frantically trying to untangle myself from a warm embrace and blankets.

"Just letting you know it's half an hour until dinner," an unknown male voice calls through to me from the safety of the other side of the closed door.

"Umm, thank you," I holler back, swiping my hair out of my face and shaking Victor awake at the same time.

We bathe and dress. While I'm brushing my hair, I realize I'm being watched. Giving him a curious look, I'm about to ask why he's watching me so intently, when he asks a simple question surprising me.

"May I brush your hair?"

"You want to brush my hair?"

"Yes. If you don't mind, that is."

Hesitantly, I pass him my brush. Except for my mum when I was a kid or a hairdresser, no one has ever brushed my hair other than me. For some reason, it feels ever so intimate. As if I'm allowing him to peer into my soul.

Chapter 33

Running the brush through my hair, he stays perfectly quiet. Looking in the mirror, I see fascination on his face though I have no idea why.

"You honor me," he informs me, looking up from my hair to make eye contact with me through the mirror.

I open my mouth to say something, I'm not sure what. Catching him shaking his head at me, I close it again.

"In allowing me this intimacy with you, this trust you have shown me. You honor me."

"We have shared much more intimate moments than this," I blurt out in confusion. The feeling of allowing him to peer into my soul comes over me again. I glance away, admitting to myself he's right.

Coming around to face me, he cups my chin in his large palm, brings my face around so we are once more looking directly at one another with no barrier of a mirror between us.

"It is different, and you know it. Even if you're not ready to admit it," he calmly informs me before kissing me gently on the lips, effectively scrambling my thoughts. Once more, he starts brushing my hair until it shines like a fiery curtain straight down my back.

With my hair loose about my shoulders, we exit the bedroom, descend the stairs, and walk into the dining room. Thankfully, we're not the last to arrive.

The dinner is a loud affair. There must be at least a hundred people around the huge table. I find it a little overwhelming. It's only when I overhear someone discussing the ball in two nights' time, I realize somehow we've missed Christmas.

"So what brings you here?" a female vampire demands. Her lips are curled back, baring her fangs. I wonder if she realizes how daft she looks.

Looking her up and down, I notice her jet-black hair is so tightly pulled back from her scalp it looks like it's pulling her skin painfully back. Her clothes are also a size too small, making the fact she doesn't need to breathe a godsend.

I look into her empty black eyes; they're like pools of oil, no emotion. No warmth. Nothing.

"Well? What brings you here?" she demands again before letting a false tinkle of a laugh escape, "Apparently, I must make you nervous, little witch, as you are obviously in thrall with me since I've rendered you mute."

A laugh of amusement escapes me and a snort follows. "No, I'm definitely not enthralled with you," shaking my head at the absurdity of the thought.

Fury races across her face. She reaches out to grab me, her fingers curled like claws. "I'll teach you some manners and your place, little witch," she hisses, going in to strike.

With a flick of my fingers, she's frozen, and I just watch her as confusion, then fear, fights for dominance.

"Why don't you take a chill pill, hmmm?" I calmly ask her. "I have no idea what has gotten your knickers in such a twist. I can tell you, though, it's boring and annoying."

"Well, this is not the entertainment I was thinking of supplying at my dinner party," Vlad calmly informs everyone while running long elegant fingers along his chin in a thoughtful manner. "I must admit it is amusing to watch Vasalina in such a quandary.

"Tell me, my dear, what you were thinking in attacking Victor's *dragoste*, his love, and my guest? Actually, I'll change the question to trying to attack her. After all, you didn't even come close to succeeding."

"I… I'm sorry, my lord. I wanted to know why she was here. She then insulted me," Vasalina replies in a trembling voice, as if acting the victim in this bizarre drama.

"Vasalina, Vasalina, you try my patience. Something I'm not known to have to start with."

"Make her answer, my lord."

"You have got to be kidding me! You try and insult me, attack me, and now you're having a childish tantrum because I won't answer your question. Which is none of your damn business," I blurt out, completely losing my temper.

I'm determined to gain control before my wolf shows herself. I can feel her pacing in anger wanting to take a bite out of the petulant vampire bitch.

A strong warm hand curls over mine, gives it a gentle squeeze. Instantly I'm calm, which is seriously scary that Victor has such an effect on me.

"My, you are a lively one. I can see why you're enamored with her," Vlad informs Victor while watching me. I can feel his mind trying to prod at mine. Without thinking, I slap the intrusive invasion away. Vlad's head snaps to the side, his fangs descend, and blue fire blazes in his eyes when he looks back at me.

Whoops, my bad. He does not look impressed at all.

Almost everyone is staring at him in confusion. Yet no one asks what happened. I do hear slight groans from my friends, who apparently guessed.

I send a mental apology into Vlad's mind, startling him.

A growl escapes him; his gaze burns straight into mine before he gains control of himself. Gives me an ever-so-slight nod of his head in response.

"Please release Vasalina." A slight wave of his hand, palm up, gives the impression of a request, yet I know it's an order.

I snap my fingers and release her. Granted, I didn't need to snap them. Sometimes though, and this is definitely one of those times, a show of power is needed.

Upon her release, she falls forward and bounces off a shield I'd placed around myself. Her nose crunches on it, blood spurting, yet not a drop lands on me.

Loud sharp inhales echo around the table. I've managed to get the "don't fuck with me" message across loud and clear.

Chapter 34

The rest of the dinner goes without any further drama. Once it's over, everyone rises to leave the room and to mingle elsewhere. To be honest, I can't wait for the night to be over.

"One moment please," our host murmurs to my group.

We pause, turn, and walk back toward him. No emotion shows on any of our faces.

"Relax, I'm not going to do anything drastic." Vlad laughs in genuine amusement. Leaning casually against the sideboard, he pulls a grape from the bunch in a bowl and pops it into his mouth.

Victor steps forward bringing me with him, so we're in front of everyone else, a silent show of authority and power.

"Tell me why you have come. You remind me of people on a mission, not on a holiday."

I let out a slight laugh, more of an exhale through my nose though. Looking at him, I come to a conclusion. "We've been led here to find answers."

"To what questions?"

"I don't know," I admit in frustration. "None of us knows what the questions are, just that we'll find the answers here."

"How intriguing and fun. Who is sending you on this quest?"

I chew my lips while thinking about it.

"Surely it's not such hard a question?" demands Vlad in annoyance.

"Actually, it is," I reply.

"Tell me, do these markings on your arms have anything to do with your quest?"

"I'm not sure, probably though. They didn't exactly come with instructions or an explanation when they appeared," I inform him with a grimace, without thinking of what I said.

"Appeared out of nowhere? I do believe you need to tell me everything. Not here though." Sweeping toward the door, he looks back at us to notice we haven't moved. "Follow me."

It's not a request, and as we need to be here, we have no choice but to comply with his order. I just hope he's trustworthy.

We follow him up the stairs. I must admit to being relieved it wasn't to the dungeons. We end up on the top floor, enter a large sitting-room. Glancing around, I realize this must be his private quarters. It's masculine and simple. A beautiful room to relax in.

"Please sit. No one will overhear us here," the prince informs us, waving a hand toward the sofas and chairs.

Once we're all seated, he looks to me, and so I inform him of everything that happened. From the murder in the woods, which led to meeting both Kheda and Victor, to being informed of finding answers at the ball here in two night's time.

Throughout my telling, I'm only interrupted once or twice for clarification. Other than that, there's complete silence. The only thing I leave out is my double magick.

Tapping a finger against his chin, he looks at me with curiosity and intrigue. "You're not telling me everything," he informs me, giving me a narrow-eyed thoughtful glance as if to drag all details from me.

I look back at him without shifting or blinking. For some strange reason, this seems to amuse him.

"Such a determined one, very strong in power. You're unusual." He declares as if I'm a recipe or something. "What is she hiding?" he demands of the others.

When no answer comes out of them, anger flickers across his face. It quickly vanishes to be replaced with a grudging respect. "You're loyal to one another. I like that. Now tell me what you are hiding."

"It has nothing to do…"

"It has everything to do with me," he thunders. Power flickers around him. I can see it vibrate.

"How strange," I murmur. In fascination, I watch the waves rippling from him.

"You see it?"

"Yes, why?" Looking at the others, I notice their puzzlement. "Do any of you see it?"

"See what, Candi?" asks Talia in confusion.

I don't answer her, instead I look at Vlad. "How come?"

"Frustrating, isn't it, having questions which aren't answered?"

I give an inelegant snort of amusement before shaking my head and unsuccessfully suppressing a smile. I mutter, "Very."

"You tell me yours, and I'll tell you mine."

I search his gaze. Finding only honesty, I give a

nod of agreement. "I have double magick. I'm both a witch and a werewolf."

This obviously isn't what he was expecting, judging by his eyebrows shooting up into his hairline. "Truly? Yes, I can see you believe this. Show me. I know you to be a witch. Show me your wolf."

I'm tempted to refuse. I'm not some gimmick to do tricks on demand. I can also feel my wolf's anger; she doesn't enjoy the thought of performing for others either.

As if sensing my fury, he raises his hands in a soothing manner. "I mean no disrespect. I have been informed before of someone being what they're not. I will not be deceived twice."

I wonder who deceived him and why? Whoever it was has left a lasting impression and not a good one. Realizing we need him on our side and we have no choice in the matter, my wolf and I agree in showing him.

Because of his demand, I spring at him, transforming midleap from human into wolf. I land in front of him with my lips pulled back over huge fangs. Letting him know just how displeased I am with him.

"*Dumnnezeul meu*, my god, you speak the truth."

I give a chuff of agreement before turning back into my human form, startling the prince further.

"May I ask how do you keep on your clothes?"

At those innocent words, I burst out laughing. The tension in the room vanishes as the others join in with a chuckle.

"It's because my magicks are separate from each other," I explain, returning to my seat.

"I must admit you've surprised me. I did not

believe it was possible."

I watch as he shakes his head as if he's still trying to grasp what he saw. He looks at me, once more completely in control.

"Now, it is my turn to explain. Vampires are, as you know, magickal, as all supernaturals are. Each of us has a power of some sort or another, some more than others."

Leaning forward, I look directly at him; I send my power out to feel his. Letting it curl around him and stroke his aura. I blink in surprise at just how powerful he is.

"You can manipulate energy, mind read, and there's something else too."

"Very good, I'm impressed. I can control others of my species. Most others, I should say. There are always some more powerful than me."

An awkward silence greets his statement. To be honest I'm dumbfounded and slightly worried. *What if he controls Victor? How would I tell?*

"It's not a power I particularly like," he admits. "One I only use on exceptionally rare occasions. Only if it is necessary to protect, as a last resort."

I look at him closely and realize he's telling the truth. I also comprehend he doesn't like the power. In that instant, I'm glad it is him who has it. A power like that in the hands of someone who enjoys it—the thought is terrifying.

We change the subject and just talk about general things. Nothing personal or intrusive. Soon, it's time for us to go and join the rest of the guests. Our host has been away too long, and we should also mingle with the others.

"Before we join the others, if you need assistance in your hunt, come to me. You may go anywhere in the castle or grounds except chambers being used, of course. It would be impolite to my guests.

"The rest you may search and the grounds too. I hope you find what you're looking for." He opens the door, and we exit.

Once back downstairs, we mingle with the other guests for a while. Slowly, I notice people slip away, either to retire for the night or stroll in the garden. I take it as my cue; I say my goodnights and head off to my room.

Victor accompanies me upstairs, making sure I'm okay. When I reassure him I'm fine and admit I want to read, he just laughs, kisses me, and returns downstairs.

I prepare for bed, climb in, and with a feeling of anticipation, I open my book. Soon, I'm sucked into the story unraveling before me.

Gradually, though, my lids become heavy, and with a feeling of regret, I close the book, placing it on the nightstand beside me. I turn off the light and cuddle down into the blankets. Before long, sleep claims me in its embrace.

****

I'm walking down a corridor. It's long and windy with no beginning or end in sight. Silence feels like a presence pushing around me, prodding me for a weak spot. I let out a growl of anger, call my fire to me, and have it swirl around my body, keeping distance between me and whatever is out there. I move farther into the corridor, following its path until I exit into a field of blood and death.

I pause in horror. The stench of the dying is

horrendous. The screams of the battle cries and injured are deafening. It's only when I spot my friends battling for their lives, I realize this is happening right now.

With a roar of anger, I blend my two magicks together. My wolf comes howling out of my body as the flames wrap around her. Opening my jaw, flames shoot from it burning those who attempt to harm my friends. Changing back into my human form, I swirl energy and magick together creating a bubble of fire. Spreading my arms wide, I call a spell as I let my fire loose.

"Protect those of mine from my power,
Let those against us fall.
Let the terror The Protectors bring
End with this night of death and pain."

My flames race over the field, swallowing some of the fighters and moving around others, leaving them untouched.

Silence once more descends, broken by the sounds of tears. I cool my fire, change it to warmth and healing. Letting it wash over the warriors and heal them.

****

With a gasp, I shoot up in bed. The smell of burning flesh lingers in my nostrils.

"It is just one outcome of the potential war ahead," Hecate informs me.

"How can I prevent it from happening?" I ask, feeling dazed and queasy by the thought of the nightmare coming true.

"I'm glad you asked. Sadly though, I have no answers for you. Danger surrounds you. The war with The Protectors is approaching."

"Can it be stopped?"

"The war? No. How it ends? Possibly. Time will tell. Sleep now, daughter of mine. Rest while you can. The Protectors are gathering their allies in unlikely places."

Without another word, Hecate is gone. Leaving me in confusion and definitely unable to sleep.

Chapter 35

I must have fallen asleep. I honestly don't remember. All I'm aware of is the feeling of a smoldering hot mouth on my breast and warm hands squeezing my butt, stroking my sides, waking me up.

"Mmm, hey," I murmur. I lift my hands up and explore Victor's muscular back, run my fingers through his hair, before grasping it and yanking his head up to mine. He gives me a wicked grin before leaning in closer to me.

Our lips slant over each other's, rubbing gently before opening to entangle our tongues together. Slowly, we make love before curling up in each other's embrace and falling asleep.

The next time I wake up, it's morning. I open my eyes to look directly into Victor's. A smile escapes him as he watches me.

"You okay?" I ask, wondering why he's watching me so intently.

"Yes."

"Why are you watching me so...?" I wave my hand in front of his face as if it explains anything.

His grin grows wider; he quickly grasps my waving hand bringing it to his chest. Trapping it between his hand and body.

"I like watching you," he admits. "Seeing you like this, naked in my arms, brings me peace I've never felt before."

"How?" I frown in my confusion only to have him reach out and soothe my forehead with his fingers, easing my frown away.

"You bring me peace. Having you near me, falling asleep with you, and waking up beside you gives me unimaginable serenity. You give me hope. Your loving me makes me love you even more. Watching you makes me know you're really here with me."

"Wow, uh, yeah, wow." My ability for eloquent speaking astounds even me. In mortification, I feel my blood rise in my face.

"I don't expect you to say anything…"

"No, I…I don't know what to say," I stammer. "I love you. It's something I've found hard to admit. I've never felt the way I feel about you for anyone else. You make me happy and feel alive, safe. I've always…"

"I make you feel safe? You're one of the strongest people I've ever met."

"Thank you. The way you make me feel, I know I can rely on you to have my back if needed. It means a hell of a lot to me." With my untrapped hand, I reach out and stroke his face, exploring the sharp angles and his soft full lips. He nips my fingers playfully, making me laugh.

"I love you more than I ever imagined I could ever love anyone," I inform him, making his eyes widen before I lean forward and kiss him.

We hold each other close, stroking each other in a loving caress every now and again. A simple embrace which means so much more.

Eventually, we rise from bed, shower, and dress and leave our room to go down for breakfast and meet up with the others.

With breakfast over, we all spend the day exploring the castle including the dungeons. Nothing jumps out at us. Though the echoes of the past are vivid. Especially with some of Vlad's instruments of torture, including poles thankfully without people impaled on them placed on tables or leaning against walls. I'm about to ask if he still uses them, before deciding I really don't want to know.

After exploring the castle, we head into the woods. Snow covers everything. The place is stunning. Every now and again, I see movement from an animal through the trees. Soon, I realize a wolf is keeping pace with us. Close enough to track, too far away to meet.

I pause before backtracking. With a slight wave of my hand, I encourage the others to carry on walking. I want to see if the curious wolf will notice if one of our group goes missing, maybe find out who the wolf is following.

By the time I've backtracked, the wolf is gone. I search for any sign, yet find nothing. Not even a scent, which surprises me. *Did I imagine the wolf?*

I quickly catch up with the others. Turning to them, I ask if any of them had seen the wolf. Receiving blank looks and no's, I become very confused. I know deep down inside myself I saw the wolf, even if there isn't a trace of one being there.

"Maybe the wolf is your spirit animal," Jezebel pipes up while continuing to walk.

"My what?" I can hear the astonishment in my voice and see it reflected on the others' faces.

"Your spirit animal. We all have one. Most don't get to meet them unless…"

"Unless what?"

"Well, I don't know; different reasons. Can be you're more acceptable, curiosity, a desire to meet, or a warning. It depends on you and your spirit animal."

"You know that doesn't help, don't you?" I mutter in frustration.

"Look, just keep a watch out. If you see the wolf again, try to follow it. Eventually, you might meet and talk."

"Have you ever met yours?" I can hear the curiosity lacing my voice, not surprising since I'd never heard of someone literally seeing their spirit animal.

"Yes, once. She was stunning and..."

"And what?" I ask, quietly wondering what she was about to say.

"Nothing, it doesn't matter. Well, I should say it's between me and her."

I want to ask more questions desperately. Yet I know there's no point right now. Looking at my friend, I have to wonder, what was the reason her spirit animal came to her and why only once.

Chapter 36

Throughout the day, more guests arrive for tonight's ball. Eventually, it's time to get ready. After I've finished bathing, I apply some makeup and then remove it as I've botched it big time. And then reapply it. Once satisfied, I dress. I add some knives to my sheaths and do my hair into a twist at the back of my head with some loose tendrils around my face.

Hearing a noise behind me, I turn to find Victor watching me. His jaw has slightly dropped, flashing his fangs while blue fire swirls in his eyes. He looks stunning in his black tuxedo with his hair in a slightly shaggy fashion. It gives him an edge of danger.

"You look gorgeous," I murmur, moving to him and shutting his jaw by pressing his chin up.

"You…"

I watch him swallow in amusement. I've never seen him lost for words before and decide to take it for a compliment.

"Stunning," he finally croaks out.

I look at him in confusion for a split second, before realizing he's finishing his sentence. Giving him a beaming smile, I say thanks and indicate the door. "Shall we?"

"It'd be my utmost pleasure." Victor offers me his arm, linking mine around his, we exit our room and descend the stairs.

The sounds of a waltz playing greets us. I have a second of panic before the pressure of Victor's gentle squeeze of reassurance calms me. Next thing I know, I'm being moved into his embrace and danced around the floor.

I think I do quite well. I only stomp on his toes four times. When the music ends, I'm led off the floor by a limping partner. Due to quick healing, his walk turns quickly into his usual fluid grace.

I hear chuckles from some of the other dancers and see sympathetic looks sent in Victor's direction. I can't help the twinge of guilt which filters through me. It thankfully doesn't last long though.

"Would you like a drink?" Tucking my fingers into the crook of his arm, he leads me to the bar.

"Please. I'll just have a soda though."

"You sure?"

"Oh yeah, I don't think your toes could take me on with a couple of drinks in me. Anyway, I'll need a clear head for later," I add, wondering what exactly I'll find out at midnight in the garden.

Time seems to go so slowly. We mingle as much as possible, and eventually, it's five to twelve. I refrain from dragging Victor into the garden. Instead, as casually as possible, we stroll out as if going for some air.

We step out into the garden and wander around. Bathed in moonlight, everything looks ethereal and otherworldly, a magical place of beauty and peace.

We come across the fountain and find two women talking beside it. Suddenly, I come to a fast halt as my arm is almost yanked out of its socket by the immovable object attached to it. Glancing back at

Victor, I'm surprised how pale he looks.

****

"Are you okay?" I ask in concern, retreating back to him and easing my aching shoulder.

"That's...it can't be though...she's dead!"

I'm surprised at the confusing babble spluttering from the normally articulate vampire. I feel confused and extremely curious. *Who is meant to be dead who's not?*

Turning back to the women, I receive a jolt of my own as I realize I recognize one of the women and assume the other woman is who he's talking about. "Janna? Holy cow, it's the Daphmire Janna," I whisper in urgent excitement.

I'm about to hurry toward them, only to be stopped once again.

"Why are you stopping me?" I hiss in frustration.

"It's Vincent's mother."

"Ugh. What? Wait, which one's his mother? I demand, feeling completely confused. "Is Jana Vincent's mother or the other woman?"

"The other one, as you put it, is my mother," drawls a testy voice from behind us startling us both. "God damn her, why couldn't she just stay away," grinds out Vincent in aggravation while glaring at me.

"What? I've never met your mother so why...hold on, your mother?" My head snaps back around to face the women once more. "Ohhh, oh, oh my god, it was her you've been taking the blame for all these years, isn't it?" I demand in excitement as I now fit the little bits of information together.

"How is it you've met me now twice, yet you manage to realize the truth so quickly while..." his voice trails off, I watch him rub his forehead as if to release tension or give him a second to gather his thoughts.

"It was your mother? Why did you never tell me? Wait." Holding up a hand as if to stop someone speaking, Victor releases his hold on my arm to step toward Vincent. "Your mother is the killer. Why did you let me believe it was you?"

"How could I tell you I'd turned my mother when she begged me to, only for her to go and massacre your whole family? In what possible way could it make anything better?"

Vincent's pain is etched across his face like a living scar. His shoulders have dropped and curve in on him as if to protect himself from a coming blow. When Victor reaches for him, I notice him flinch as arms wrap around him in a hug instead of attack.

"Knowing it wasn't you who killed them would have meant everything to me. Does mean everything. I've missed you every day. You're my brother."

"But my mother…"

"Your mother is not you. You can't blame yourself for the choices and decisions she has made. You're her child, not the other way round." I see a look of confusion on his face as he draws back so he can look at Vincent before continuing, "All this time you've been cleaning up after her? Surely not…"

Silence descends on our small group as no further words are uttered on the realizations which have come to pass.

"You feel guilty. Is that why you've tried to keep her existence a secret?" I ask, though a part of me knows I'm right.

"Yes. If I hadn't changed her..."

"Look, I'm not being funny here; you can't be her cleanup crew. Obviously, it hasn't been helping. I think it is past time you started living for yourself. Cut the apron strings, so to speak. Though they are in reverse, which is odd," I add, scrunching my face up like a confused rabbit as I think about it. Hearing chuckles from the hugging vampires, I make an effort to relax my facial muscles.

"You're cute and rather wise for one so young," Vincent informs me in such a matter-of-fact fashion, I feel the honesty of his words reverberate through me. More as if he's declaring it to the world than to me.

I give a nod of thanks as my attention once more returns to the fountain. Without a second thought, I remove my skirt, turn it inside out, and attach it to my shoulders. Swiftly, I move forwards, keeping to the shadows, drawing them closer to me.

Once I'm in hearing distance, I lower myself down to a crouch.

"It doesn't explain why you have come here, Rose."

"Janna, I've told you already. I've come to apologize for the havoc I've wrought. Why don't you believe me?" whines Rose in a petulant voice.

"Enough." Swiping a hand through the air as if to slice through any further comments, Janna frowns at the woman in front of her. "You have created mayhem wherever you go, leaving your son to clean up and take the blame for your actions. Your behavior is despicable and selfish. Now answer me truthfully, what have you done with Roísín?"

A cackle of a laugh escapes from Rose, causing

shivers to creep up my arms. Her laugh sounds insane.

"I've, hmmm, how should I put it," purrs Rose with a pleased look smeared across her face, while tapping a finger against her chin. "Sold her. Yes, that's the best way of putting it."

"You've what?" demands Vincent striding forwards to grasp hold of his mother and shake her.

"Sold her," she screeches in his face causing spittle to fly from her lips.

"Why? How could you do...?"

"Easily, you were leaving me for her. I knew she was dangerous from the moment I saw that, that... harpy!"

"Where is she?" Growls Vincent, shaking his mother furiously as if the action can loosen the answers from her, I see fear and agony ripple across his face.

Who is Roísín and why would Rose sell her and to whom?

"You'll never know because I'll never tell," Rose sing-songs her answer with a gleeful laugh.

Standing up, I've decided I've had enough of this woman; I'll bloody well make her tell the truth.

"Hecate, Goddess of the Underworld, Crossroads, and Witches.

I call on you to find the answers this woman withholds.

Hear. My. Cry."

Flinging my arms in the air, I step forward to the gasps of the three by the fountain and the loud boom of thunder reverberating through the sky.

"What are you...?"

The howling wind brings the forms of Hecate and her hounds with it.

"Tell me the truth, Rose O'Sullivan, or I shall make you regret the day you were born." Echoes out of the wind startle her, making Rose look warily into the wind until she hisses in alarm when Hecate appears with her hounds snarling, baring their teeth.

"I...I..."

"Now!"

"The Protector's humans. I sold her to their humans."

"Where?"

"They have a farm in Montana. A recruitment farm where they train to catch supernaturals."

"Wait, what?" I blurt out, feeling completely baffled by everything.

"I had feared this was coming to pass. Rose O'Sullivan, for your treachery against your son and your victims, I remove your eternal life as a vampire.

"You shall from this day forth live as a human. Unseen by all supernaturals and helpless to all humans. You shall be the prey you've always hunted."

A crackle of power flies from Hecate wrapping around the screaming woman, dragging from her, her vampire essence. As Hecate pulls back her power, we no longer see Rose. She simply vanishes from our sight.

"Go to Montana. Find Roísín. And be safe. This treachery goes deep."

With a final nod, Hecate and her dogs vanish leaving behind a gaping Daphmire and vampire. Victor comes up behind me; taking my hand in his, he gives it a squeeze.

"So Montana, then. Who is it we're going to rescue, and why was she sold?"

"She's our daughter, Vincent's and mine," Janna

answers, looking at us with tears rising in her vision.

"What? Wow, okay. Really?" I splutter out, feeling completely floored by this sudden turn of events. "Does she have double magick too?"

"What? No. Hold on, you said too, meaning someone already has. Who?" Janna demands prowling closer to me.

I stare at her, drinking in the sight of the woman who I've been seeing through history. A woman I'm descended from. Who by rights shouldn't be alive. Both of us being hunted just because we exist.

"I have," I inform her.

Chapter 37

Silence greets my answer. As if both Vincent and Janna have turned to stone. I look at them with my head cocked to the side, wondering how they met and became lovers. They look good together, happy.

"Are you telling me you have two types of magicks?" demands Janna, breaking into my contemplation.

"Hmm? Yes. I do."

"What are you, then, other than witch? What else are you?" she clarifies her question, with distrust reverberating in her voice.

"Wolf. I'm a witch and a wolf." I can see this line of questioning carrying on for a while so decide just to end it by turning into my wolf form.

"Holy cow, you really are the double magick one. I'd assumed you were lying. Others have…"

Changing back, I look at her curiously. "Why would someone pretend to have two magicks if they don't?"

"To try and get close to me, I guess. How do you know who I am?"

"Weird dream-like flashbacks, out-of-body experiences kept happening. It would show me what you were doing and where you were," I reply, getting confused by my own explanation.

"She kept literally disappearing. When she came

back, she had new clues to follow," adds Victor in a no nonsense voice.

"Your body vanished? Blimey, that could have been dangerous," mutters Vincent under his breath.

"Dangerous, annoying, oh, and embarrassing," I add with a slight shudder. "Anyway, so your daughter, Roísín, was kidnapped by your mother and sold to humans in Montana. Who work for *The Protectors*, is that right? Why would she do it?"

"Maybe we should go inside and have this conversation. I don't fancy it being overheard." Without waiting for an answer, Vincent walks back toward the castle. Janna, Victor, and I quickly follow. I change my cloak back into a skirt as I follow the others back to the castle.

Upon entering, I spot Nancy and indicate she should get the others and follow us. Twenty minutes later, we're all upstairs in Vlad's rooms once more. He'd seen us gathering and, on the condition he was coming too, allowed us the use of his rooms for our conversation.

Once everyone's settled, Janna begins her story.

"I am the first Daphmire. My mother was a powerful witch and my father a vampire. My mother had foretold of my coming and of the birth of the one with double magick." Taking a sip of wine before continuing her story, she glances at me as if still surprised at my being here.

"Many have attempted to kill me even before I was born. Accidents were set up and attempted in the hopes my mother would be harmed and miscarry. The fear *The Protectors* have wrought has been going on since time began. They are power hungry and vicious.

"Many tried to kill me in order to save their families from persecution. An act of folly and stupidity." She huffs in aggravation, shaking her head as if still trying to understand why someone would attempt it.

"Anyway, once I was born, we moved around quite a bit. We never stayed anywhere too long until finally my mother built a home and cast a protection spell over it." A shudder ripples through her, and her skin pales at the memories she's retelling us.

Looking up, she glances at Vincent, who takes her hand in his and gives it a gentle squeeze. They share a smile between them before Janna continues her story.

"My mother steeped the support beam in blood. By steeped, I mean a town was slaughtered so she could do the protection spell.

Holy fucking hell, a whole town was slaughtered? Oh my god, it's Victor's bar counter, I know he said it was spelled in blood. I never guessed a whole flipping town though.

I'm dragged out of my thoughts when I'm nudged by Nancy. Quickly looking up, I notice Victor's looking a little shocked himself.

"We lived in peace for years. I met and fell in love, married, and had two children. Twins." She gazes at the wall in front of her for a while. I'm guessing her thoughts are with her family. I remember she had to send her kids away to keep them safe.

I wonder what happened to her husband, and why it was necessary to send her children away. What happened to make the need to send them away so great?

"Demetri, my husband, was taken. His brother

Vlasim, your sire"—she nods at both Victor and Vincent—"came to us, warned us. He helped send away my children. From thence onwards, I trained in warfare completely. I was determined to find and rescue Demetri.

"I failed."

"Holy hell," Talia mutters, breaking the silence.

I turn to look at her, noticing everyone gazing in fascination at Janna. Hooked on her story, though a few look slightly pale.

"I never found him." A slight grimace crosses her face at the memory flitting through her head. "Vlasim told me he'd come close to rescuing him. The torture being inflicted was so horrendous it would make Vlad look like a boy scout.

"We were set to storm the castle he was being held in. A battle broke out before we could reach it; by the time we got there, he had been moved. It was the closest we ever came to rescuing him.

"I've never heard of any sign or mention of him since that day. It was like he vanished from history. I'd managed to lose everyone in a matter of months. My husband and my children; my mother gave up afterwards.

"She destroyed the house she'd built, giving Vlasim the support beam and an eye-chart codex before simply leaving. It was the last time I saw her too."

She falls into silence for a while. Lost in her memories, her sight fixed on the wall without seeing it. Yet sorrow radiates from her. I can literally feel her pain lashing out until she reins it in and it eases. I watch her blink a couple of times, glance at Vincent, and smile at him.

Once more, he gives her fingers a reassuring squeeze and a gentle smile, and a look full of love and devotion flickers across his face.

"For five hundred years, I was alone. Well, mainly alone, I should say. I did for a short period fall in love again. Hector was one of my warriors; I was going on a mission and sent him away.

"I shouldn't have. He and the other warriors with him were ambushed and killed. Afterwards, I drifted between wars, fighting and searching for the one my mother proclaimed will stop this war with *The Protectors.*

"Hearing of a killer hunting prostitutes, I decided I needed a distraction. What I hadn't expected to find was love."

"Was this when..."

"Yes, this is when we met," answers Vincent. He looks at us long enough to acknowledge the question before returning his gaze to the woman he loves.

"I came across him trying to clean up after his mother. Obviously, at the time I didn't know this, so decided to observe him. It was during the next killing I witnessed him stopping her and trying to help the victim. I realized there was a lot more going on than I first knew.

"This was also when I first saw you, Victor. You and Vlasim came rushing onto the scene and chased after Vincent. While his mother had already hunted down her next victim.

"A sorrier mess I've never seen. Quite confusing too. Later, I hunted down Vincent and forced him to tell me exactly what the hell was going on. Why two vampires—I hadn't told him I knew one of them—were under the presumption he was the killer."

"You never did understand my guilt, which is amusing, since neither did Victor when the truth came out." Vincent chuckles, shaking his head.

Looking at him, I wonder if he's thinking of the lost years which could have been avoided if only his guilt hadn't gotten in the way. *What a waste of a good friendship. I'm glad the truth has been revealed. They need each other.*

"I can't believe the years I wasted…Never mind though, we're now altogether, which is the main thing."

"Exactly. Anyway, where was I? Ah yes, so once I found out the truth and was unsuccessful in convincing him to tell you about his mother, I opted to help him instead. Granted, Rose didn't appreciate it or make it easy."

"She can be a stubborn one at times." At the wiry look he receives for this comment, he gives a slight shrug and nod of his head. "She's my mum…"

"So when did you have your daughter?" I ask trying to steer the conversation back on track.

Sorrow flickers across their faces, and I feel like kicking myself. For a second, I'd forgotten their daughter has been kidnapped and sold by his mother. "I'm sorry…"

"It's not your fault. It's not as if you kidnapped her, after all. That was my mother." The bitterness and regret in Vincent's voice is also reflected in his expression.

How could his mother do such a cruel and evil thing to her child and grandchild?

"Why did your mother do such a horrible thing?" Selena asks in a quiet voice.

"To get back at us. When we met and I realized exactly what was going on, I decided to help. Okay, help is probably the wrong word. I decided to…"

"Convince me of the errors of my ways and live for myself."

"Exactly." A gurgle of laughter erupts from Janna surprising me.

"Anyway, after a century, I somehow managed to persuade him to stop. All those years he'd spent protecting her by cleaning up after her wasn't stopping her. So my logic was, if he stopped, she would have to learn to take control and responsibility for her own actions.

"It seemed to work, as for a long time we didn't hear from her or of murders which could be hers. Eventually we married."

Once more, we witness the look of love and devotion they share with each other. I hear a couple of the girls let out barely audible sighs of longing.

I glance at Victor to find him watching me with a contented smile on his face. I feel the slight blush rise to my cheeks, and his smile grows bigger, warmer…

"Anyway, ten years ago, I became pregnant and had Roísín. Everything was wonderful until…"

"My mother came back into the picture." His shoulders appear to slump as if the weight of the world has landed on them. Sadness cloaks him.

"It's not your fault we were both fooled. The year after she was born, Rose found us. She acted contrite and wanted to be there for us. At first we were leery. Slowly though, and I do mean slowly, we allowed her access.

"Six months ago, she kidnapped Roísín. Tonight is

the first time we've seen Rose since that day."

Turning his head to look at both Victor and I, Vincent picks up the story. "When I saw you two at the graveyard in Whitechapel, I was following a lead on my mother's possible whereabouts. She'd been spotted there the week before. When I arrived, I couldn't find any sign of her, and then I saw the two of you.

"I couldn't lose the chance of speaking to you. I also knew if you'd seen her you would mention it what with you thinking she was dead and all."

"Yes, I'd certainly have mentioned seeing her. I almost had a heart attack when I saw her tonight," Victor replies.

"So let me get this right," I butt in, "since you turned her, you've done everything possible to keep her a secret, including taking the blame for her being a serial killer."

"Ugh, yeah..."

"After way too long playing clean-up duty, you realize you've had enough and decide to actually live your own life, find happiness, and start a family. Correct?"

"Well, yes..."

"Suddenly, she reenters your lives after a century of no contact, yet a year after the birth of your daughter..."

"You really know how to speed up and make everything as blunt as possible, don't you?"

"Yes, I do. Now back to the situation at hand. Did you ever find out how she found you?"

"How?" asks Vincent in confusion.

I watch as they share a confused look between them.

"Yes, how. For the greater part of your existence, you've been hunted because you're a Daphmire, so it's not as if you advertise your whereabouts. You also mentioned you've had no contact with your mother for a century.

"So how, a year after the birth of your daughter, did she wander back into your lives knowing exactly where to find you?"

"I." Vincent shakes his head in bewilderment, it's obvious he doesn't know how to finish his answer.

"Which brings me to the conclusion, she was keeping watch on the two of you. Had planned on the moment of your daughter's birth how she was going to exact her revenge upon you both. In the cruelest fashion possible."

"So what now?"

"Now, we rescue your daughter. We need to book flights to Montana. Do you have a picture of her with you?"

"Yes, well, in our rooms anyway. You're going to help us?"

"Of course we will. I think we should all get a good night's sleep. And tomorrow, we'll book our flights and set a plan in motion. Agreed?"

"Agreed," everyone choruses except Cedrix.

"Actually, since we're going back to America, Jezebel and I should head back and sign her in before she's classified as skipping bail. We can meet you in Montana afterwards."

"Wait a sec…" Jezebel erupts in annoyance.

"It makes sense. You know it does," I quickly interrupt her.

After a few minutes of arguing, she relents and

agrees to meet up once she's sorted out her own affairs. After all, there's no point in having the cops after her if it can be avoided. Especially when we'll be trying to rescue a child.

Decision made, we all head off to our rooms. A sense of excitement and anticipation resonates amongst us. It's been a long time since we've been on a mission, never mind rescuing a young girl.

Once back in our room, I turn to Victor and kiss him. Releasing him, I look into his beautiful eyes and can't help smiling.

"I'm glad you now know the truth. Your friend— your brother—has always had your back."

"So am I. I just wish he had confided in me. I could have helped him."

"You are now, which is what matters."

We undress and crawl into bed. I curl up against him, wrap my arms around him, and drift off to sleep. My last waking memory is of his hand stroking my back over and over again.

Chapter 38

I wake up wrapped in Victor's embrace. His arms tighten for a second around me, pulling me closer if at all possible, when I shift slightly back to look at him. I can't help the little smile which flickers across my face as I wonder if he realizes how a simple action makes me feel safe.

Silly, really. After all, the slight tightening of his arms is just reflex. As for feeling safe…the fact I do feel this way with him, I still find confusing and wonderful at the same time.

I place a kiss on his chest, run my fingers over his beautiful body, and wake him up with gentle touches and kisses. We make love slowly before getting showered, dressed, and packed. Afterwards, we head on down to have breakfast.

When everyone's fed, we take a walk in the garden and discuss our plans. All agree the sooner we can fly out, the better it'll be all round. Janna offers to fly us out in her plane.

I must admit I feel kind of in awe over the fact she not only has her own plane but can fly it herself too. Everyone quickly agrees. After all, this way will be quicker and more comfortable.

Our carriages are brought around to the front. I'm surprised they're still here, to be honest.

"They are kept here, so no questions will be asked

about them returning here. After all, the non-supernaturals only see ruins. This way we have them here and can influence them into believing they took you much farther," Vlad informs me.

"Huh, makes sense. I was wondering how we could convince them to return," I admit, feeling slightly daft I hadn't figured it out.

Janna gives the coachmen directions to the airfield we'll be heading for. Apparently, it's a private one off the beaten track and a couple of days traveling to boot. My butt tenses just at the thought of the long bouncy ride ahead.

Before leaving, I remind everyone to be careful what they say while in the carriages. At this, I receive startled looks from Vlad, Janna, and Vincent, so quickly inform them of how Victor found out we were being listened to.

"I'll warn my other guests. Thank you for letting me know this… situation."

I can't help but feel a little worried for the remaining coachmen. Only for a second, though, as my main concern quickly returns to our remaining journey and what we'll find once we land in America.

Chapter 39

The journey by coach is as tiring as expected. Which is surprising if you think about it as we're sitting on our asses the whole time. We had to stay one night at Janna's due to the full moon.

It wouldn't have been good if two werewolves transformed on the plane. Also, I needed to change and rejoiced in the run. Jezebel and Jasmine also shapeshifted into their animal forms.

By the time we all had come back, the flight arrangements and permissions to use the air space are approved.

Early the next morning, we board the plane and soon are in the air. I read and snooze for most of the flight.

At last we arrive. As I'm about to exit my seat, we're informed this is only a pit stop to refuel and for Cedrix and Jezebel to disembark. I press my nose to the window trying to drink in everything I see as I've always wanted to visit New Orleans.

A feeling of disappointment washes over me when all I see are other planes. With a little huff, I turn back to my book. Sensing someone watching me, I look up to meet gorgeous silvery green eyes.

"Have you ever been here before?"

"No, I've always wanted to, though. I did want to explore, not just see other planes, mind you."

"Maybe we'll come here for a holiday sometime. If you'd like?"

I give him a beaming smile and wiggle in my seat happily at the thought. "Oh yes, I'd love to."

"As soon as we can then," promises Victor, bestowing on me a smile that makes my bones turn to mush and my heart accelerate.

"Damn, he's hot," T.T. blurts out.

A moment of silence greets her statement before I look at her with a simple, "Yep, totally agree," before bursting out laughing at the man in question's scarlet cheeks. "Ah bless, you've gone all red and embarrassed," I tease him causing him to squirm in his seat.

"I never knew a vampire could blush." Kheda chuckles, causing further amusement between the girls.

"Okay, okay, enough of making me blush, guys. I do believe it's feeding time."

"What?" squeaks T.T. looking concerned.

"Behind you, food is being brought out," I inform her, trying desperately not to laugh at the relief crossing her face.

"Ohhhh, okay."

"We're only stopping long enough to eat," Janna informs us, coming out of the cockpit with Vincent behind her. They both head straight for the food being laid out.

"We ordered this to be brought onboard just after we landed," Vincent explains, indicating the retreating delivery people.

"I never knew you could do that," I blurt out, watching the men and women exit the plane and cross back into the terminal building.

"Normally, you can't," Janna admits. "We know the deli owners and have a contract with them."

"Okay." I must admit this answer leaves me more curious than anything else and confused to boot.

We all grab something to eat and drink. I notice Victor's looking a little pale. I must give him some of my blood next time we land and are on our own, unless he doesn't mind following me to the bathroom for some privacy.

Catching his attention, I give a little nod in the direction of the bathroom then walk toward it. A couple of minutes later, he follows me inside.

"You okay?" The concern on his face and in his voice is endearing, and I can't help the smile from flickering across my lips.

"I'm fine. You need to drink though," I reply, moving my hair away from my neck and tilting my head to the side, giving him better access.

"Are you sure?"

"Drink, you need it, and no, I don't mind."

He looks at me a while longer. I can feel the muscles in my neck beginning to cramp due to the angle. When he finally lowers his head, he places an open-mouthed kiss on my neck before sinking his elongated fangs into me, making me groan in pleasure.

My arms circle him, one clasping the back of his head keeping him locked to me. A large strong thigh slips between mine; his arms lift me up, and I wrap my legs around his waist, right before I bite him on the shoulder, making him shudder as I sip the droplets of blood which escape from him.

"I love when you bite me," he informs me through the bite link.

"Mmm, good, 'cause I can't help it. I love the taste of you in my mouth." I feel the blush rise into my cheeks as I realize the double entendre I'd unintentionally uttered.

"I love being inside you too," he informs me with amusement lacing his mental words. I also feel his smile curve against my neck and know he also means more than his blood.

I can't help it. I burst out laughing, which is muffled around his neck. We both stop drinking from each other. He places a kiss on my shoulder, whispering, "Thank you."

"There's no need to thank me," I inform him.

"Without me asking, you knew I needed blood. You give yourself so willingly. You'll never know how much I appreciate your generosity with yourself and especially your blood."

"It's…"

"Don't tell me it's nothing," he sternly growls at me. "Your gift is not nothing! Your blood is powerful. A few sips from you sustains me for longer than any other blood possibly can."

"Well…"

"Makes me not need to feed as often. I hate the need to feed," he admits, resting his forehead on mine. A slight smile curves his lips. "I've never admitted it before."

"There's nothing wrong with your drinking blood. You shouldn't be embarrassed about something that's just natural."

"It's not natural."

"It is to vampires," I gently chide him, unlocking my legs from his waist and sliding down his body so I can stand up.

"I know. It's just I can't stand the cravings and the driving need for blood."

"Drinking blood is your main source of food. Get over it," I growl at him. "Seriously, I can't believe you're embarrassed about needing to eat!"

"I'm not…"

"Really? Or have you just not thought of it like that?"

"I… never thought of it like that."

"Why are you embarrassed, or is it you don't like it?"

"To be honest, I think it's more a fear of losing control and becoming a ravenous beast. Of drinking too much, becoming a killer. The drinking I enjoy."

"Ah, I see," nodding my head in understanding. "You fear becoming like, well, Rose, though you had thought it was Vincent all this time."

A startled look crosses his face followed by dawning realization. Shaking his head, he lets out a startled bark of laughter, opens his mouth to say something just as Janna's voice crackles over the loudspeaker.

"Kindly take your seats. We're about to take off."

We exit the bathroom and hurry back to our seats. I ignore the smirks I receive from some of the girls, strap myself in, and glance out the window. A few minutes later, the sounds of the engines start up, and we're moving. Our speed slowly picks up and becomes faster until we lift off.

The flight takes a little over five hours. By the time we land, everyone is exhausted. Jet lag is hitting us fast.

We disembark and once more spell our weapons,

just in case we get stopped.

T.T., Felicity, and I quickly cast our spells on everyone's luggage. Once done, we continue on without any hassles. We opt to hire cars in order to get around.

Altogether, we hire four cars. The woman at the desk gives us all beaming smiles and "Have a great vacation," after telling us where we can collect the cars and giving us our paperwork.

With tired smiles, we head out of the airport, collect the cars, and drive to a hotel. After we've all checked in, we agree to get some sleep and meet once we're up. No specific time, just when we awake.

I feel like crying when I see the large comfortable bed. I'm so tired I can almost hear the bed's siren call.

"Oh, thank god," mutters Victor from directly behind me.

I turn and see a look of longing on his face as he glances at the bed. He drops his bag on the floor, kicks the door closed behind him, and starts stripping.

I just stop midyawn to drink in the sight of his beautiful body being bared to me. A happy sigh escapes me. I can't help it. It does, though, catch his attention. Sadly, he stops undressing. His belt unbuckled and his jeans opened, his hands rest on his hips.

"Oh, please don't stop," I beg, indicating with a wave of my hand and an appreciative look I want to see more.

"You're exhausted as am I. Do you really have the energy?"

I notice his erection playing peek-a-boo over the top of his jeans as it pushes its way out. I lick my lips as they feel suddenly dry.

"Mmm-hmm." My extensive vocabulary astounds me sometimes; thankfully, he ignores my eloquent words and extends his hand toward me. I grasp his hand and let him pull me into his embrace. We're just about to kiss when I let out another jaw-breaking yawn.

"Damn. You need sleep, my beauty. Come on, let me get you to bed."

"Mmm, yes, bed," I murmur seductively around another huge yawn. Ugh, who am I kidding; seduction left the building when I almost cracked my jaw with my first yawn.

A chuckle escapes my half-naked sex god.

If I had the energy, I would be offended. Mind you, if I had the energy, this would be a completely different situation altogether.

I half collapse against him, mainly so I can have a tired, quick grope of him. Also, so I don't go sliding to the ground in a heap at his feet. I do believe my body is shutting down on me.

My eyelids flutter closed. I feel his arms wrap securely around me...

Chapter 40

I'm not sure what time it is or how long I was asleep for, but what I do know is my eyeballs feel like grit has embedded in them. My mouth, ugh, it is drier than the Sahara Desert. I'm positive I have a couple of days' worth of morning breath gone wrong. I give a tentative sniff, Smelling the musky scent of sleep and sweat, I wrinkle my nose.

Basically I feel like crap. Rested crap granted, yet crap all the same. I need a shower and to brush my teeth at least four times.

With a plan in mind, I flop out of bed and land on the floor. For a minute, I stare dumbfounded at my situation. I feel weak, pathetic, and wanting to cry. The sudden urgency to relieve my bladder now I've decided to move has moved beyond the critical stage.

With momentous determination, I somehow get my feet under me. Sway to a standing position and half throw myself off walls into the general direction of the bathroom. I face plant only a couple of times. So I'm quite impressed with myself.

Spotting the item of my current desire, I let out a groan of relief when my ass lands on it. A second later, I remember I haven't cleaned it, and I shudder in revulsion. Once finished, I check out the shower.

Half an hour later, I'm squeaky clean with fresh minty breath. My stomach lets out a yowl of a reminder, which is when I notice I'm on my own. I'm not sure how I didn't realize this sooner.

Once dressed, I'm ready to face the world or at least any part of the world that will feed me in the next twenty minutes. I don't have far to go, just downstairs. I plop into a booth and order pancakes with extra sausages and bacon and maple syrup on the side.

I've just finished eating when the others start trickling into the restaurant. Slowly but surely everyone starts looking less like death warmed up and more like people with a pulse, once they're fed.

We're missing two members of our group, both vampires. I'm just starting to wonder where they are, when they stroll through the door, spot us, and head over to join us.

"So what's the plan?" asks Nancy, glancing in turn at each of us.

"How about we do a little sightseeing today?" I pipe up. "Find our way around the place," I carry on before the unhappy parents can say anything.

"Oh yes, that is a good idea," Janna admits rather reluctantly.

Leaning toward her, I quietly add, "There's no point in rushing into a rescue mission if we don't know our way around, especially how to extract ourselves with the least amount of noise and notice."

I watch the relief flicker across her expression as she nods her agreement, and I see her steely resolve from within as it strengthens her.

Damn, no wonder her enemies fell before her during battle. I'm glad she's on our side.

We pay and leave. We start off by simply strolling about the place, then buying a couple of maps and sightseeing. Basically, doing the whole tourist experience including buying some trinkets.

Soon, we return to our cars and take separate trips out in different directions. Scouting prospective areas where a training camp for killing supernaturals could be located.

The thought makes me want to laugh. *How the hell do they recruit?*

"What are you thinking about?" Victor asks me. Curiosity laces his voice as he glances quickly at me before returning his attention back to the road.

"Recruiting people to kill supernaturals," I answer with a burst of laughter. "Can you imagine their pitch? 'Hi, we're currently recruiting for the position of killer. It's okay though. It's only the supernaturals you'll be hunting!' "

At my ludicrous sales pitch, I receive a full-blown shout of laughter.

"Yeah, my sentiments exactly." Shaking my head in amusement, I return to looking out the window. "Slow down."

"What?"

"Slow down. I think…" I trail off as I stare intently at the snow-covered scenery.

A distant farm has caught my attention. Nothing about it stands out, yet my hackles rise just from looking in its direction.

"There's something very wrong about this place," I mutter as we drive by slowly.

"Do you want to go and have a look around?"

"No, keep going straight," I reply as I take out the map and unfold it. A wink of light flashes briefly from the direction of the farm. I point further down the road before looking back at the map.

"I do believe we're being watched," I mutter, to which I receive a grunt in reply. I've seen that particular flash umpteen times on missions. Binoculars can be quite obvious when the sun glances off their lenses.

We follow the road along until we reach some woods. Getting out, we stretch our legs for a while by entering the woods and following the rough path until we reach a stream. Glancing over to the other side, I notice another road leading to a housing estate.

"Ah hell, we should be over there," I exclaim in exasperation.

I see Victor turning toward me; thankfully, he just laughs at me. "I knew I shouldn't have let you read the map. You're terrible at directions."

"Well, I did fail geography for a reason," I tease back before we turn and head back to the car.

The rustle of someone moving in the woods comes again. They're fairly quiet, just not quiet enough for supernatural hearing.

Chapter 41

I get teased for my lack of direction, and we mess about playfully as we make our way back to the car. The whole way we're being followed from a distance.

When we reach the car, I hear a distant, "They're just lost. Stupid bitch can't read a map."

Climbing into the car, Victor takes the map from me, looks it over before handing it back. A few minutes later, he turns the car around and heads back down the road.

We stay silent for the rest of the journey. Eventually, we make it back onto the road and head toward the other side of the river.

The place looks like one of those ghost towns I've read about. If it wasn't for the fact it's snowing, I wouldn't have been surprised if tumbleweeds rolled by.

A dog barks in the distance, and a crow caws from the roof of a nearby house. A shiver ripples down my back. This place gives me a serious case of the heebie-jeebies.

"Jesus, this place is creepy," mutters Victor from beside me.

We take a walk around. Chatting about nothing in particular, I'm under the presumption anyone could be listening. Eventually, we come across a barn and slowly poke around it.

Letting out a giggle, I allow myself to be dragged

inside as if we have been looking for a warm dry place to get frisky with each other.

We quickly realize this is the perfect area to hide a car while someone crosses the stream to rescue Roísín. If she's still in the farm across the river.

I let out a scream before darting out the door.

"Hell, no, I just saw a rat, for crying out loud."

"He won't bother us," laughs my would-be lover.

"Sure, right, it's not you who has to take her pants off completely!" I declare before storming off in a huff back to the car.

I hear a spluttered laugh quickly muffled. I'm not sure if it's Victor or someone else. I hurry back to the car, unlock it, and hop inside slamming the door behind me. A few minutes later, I'm joined by a contrite-looking partner who's unsuccessfully smothering a grin.

"Is this our first argument?"

"Just drive," I mutter back.

Once more, he turns the car around and heads back down a road. This time we carry on back toward town. Halfway there we pull over, climb out, and search the car inside and out for any form of device. Near the front tire, we eventually find a small tracking device, left during our traipse through the woods.

Finding a big enough branch, we knock it off leaving both the device and the branch in the road. Once they come searching, it'll look like a simple natural removal. Especially as we drive over the branch and feel it scrape the underside of the car.

Once back at the hotel, we search out the others and tell them what we discovered. We quickly find out they didn't find anything interesting. No one was followed or bugged.

"We did find a place to stay though," Selena informs us. "It'll be far enough away from here no one will recognize us, yet close enough to get to so we don't have to go too far out of our way once we've rescued your daughter."

"Will it fit all of us?"

"Yes, it's an old abandoned manor house. It's for sale and is also off the beaten track, so to speak."

"In other words, it's perfect for our needs," I agree.

"Exactly. How about we grab something to eat and set out a plan of action?"

An hour and a half later, we've eaten and scraped together a plan of sorts. Honestly, I'm not impressed at all, but mind you, no one seems to be.

What we've managed to do is gather together half-assed ideas and glue them together with a prayer it'll work. We're going in blind, and we all know it.

We have no idea how many people are on the farm, where the kid is being kept, and what exactly the situation is.

The words "up a creek without a paddle" and "you're so screwed" keep bouncing around my head, so not helpful especially when I hear my brain making wonderful whistling sounds mimicking a bomb falling from the sky before exploding.

"Ugh, this has to be the crappiest plan in the history of crappy plans," I moan behind my hands covering my face.

"I agree, but it's all we got." Vincent apologizes.

"Yeah, it doesn't help. Look, how about we try and find out information on the farm tomorrow. If nothing turns up, we can always go ahead with this idea tomorrow night."

"I see where you're coming from, I honestly do, and I agree. It's just the idea of leaving our daughter there for one more night..." Janna trails off. Anguish is clearly written all over her face.

"Okay, fine. We have a couple of hours before we can do anything. Let's try to find out as much as possible. Use whatever means necessary to gain the information we need," I instruct. No way in hell am I going in completely blind.

Four hours later, darkness has descended, and we've gathered together a little more information. Not a lot, though what we have might just make a difference. I'm still not happy though.

Selena, Nancy, and Vivian pile into the car Victor and I had used earlier, then they drive off to what we're classifying as our safe house. In the boot is everyone's luggage.

T.T., Felicity, Jasmine, Kheda, Vincent, Janna, Victor, and I divide ourselves between the other three cars.

Every person on this part of the journey is vital. We all have a part to play. I just really don't like mine.

Slowly, we drive off toward the shed we found. When we eventually meet near the housing area, we turn off the car lights, making the journey more treacherous in the pitch darkness.

After we finally arrive, I climb out of the backseat and open the doors, while the three cars reverse back into the shed. Once they're inside, I quickly enter and close the doors behind me.

I hurry over to Janna and ask for one final look at the picture of her daughter. The idea of accidentally rescuing the wrong child has crossed my mind for a fleeting second. A moment of guilt flashes through me at the idea of other kids there. Shoving it to the back of my mind, I opt to concentrate on the mission ahead.

Jasmine and Kheda slip into a dark corner to change and transform privately into their other forms. Victor waits until they're done, so he can collect their clothes and wait in the driver's seat of the car they'd driven.

Both will be returning in wolf and dog form to the safe house. With a final look at everyone, I transform into my wolf form. I feel a gentle brush of fingers against my fur and look up into Victor's worried gaze.

"Be safe. If you sense anything wrong, come straight back to me."

His concern makes me feel better. I give him a gentle bump and a quick lick of his fingers before I slink out of the shed.

I hear T.T. and Felicity start their chanting, keeping the shed protected from prying eyes. After Jasmine and Kheda transform, they'll circle this side of the river in case I need their help.

Victor will be their getaway driver. Vincent and Janna will be ready to collect their child to help soothe her and get her to safety.

While me, I'm the collector. The only one who can change into a wolf and back to human for my magick. Both my forms will be needed on this suicide mission. Sometimes it really sucks to be me.

Chapter 42

Swiftly, I run toward the river and keep to the shadows as much as possible. Being a white wolf means I really stand out here, though I do blend in nicely with the snow.

I sniff the air, my nose twitching for any scent of human or other. Finding nothing to concern me, I carefully cross the river. Once on the other side, I shake my paws before continuing carefully though the woods.

From somewhere above, an owl hoots. I stop for a second, my ears pricked and swiveling. Everything is silent as if the forest is waiting to see what will happen next.

Once more, I continue to my destination. Weaving around the trees in no particular fashion, every now and again I pause, sniff the air, and listen before carrying on.

Reaching the edge of the trees, I flatten my belly against the ground and watch curiously for a while. All is quiet, though I sense movement near the house and sheds.

I'm just about to creep forward when I hear a man's voice. I can't make out what he says, though. I'll need to get closer, much closer. Something I'm not in a rush to do.

I opt to pace around the edge of the tree line. This way I'm at least moving, and hopefully, I'll be able to hear or see something helpful to me. After what feels like an eternity later, I finally see some movement. A large man is coming out of the barn. He looks mean and very, very dangerous. Someone I wouldn't want to meet in a dark alley, never mind trespassing on his land.

I hunker down once more. Watching the barn entrance and the man as he comes and goes between the barn and another outbuilding nearby. I can hear him talking to someone. Though I keep my ears pricked for the slightest answer, I never hear anyone else.

If it weren't for his tone of voice, I would assume he was talking to himself. It's the pauses between his words and the slight rise in tone as if asking a question and waiting for a reply which gives me reason to believe, though I can't see or hear another person, there is at least one more individual there.

With a sinking feeling in the pit of my stomach, I realize I'm going to have to move closer. If I don't, I could be waiting here all night.

****

I creep forwards keeping myself as low as possible, blending with the snow-covered fields. I sense fear from the barn. Pausing, I sniff once more. The ripe smell of fear is strong. *If I haven't found who I'm looking for, I definitely have found someone in need of help.*

Once more, I lie down and watch. Again the man leaves the barn to enter the woodshed building. I'm not too sure what it is, only that it's bigger than an outhouse, yet smaller than a shed. Again, he speaks to someone. This time I hear a faint reply. I have no idea if it is a man or woman who answers.

Spying some windows around the side of the barn,

I decide to check them out. If I don't need to go inside, I'd rather not. Quickly, I stand up and run to my destination. At the farthest window from the barn door, I pause to listen more closely this time.

Hearing quiet sobs from within, I stand on my hind legs to peer in through the window. Inside looks more like stables than a barn. In one stall, I spot a young girl chained to the wall crying. Though dirty and hungry-looking, I can still tell I'm looking at the girl from the picture. Roísín.

I decide I need to look through another window to try and find out if there is anyone else inside chained or not. Pushing away from the window, I move again swiftly around to the next window, situated around the corner.

Seeing the outbuilding, I hesitate before standing on my hind legs to peer through the window. This time, I see a young girl strut into the barn. Curiously, I watch her wondering what she's going to do.

She marches into the stall holding Roísín, says something, and before any answer can be given, slaps her across the face causing her to cry once more. My lips pull back over my fangs. I just barely manage to not let out the growl rumbling inside me.

Before I can do anything else, a rope whistles through the air, drops around my head, and tightens. Next thing I know, I'm being yanked to the side and land heavily on my shoulder. A yelp of pain escapes me before I can hold it back.

I can't believe I was stupid enough not to notice him! I chastise myself. With a grunt, I clamber to my paws and pull back, wiggle, and try to escape the rope while staying in wolf form. Under no circumstances can

I let them know I'm anything other than a wolf.

I let out a vicious growl, baring my teeth at the man I'd seen earlier. For my trouble, I get yanked once more. My paws lift off the ground, and I fly forwards from the brutal action.

On my landing, I face plant into the snow, thankful for its cushioning softness even as a cloud of the powdery stuff puffs into the air. Before I can lift my snout up, the man is on me, tying my snout closed and securing my paws to each other.

Oh great, he would know how to secure an animal, wouldn't he! I didn't even get to bite him.

He picks me up dumping me across the back of his shoulders. A shiver of fear ripples through me. This man is strong, knows exactly what he's doing, and is efficient. A dangerous combination if you're on the receiving end of it.

He brings me round to the front of the barn. Once inside, he enters a stall opposite Roísín's. He quickly removes me from across his shoulders, secures my neck in a choke chain, and removes the ropes securing my paws and muzzle before stepping backwards.

I pant there for a second before trying to pull my head out of the choke chain, an impossible task. All I manage to do is hurt my neck and swing myself around. Snapping and snarling, I'm feeling very pissed off. I growl at my captor, who's watching my antics from the stall door with his hand on a chain.

Next thing I know, he gives me a nasty smirk as he pulls the chain. My collar suddenly yanks me up. In a panic, I realize the chain is attached to the choke chain. Soon, my front paws are off the ground, leaving my hind paws barely able to find purchase.

I watch in a state of panic as the man secures the chain before turning away, whistling as he goes.

Chapter 43

The girl tormenting Roísín appears in my stall. Walking toward me, she looks me up and down.

"Oooh, you're beautiful. I've never seen a silver wolf before," she coos, before trying to pet me.

I bare my teeth at her in response, letting a growl lose.

"Bitch, my father will teach you some manners!"

I roll my eyes before I can help it. I mean, really, what a daft thing to say to a wolf chained to a wall.

"Oh my god, you just rolled your eyes at me," she gasps in surprise as her own round comically. "Didn't you?"

Looking at the girl from my precarious position, I wonder what she would do if I actually answered her. Somehow, I just barely refrain myself from answering and rolling mine at her again.

The bloody chain is driving me nuts. All I want to do is transform into my human form and get it off me. To do so, I need this annoying child to fuck off.

I have a vision flick through my head of the girl's father returning to find her in the choke chain instead of me. The idea appeals to me.

Without making it obvious, I glance around as best as I can, looking into the corners. This whole setup stinks of a trap. I look at the girl more closely from the corner of my vision and realize she keeps glancing up, behind me.

Is there a camera watching me? I let my paws skid out from under me, almost choking myself in the process. A whine of pain escapes me.

As if she's been given a signal, the girl loosens the chain by the door slightly, so I can sit up straight instead of dangling in the air. I pant in relief. I watch the girl saunter out of the barn whistling as she goes. Just like her father did.

Now would be the time to transform back into my human form. Instead I let my wolf go crazy. Lashing about the place, I whine and growl trying to break free. Until in exhaustion, I slump forwards, choking myself on the chain.

A whimper escapes me just as the girl's father rushes into the barn, hurries to my stall, and removes the chain from around my neck.

With a burst of energy, I leap up knocking him down and flee from the barn as fast as I can.

There's another man outside. I dash past him. My paws eat up the ground. I hear a shout from behind me, a click, and a gun goes off. I trip, tumbling to the side. A bullet smashes into the ground where I was a moment before.

Leaping to my feet, I run faster into the trees, heading straight for the river. My sides are heaving from my exertion, my panting loud in my ears. I'm positive my poor heart is about to jump out of my chest in fright.

I reach the river, cross it, and slink my way back to the others. We need a new plan. And we have no time to make it good. I feel awful having to leave Roísín behind. Deep in my heart, though, I know if we're all to get out of this alive, I needed to leave her. Only for a short while, though, just long enough to gather help.

Chapter 44

A plan of sorts is in motion. Well, plan is the wrong word. We're planning on destruction. Fast, completely tear the place apart and destroy everything. Oh, and of course rescue the kid. That's our plan.

Victor, Vincent, and Janna are each in one of the cars. This time, though, they're driving toward the farm. We leave Kheda and Jasmine to circle the farm from different directions, while Felicity, T.T., and I plan on blasting spells.

Felicity concentrates on all things electrical. Her job is to literally disable them. We can't have any live feed being sent out or recordings. T.T. heads for the barn as her job is to rescue Roísín. My job, I'm the distraction.

I stride out of the woods with the others flanking me from behind. Gathering power, I form a fire ball into my hands. *"Just destroy and melt, but harm no animal or person,"* I whisper before flinging my fire balls, straight for the woodshed.

Mayhem quickly breaks out.

Shouting and screaming, running feet and curses as the man from earlier charges out of the outbuilding. Seeing a fireball whipping through the air in his general direction, he makes a break for it, charging toward the woods. A minute later, I hear a deep-throated growl and a shout of surprise.

From the direction of the house, lights turn on only to blink out. I quickly fling in rapid succession more fireballs as I speed up my pace.

"What the fuck!" shouts the man who had captured and chained me up earlier. He pauses midstride to gape at me. Fear flickers across features which would be handsome if it weren't for the anger, hatred, and greed which have grooved lines of discontent into his face.

A snarl of anger erupts from me. I gather my energy and whip it toward him. Steel bands of wind wrap around him and squeeze. Once he passes out, I release the wind, reluctantly. I'm not here to kill, just destroy and rescue.

Soon the house and woodshed are burning brightly. Wood snaps and windows explode as they're consumed.

Talia hurries toward the barn, rushes inside, and a few minutes later exits with two young girls.

"Let me go," screeches the girl from earlier, trying to scratch and bite my friend. "Daddy," she shouts upon seeing him collapsed on the ground before bursting into tears.

"Enough," I bellow. Good god, the kid is a nightmare.

She pauses at my sudden shout. Peeks at me curiously as if unsure if she should obey. Something inside her seems to encourage her to keep quiet. She stops fighting. A simple act I don't trust for a second. Receiving a wary look from Talia, I'm glad I'm not the only one the girl isn't fooling.

I notice Kheda and Jasmine arrive. The girl gives a squeak of surprise, not taking her eyes off the huge black wolf prowling closer. I must admit Kheda is a formidable-looking wolf.

They have a quick sniff around. Finding no one else, they come back to our small group. Jasmine comes over to Roísín, gives her a quick lick across her cheek making her smile.

"Are you going to take me away from here?" she asks in a quiet yet strong voice.

"We're taking you to your parents," I reply, bending down slightly to make eye contact with her.

"They didn't want me. It's why my grandmother brought me here." Her chin trembles as she speaks, but she doesn't cry, though.

My heart feels like it's breaking. It would be bad enough to be kidnapped and sold, but to believe your parents gave you away because they didn't want you...

"Your grandmother took you. Your parents have been searching for you ever since," I inform her.

The other girl apparently decides now is a good time to make a break for it, as she yanks her arm from Talia's grip and dashes not to her father, but toward the woods in the same direction as the other man had run.

Kheda makes a move to chase her.

"Wait, track her. The other man went in the same direction. They obviously have a place to go, and we need to find it."

We move toward the road. I drag the unconscious man with me. At a far enough distance, I drop him. I blast another stream of fireballs this time sending them toward the barn. In great satisfaction, I watch it be consumed by my fire.

A loud groan echoes from it before it crashes to the ground sending out sparks and flames. Soon, there will be nothing left of any of the buildings.

Chapter 45

Fifteen minutes later, we've moved closer to the flames. It's bloody cold, and we're still waiting for the others to turn up. I've cast a spell on the escaped girl's father to keep him unconscious but warm. I don't want to cause his death or illness.

Kheda pops out of the woods, gives a yip loud enough for us to hear but not so loud as to gather unwanted attention.

Leaving Jasmine, Felicity, Talia, and Roísín, I hurry toward him. He leads me past the man who had run earlier who is still alive, just unconscious on the ground. I cast the same spell on him as I had on the other man, before hurrying after my guide.

Eventually, we come across a long building built of wood, mostly camouflaged by the surrounding trees and greenery. Screams of pain and exhaustion escape from the building.

"Why people build a secret torture place only to not make it soundproof is beyond me," I mutter. I receive a chuff as an answer from the wolf beside me.

I'm feeling slightly baffled about what to do. After all, if someone is being tortured then someone is doing the torturing. I also know the girl is inside too. So how many people are in there? I have no way of knowing.

I opt on playing it by ear. Gathering power, I create a net of magick, surrounding the building under, over, and around it. Just in case they have escape routes other than the one door we can see.

Once done, I gather more power to me. Centering myself, I blast the door open. The impact of my power shatters the door into flying splinters. I quickly transform myself into my wolf.

Curses of surprise erupt followed quickly by exclamations of "It won't open!"

Apparently, there was another exit.

Kheda and I stalk toward the opening. One silver and one black wolf both with fangs bared peer inside.

Men, women, and children are shackled to the walls. Each have cuts, burns, and bruises.

I let out a howl of fury. Snapping and snarling, I attack the man closest to me. My teeth close around his leg. I shake my head furiously; hearing his screams, I only stop when I hear his leg snap.

Someone grabs a knife, slashing it toward Kheda. I open my jaw and a ball of violet fire erupts from me, singeing the man's hand, wrapping around it until he releases the knife with a cry of agony.

Others dash past us only to find, out even though they can exit the building, they can't escape. My barrier bounces them back into the clearing.

Transforming back into my human form, I release the prisoners. They are all supernaturals. A couple of vampires pounce onto their captors, ripping into them and drinking their fill.

Then they allow the other prisoners to drink a little of their blood, helping to heal them.

A witch places a trembling hand on my arm. Tears cloud her vision. With a trembling smile she tells me, "I don't know how you found us, but thank you."

"You don't need to thank me. How did they capture you?"

"Some of us were kidnapped by family members and sold. Others were hunted."

"Bloody hell," I mutter in disgust, shaking my head. Kheda bumps up against me, looking back toward the door.

I walk outside into a scene from a disaster movie. The captors are being attacked by their prior victims. Unable to escape, they're easy targets. I remove the barriers containing everyone inside.

A flashback of Jasmine's rescue from our days in the army pops into my head. With a shudder, her broken, battered, and abused body swims in front of me and the retribution we sisters in arms brought down on her captors.

I won't interfere with the retribution being brought here. They need it. To take back the power which was stripped from them. It'll help them through their coming nightmares.

Kheda and I slip away. Others, realizing they can now escape, simply run. Some of them are captives unwilling to take revenge or just too desperate for their freedom. Others are some of the men and women who held them captive determined to escape with their lives.

I change back into my wolf form, and together Kheda and I race back to the others. As I pass the unconscious man on the ground, I release my spell, giving him a fighting chance at survival, something he hadn't given the others. If he dies, I don't care.

I do the same for the man who had taken me earlier only because he has a daughter to save. I have no idea where she is. I haven't seen her since she ran into the woods.

Thankfully, our rides are waiting for the two of us to hop inside. I transform back into human form, close the door behind Kheda, and then jump into the car waiting for me. Once in, we quickly drive off, leaving behind a greater disaster than I ever imagined.

Chapter 46

I've never been as happy as I am right now when I realize we've arrived at the safe house. To say I'm exhausted is too mild a word. I feel drained, physically and mentally. I hear crying from somewhere behind me. I'm guessing it's a happy reunion going on. The poor kid will need some major reassurances.

The house has no furniture. Being as it isn't in use, I shouldn't be surprised. Though for some reason I am. It feels full. I have no idea why. Glancing down at the floor, I notice it's been cleaned. Next thing I know, I'm closer to it than I expected. My face and body hurt for a split second before my eyelids slide close.

****

Sunlight blazes across me, and I hear the annoying sound of people chatting. I crack open an eye and groan as I'm blinded by a bright beam of light shining through the windows.

"Ugh," I groan, throwing an arm over my head.

"You awake?"

"No," I grumble back to the cheerful voice above me.

"Yes, you are. You just answered me," laughs a little girl.

What the hell is a kid talking to me for? As soon as the thought flickers through my head, the events of last night start flashing back to me.

"You saved me. You also left me; at least you came back, though."

I peek at the girl chattering to me. She's had a bath. Bright golden hair and big blue eyes in a heart-shaped face greet me. I feel like groaning again. She's so shiny. My eyeballs are really sore.

"Realized I needed a different exit strategy," I mutter in response.

"Come on, breakfast is ready," she informs me with a beaming smile.

At the mention of food, I perk up. Slowly, I clamber off the ground and wobble in the direction she informs me is the bathroom. Once freshened up, I find the others in the kitchen.

Someone had gone out for food, bringing back easy to assemble items. Nothing which needs heating and takeaway coffee. Everyone sits on either the floor or the counters.

In silence, we eat. Well, the adults eat in silence while Roísín chatters non-stop. I feel bemused, to be honest. *How can anyone be so chirpy so early in the morning?*

Looking around, I again sense the place being full.

"How did you find this place?"

"Umm, by accident, to be honest. We just took a wrong turn and found it."

"Do you sense anything?"

"Like what?"

"As if the place is full of, I don't know, just full of furniture I guess."

"No."

I glance up to see puzzled expressions looking at me.

I push out a little power and see it move over and around shapes that aren't there.

"Reveal," I command.

A table and chairs appear in the kitchen, as well as the other usual items expected.

"You mean we've been sitting on the floor for no reason?" Kheda asks with a slight grin pulling at the corners of his mouth.

I give an inelegant snort from where I'm sitting on the floor looking up at him, while he sits on the kitchen counter.

I stand up and walk through the now fully furnished house. Thick drapes cover the windows, and I let out a groan of exasperation. There was no need for me to be blinded by the sun earlier.

I feel something pulling me upstairs. I follow where I'm being led to until I face a wall. The feeling pulls at me again, directing me through the wall.

"Hold on," I mutter in exasperation as I test the wall and surrounding area. Looking at a wall lamp, I let out a chuckle. *If I pull on it, will it open a passage just as in all those films I've seen before?*

Grasping it, I twist it. It doesn't open a passage; it does break from the wall though. "Whoops!" I quickly drop it on the floor. This time I feel a shove from the back and fly into the wall.

Chapter 47

I'm startled when I pass right through it to the other side. Turning around, I see the corridor and the others gaping at where I was a few minutes before. To them, I must have vanished.

Poking my head out where the wall should be, I startle the crap out of them. Giving them a wicked grin and a wink, I laughingly inform them I'm okay. I then stick a hand out and beckon them forward.

Sometimes, I really amuse myself.

Without seeing if they're coming, I turn around and venture into the room. Before me covering the whole of the far wall is a family tree. Starting from Janna's great-great-grandmother and ending with Roísín.

Apparently, I'm descended from Janna's son through my mum's side and Janna's daughter through my father's. My father, I'm surprised to see, had a brother—has a brother as there is no death date by his name. My uncle also has a son and a daughter. I've never heard of any of them. I stare at the date of his daughter's birth, a date I know well as it is also written beside my father's name.

My cousin was born the same day my father was murdered. Blinking away the tears threatening my vision, I look closer at the family tree. It doesn't take me long to realize I am the only one in the complete family history who is related on both sides to Janna.

273

On a stand near the back wall, a huge book lies open. I pause for a second before crossing to it, it takes me only a second to figure out I'm looking at the book of Prophecies.

"Holy shit in hell," I whisper softly as I stare at what we've been searching for.

"I know one of those notes said, 'All answers will be revealed.' I never expected this though," Victor says from beside me, making me jump and squeal embarrassingly loudly.

"Dang it, Victor, one of these days I will put a bell around your neck," I threaten.

"What is it you're reading," enquires Jasmine as she unsuccessfully tries to smother her laughter.

"The Prophecy," I reply. *I can't believe it's here.*

"What does it say?"

"And the Double Magick one will be born stronger than any other.

Gather unto thyself allies to fight in preparation of the coming of the Triple Magick one.

When the Double Magick one fails to rise again, there will be two Triple Magick ones, to end the battle against the supernatural's enemies.

For as The Protectors meld their blood, making all one, the Triple Magick ones shall destroy them all with one swift pulse.

And once more all races shall live in freedom and love as all magicks will grow once more."

I stare in total confusion at the words before me. "What the hell does that mean?"

"It means you have a war on your hands. All of *The Protectors* will be hunting you and anyone fighting with you. It's time for us all to fight. To end this persecution.

"I refuse to have my daughter fearing who she can love in case of retribution by death," Vincent informs us, placing a hand on Roísín's shoulder and giving it a gentle squeeze.

"I'm with you to the end, though we will need to gather more allies," Janna agrees, once more looking like the fearsome warrioress she is.

Nancy's cell phone rings. Quickly she speaks to the person on the other end. "Jezebel, stay where you are. I do believe we will be coming down to New Orleans as soon as possible."

Silence permeates the room as Nancy listens to what's being said on the other end.

Giving a wicked grin she replies, "We've found the Prophecy. It's time to prepare for war against *The Protectors.*"

A word from the author...

Born in Dublin, I moved to England, then finally back home to Ireland. I now live in West Cork, but want to move to America.

In October 2010, I self-published a book of poetry called *Different Kinds of Emotions*.

But I always wanted to write down the stories in my head, until finally I did. My first novel is a paranormal fantasy called *Double Magick in the Falls,* book one in the Candi Reynolds Series.

When I was a child, I fell in love with books, amazing stories filled with mystery and intrigue, danger and fantasy. This love has progressed into a passion with me. I also like photography and cemeteries, the older the better.

http://aprilhollingworth.wix.com/april-hollingworth
https://www.facebook.com/aprilhollingworthauthor
https://www.goodreads.com/author/show/4759078.April_Hollingworth
https://twitter.com/No1Bitchmaster

Thank you for purchasing
this publication of The Wild Rose Press, Inc.

If you enjoyed the story, we would appreciate your
letting others know by leaving a review.

For other wonderful stories,
please visit our on-line bookstore at
www.thewildrosepress.com.

For questions or more information
contact us at
info@thewildrosepress.com.

The Wild Rose Press, Inc.
www.thewildrosepress.com

Stay current with The Wild Rose Press, Inc.

Like us on Facebook

https://www.facebook.com/TheWildRosePress

And Follow us on Twitter
https://twitter.com/WildRosePress

www.ingramcontent.com/pod-product-compliance
Lightning Source LLC
Chambersburg PA
CBHW060525260626
47161CB00003B/764